# Bitten by Design

## By

## Annabelle Jacobs

# Copyright

Cover artist: Natasha Snow
Editor: Sue Adams
Bitten By Design © 2017 Annabelle Jacobs

## ALL RIGHTS RESERVED:

## WARNING

# Acknowledgements

A huge thank you to these wonderful people: alpha reader Jay Northcote, beta reader N.R. Walker, cover artist Natasha Snow, editor Sue Adams, and proof readers Kirsty Bicknell and Lily G. Blunt.

# Chapter One

The taxi pulled up outside Seb's flat just as his phone started to ring. No doubt it was Jared checking he'd got home okay. A quick glance at the screen confirmed it. He'd also managed to miss a text from his sister, and he opened it to read while the driver fiddled with his meter.

*Forgot to let you know we got here. Sorry. Hotel fab, nightlife fab, chat soon xx*

Seb grinned at the screen, more than a little jealous, but glad she was having fun.

"That's twenty-two fifty." The driver pointed at the meter and then looked back at him expectantly.

Seb shoved his phone in his pocket and pulled out his wallet instead. It took two attempts to get the right money out; his head spun as he tried to focus on the notes. Bloody Jared and his insistence on *just one more drink*. "Here you go." He handed over a twenty and a five. "Keep the change."

His phone rang again as he climbed out of the cab and almost lost his footing on the slippery pavement. The rain had only just stopped, leaving the smooth concrete a little hazardous—stupid British summers. In hindsight, the shoes he'd worn weren't one of his better decisions. The soles had virtually no grip—and it had nothing to do with the fact he was drunk.

"You all right there?" The driver had his window half-down, smirking as Seb gingerly took another step.

Seb waved him off with a laugh. "Yeah, thanks."

As long as he could get from the kerb to his front door without breaking his neck, he'd be golden. He waited for the guy to drive off before attempting the walk up the steps—no point in embarrassing himself further. If he had to fall on his arse, he'd rather do it without witnesses.

With a sigh of relief, he unlocked his front door, thankful he didn't have a shared entrance considering the state he was in, and he half walked, half fell inside, kicking the door shut behind him as his phone rang again.

"Shit." Jared, probably doing his nut. Seb answered on the third ring. "Sorry!" he cut in before Jared had a chance to speak. "I'm home. Don't get your knickers in a twist."

Jared huffed in his ear. "Fuck off. You know why I'm calling." He sighed again.

Seb slumped onto the bottom step of the stairs and closed his eyes.

While taking over Jared's flat had seemed a good idea at the time, two months down the line, being this close to Primrose Hill pack territory made Jared—and Nathan to some extent—twitchy. Their alpha, Steven Newell, was not exactly friendly.

Another sigh from Jared's end. "Why didn't you answer the bloody phone, then? I was two seconds away from coming over there."

Seb rolled his eyes. That was all he needed— Jared, Nathan, and probably Luke turning up and making a scene. "I was just getting out of the taxi when you called, and then I slipped. I'm just drunk, J, not in mortal peril. No need to call in the cavalry." He stood and quickly grabbed onto the banister when the hallway spun around him. "Shit. I really need to get to bed."

Or maybe to the bathroom… that last pint sat heavily in his stomach, giving every indication that it might well come back up. "Call you later, okay?"

Very carefully, Seb turned round and began to climb the stairs, still holding his phone next to his ear.

"Yeah. Just…."

Slowly, one step at a time, Seb carried on upwards while he waited for Jared to make his point and go already.

Something scraped across the outside of the front door and Seb froze midstep, suddenly feeling a lot more sober.

It sounded again. *Louder this time.*

"What was that?" Nathan's voice.

Seb frowned down at his phone screen, momentarily distracted from whatever was outside. "Where'd Jared go?"

"Still here. You're on speaker."

*Ugh.* "You know I hate it when you do that without telling me."

"Yeah, sorry. But seriously, what the fuck was that?"

Jared's voice was far too serious for Seb's liking. *Imagine if he knew it wasn't the first time I heard that sound?* "Nothing. Just the wind, probably."

"Really? Because Nathan thought it sounded a lot like—"

A low rumbling growl filled the space around him, so clear that for a second Seb thought it had come from the phone. When another followed hot on its heels, accompanied by another scrape of what he assumed were claws across his front door, Seb turned around slowly.

"Seb?" Jared hissed, low and urgent.

"Yeah," he whispered back, well aware that whoever was outside was probably listening.

"We're on our way."

*Thank God.* Normally, Seb would have told him not to bother, that he was fine. He had a fair idea of who was out there. Well, not *who* exactly, but it would be the same ones who always did it. Normally he ignored it; nothing ever came of it, but for some reason this time felt different. Whether it was the alcohol flooding his body or the fact that it was two in the morning and the street was otherwise deathly quiet, Seb didn't know. But he was willing to admit he was really fucking scared.

He kept his gaze fixed on the front door, unable to look away. The small semicircle of glass in the top had never seemed more frightening. When a shadow fell across it, Seb gasped, stumbled backwards, and lost his footing on the stairs. With his coordination already compromised from the beer, he reached for the banister but missed by a mile. At least the alcohol numbed the pain as he tumbled forward and fell in a heap at the bottom, phone still clutched in his other hand.

Now a lot closer to the door, he ignored everywhere that hurt, and with his heart pounding hard against his ribcage, looked up at the glass and listened. One, two, three seconds passed, and nothing. *Fuck.*

He waited another few seconds before forcing himself upright with a wince. *Ow.*

Seb had his phone held face down on the carpet, and when he brought it to his ear, Jared's shouting filled the air.

"Seb! *Sebastian!* Fucking hell, he's not answering. We—"

"Don't ever call me that if you expect an answer." Leaning his head back against the wall, Seb focused on Jared's sigh of relief and not the throbbing in various parts of his body. That could wait.

"Thank fuck." Jared sighed again and Seb closed his eyes and pictured his best friend running a hand over his face and pacing. Unless they were in the car already. "You okay? Are they gone?"

Ignoring the first question, Seb chanced another look at the door. Still nothing, and it felt like whoever had been out there was gone. "Yeah, I think so."

"And are you okay?" Jared repeated.

"Fell down the stairs."

"Shit."

Nathan snarled in the background, but that was kind of comforting when it was on Seb's behalf. He smiled at the thought, then abruptly shivered as the cold from the wall seeped through his shirt. It was only September, for fuck's sake. Now the adrenaline had started to fade, everything else came into sharp relief: the hard floor, the cool hallway, and the aftereffects of too many beers. He felt like shit and in no way wanted to move, but he couldn't stay at the bottom of the stairs all night.

Despite all that, it was far too easy to keep his eyes closed and drift away.

*I'll move in a minute.*

"Seb?" Jared's annoying tinny voice snapped him out of his doze.

"Hmm?" Blinking away sleep, Seb put the phone closer to his ear. "Sorry."

"Look, we're almost at yours. I've got my spare key, so you don't have to come down."

5

Seb laughed, but couldn't be arsed to explain that he hadn't actually managed to get back upstairs. "Yeah, okay."

It must have been longer, but it felt like only a minute later when Jared opened the door and kneeled next to him.

"Jesus, Seb." Jared smoothed the hair away from his forehead, and Seb leaned into his hand.

"Ow," he mumbled when Jared touched a sore spot.

"That's a nasty bump you've got there." Jared touched it again, much softer this time, but Seb still frowned and tried to bat his hand away, which only made his wrist hurt, and he quickly stopped.

With another muttered curse, Jared stood. "I'm calling Tim."

*Oh, the hot doctor. Shame he's a shifter.* He waved the hand that didn't hurt in Jared's direction. "No need. 'M fine."

Jared snorted. "Of course you are."

"Just drunk."

"Mm-hmm." Jared turned away towards the still-open front door. "Nathan, get in here and help me get him upstairs."

Seb shivered again as a gust of wind ruffled his shirt; he frowned. No wonder he was cold, the front door was bloody open.

Nathan appeared next to him moments later, and the next thing Seb knew, he was gently lifted off the floor.

"I can walk," he muttered.

Both Jared and Nathan ignored him.

"Everything clear out there?" Jared asked.

Nathan grunted in affirmation. He adjusted his hold on Seb as they manoeuvred into Seb's bedroom. "Their scent is all over the place. I doubt very much this was the first time they've been here."

Seb groaned, aware enough to know what was coming as they lowered him onto his bed.

"Yeah, you fucking should groan," Jared grumbled as he carefully unlaced Seb's shoes. His tone was a sharp contrast to the gentleness of his actions.

As Jared eased Seb's left shoe off, pain rocketed through his ankle and he hissed.

"Fuck, sorry. We'll discuss this when you're sober."

*Talking of which…*

Seb opened one eye, wincing at the harsh overhead light in his bedroom until Jared huffed and turned it off, opting for the muted glow of the bedside lamp instead. "How come you're not wasted?" he asked Jared. "We drank the same."

Jared shrugged. "I guess what little bit of shifter DNA I have dilutes the effects quickly." He unceremoniously undid Seb's belt buckle, followed by the button on his jeans. "Or maybe it was hearing a shifter outside my best friend's door and then him dropping the phone with a pained cry."

He tugged on Seb's zip with a little more force, and Seb slapped his hand over Jared's. "I didn't drop the phone."

It made sense in his head, but judging from the look Jared gave him, perhaps it wasn't the correct response. "And stop undressing me with your boy in the room."

As expected, Nathan glared at him. He hated when Seb called him that, so naturally Seb tried to slip it into conversation as much as he could get away with.

"Behave," Jared chastised, but he motioned for Nathan to leave them alone. When he took Seb's jeans off, he was as careful as he could be, but it still hurt. "Anywhere else hurt? Or is it just your head and ankle?"

Seb pointed to his right hand. "Wrist's a bit sore."

He settled back into the pillows and closed his eyes. Hopefully, Jared wouldn't try and take off his shirt, because he was far too comfy to move.

"Seb?" A gentle shake on his shoulder. "Hey, Sebastian?" Soft fingers tilted his chin up. "Can you open your eyes for me?"

With great effort, Seb opened one eye and struggled to focus on the man in front of him. Curly black hair and blue eyes were all he could make out with his vision still a little blurry. Blinking rapidly to clear it, he smiled as recognition dawned.

Doctor Tim Walters. The Regent's Park pack doctor.

"There you are." Tim smiled back at him and let go of Seb's chin to inspect the bump on his head.

"Ow."

"You've got quite a lump there, but I don't think it's serious. At worst a very mild concussion."

The throbbing in Seb's temple begged to differ. He had to swallow a couple of times to get moisture into his mouth. Wow, that was unpleasant. The nasty taste along with his furry tongue made him grimace.

Thankfully, Tim handed him a glass of water. "Here."

Cold and refreshing, so he emptied the glass in four swallows. *So much better.* "Thanks."

Seb handed the glass back and slumped against the pillows with another groan. "Are you sure it's nothing serious? My head fucking kills."

Jared's voice piped up from the other room. "That would be all the alcohol you drank."

"Ugh. They're still here, then?"

Tim grinned at him, and Seb's gaze caught on how full his lips were. "Yes, they were worried when you passed out."

Seb glanced down to where Tim had one hand on the bed covers.

"May I?" Tim tugged the edge of the quilt to show what he meant. "I wrapped your wrist while you were sleeping, but I didn't want to check your ankle until you were awake." Seb nodded for Tim to continue and he slowly pulled the sheet back. Then frowned. "That doesn't look too good."

As soon as Tim said it, the pain in Seb's ankle made itself known, as though it had been waiting for a doctor's confirmation that it should hurt. With a wince, he pushed himself up on his good arm for a better look. "Oh." Even from that awkward angle, Seb could easily see the swelling around the top of his foot and ankle and the slight discolouration. He watched closely as Tim carefully ran his fingers over the area. "Is it broke—ow! *Fuck.*"

Tim immediately stopped his gentle manipulations and sat back with a soft smile. "I suspect so. You'll need to go to the hospital to get it sorted." He pulled his phone from his jacket pocket.

Nathan and Jared appeared in the doorway, looking more worried than the situation warranted. Well, Seb thought they did, anyway.

"Hey." He waved at them and managed a weak smile.

A wave of nausea rolled through him and he quickly shut his eyes, clenched his teeth, and breathed carefully in an effort not to throw up. Being sick in his bed, with an audience, was not on his list of things to do tonight. Or this morning, or whatever it was.

His skin felt clammy and he'd give anything for a cold flannel, but the threat seemed to have passed. For now, at least.

When he opened his eyes again, Nathan stood grinning at him from the door, but Jared had moved close enough to crouch next to the bed.

"I've emptied out the bin in case you're sick. You went all pale and sweaty, so—" He looked back at Tim, who was typing something on his phone. "You sure it's not a bad concussion?"

Tim set his phone down on the bed; his gaze landed on Seb again. "Almost certain, but they'll check it again at A&E. How much did he have to drink?"

Tim had addressed Jared, and Seb huffed in annoyance. "I'm right here, you know."

"Sorry." Two spots of colour appeared on Tim's cheeks and he quickly stood, fussing with his bag. "How much did you drink tonight, Seb?"

"Um…." Seb tried to recall the exact amount, but even the thought of alcohol made his stomach churn. "You answer him, J."

Seb ignored Nathan's laughter and tried to focus on Tim instead. He might be a shifter, which automatically ruled him out as far Seb was concerned, but he was nice to look at, and Seb always appreciated a pretty view.

"I reckon about four pints and four shots, so not loads, but—" He poked Seb in the shoulder. "—did you eat today?"

"Yeah, course." He'd had cereal for breakfast, a sandwich at lunch, and then some toast before he went out.

Nathan was watching him as if he knew Seb was being economical with the truth, but he didn't comment.

"You've downed that much before and not got ill." Jared ruffled his hair. "Maybe you're getting old."

"Fuck off, I'm twenty-six. Same as you."

Tim stood and cleared his throat. "I'd really like to get you to hospital and have that ankle looked at."

Seb wiped at his clammy forehead and frowned. A trip in the car was not what he needed right then. "Can't it wait until morning, when I'm not in danger of throwing up everywhere?"

"I'd rather go now." Tim checked his watch. "My brother's on shift until seven, so we won't have to wait."

Seb raised an eyebrow. "Isn't that favouritism?"

"Yep." Tim grinned, momentarily distracting Seb with how white his teeth were.

Seb strained to see if they were pointy like Jared's sometimes got, but they looked normal as far as he could tell. That made sense. Jared seemed to have shitty control over his leftover shifter traits. Nathan's control was much better, and if Tim was anything like him, he probably needed to be angry or—

"You feeling okay?" Tim snapped his fingers and Seb startled, mortified to realise he'd been staring at Tim's mouth.

He swallowed down his embarrassment and wiped at his face again. "Sorry, just spaced out for a sec. Still feeling a bit dodgy, to be honest."

"We'll take a bowl in the car." Tim laughed as Seb grumbled, and then he turned to face Jared. "You two might as well go home. I've got my car outside, and we could be at the hospital for a while."

Jared started to protest, so Seb decided to nip that in the bud. "It's all right, J. I'll be in Dr Walters's very capable hands."

For some reason that sounded dirtier when said out loud. Judging by Jared's smirk, he thought so too.

Tim smiled. "Call me Tim, please. Dr Walters makes me sound ancient."

"Seriously, I'll be okay with *Tim*," Seb added. "There's no point either of you waiting around."

"But we still need to discuss what happened tonight. Jesus, Seb, there were shifters…."

Seb sighed. He hadn't wanted to admit to this, but his head ached, his limbs ached, and he just wanted to get this hospital trip over and done with. And if Jared and Nathan came along, they'd probably take the opportunity to question him endlessly, and he couldn't face it. Not tonight. "Look." His voice came out surprisingly strong considering how delicate he felt. "It's not the first time something like that's happened." Admittedly they'd never lingered around his front door before, but whatever. "Nothing ever comes of it. They just like to remind me they're close by, I think."

Jared's expression went from worried to outraged in the blink of an eye. On second thoughts, maybe Seb should have kept quiet. His mental reasoning wasn't the best at present.

"That settles it." Jared glanced from Seb to Nathan and then back again. "You're definitely *not* going to the hospital on your own."

"Jared—" Nathan's tone held a warning, but Seb struggled to understand what it was for.

Either oblivious to it or choosing to ignore Nathan, Jared carried on. "I can't believe you didn't tell me about this before now."

"It's nothing—"

"It's not nothing!" Fisting his hair with one hand, Jared closed his eyes as though trying to rein in his temper. "Do you realise how much danger you could be in?"

Nathan tried again. "I don't think they'd actually do anything to him, J. The repercussions would be—"

"I don't give a fuck about the repercussions, Nathan! Seb could be dead by then. And no way is he leaving this flat with no one to protect him when God knows what could be waiting for him out there. It's not fucking safe!"

Even in his fuzzy state, Seb was aware that Jared was overreacting. Jared worried about Seb, yes, but not like this. Never over-the-top protective and unreasonable.

A low growl rumbled through the ensuing silence. Seb felt it deep in his bones.

"He won't *be* on his own." Tim leaned against the wall, body rigid and hands clenched into fists.

His top lip curled slightly and Seb noticed with some interest that yes, his teeth did go pointy like Jared's.

Every time Seb had run into the doctor at Jared's place, he'd always appeared easy-going, happy. In fact, he displayed so few of the traits Seb associated with shifters—aggression, arrogance, possessiveness—that sometimes he almost forgot that Tim was one. Seb had never seen him look like he did now, all coiled power and confidence, and maybe a little pissed off too.

The sudden change in Tim's demeanour was startling and a little disturbing, and it might be the alcohol talking, but Seb found it really hot too. His dick stirred in his boxers and he hastily rearranged the quilt in case anything might show.

The movement made his wrist twinge and he sucked in a breath at the stab of pain. On the plus side, it took care of his burgeoning hard-on.

Jared's mouth fell open, seeming as shocked as Seb by this turn of events. So obviously, he'd never seen this side of Tim either, but Nathan appeared resigned, almost as if he'd known it was going to happen.

Tim flexed his fingers. The smear of blood on his palms was a clear indication that his claws had lengthened too. *Really pissed off, then.*

Tim cast a wry glance at Nathan's hulking form. "I might not look as intimidating as some." Compared to Nathan, Tim wasn't as broad or as tall, but he was still about six foot, and Seb would bet good money that underneath his slim-fitting top, he was all lean muscle. "But I assure I can protect Sebastian just as well as anyone else in my pack."

*Oh.* Seb hated his full name. *Usually.* But something about the way Tim said it made him feel all funny inside, and it definitely wasn't the beer this time. It might be the roughness of Tim's voice, thicker than normal and affected by his lengthened teeth, but whatever it was, Seb liked it and didn't feel the need to correct him.

Jared raised an eyebrow at him but said nothing.

While Nathan and Jared were busy having some sort of silent conversation, Seb let his gaze linger over Tim's shoulders, noticing the way the material clung in certain places when muscles flexed as Tim stood and stretched out his hands. Yes, Seb had no doubt Tim Walters could protect him. His gaze wandered higher to Tim's face. One moment he was looking at blue eyes, full lips, and a strong jawline, the next he was faced with a snarling shifter—all sharp teeth and menace—*Fucking hell.*

Seb's breath caught in his chest, all his aches and pains forgotten in that instant, but before he had chance to utter a word, Tim was back to normal.

"Was that really necessary?" Nathan ground out, his voice rougher than usual.

Seb didn't miss the way he'd moved closer to Jared.

Tim shrugged, unrepentant. "I think so." He stood tall, shoulders back and chin tilted up. Jared had apparently done a good job ruffling his feathers, or, more appropriately, his *fur.* "I might be the pack doctor, and that position requires me to heal people rather than hurt or intimidate, but I am still a member of this pack, first and foremost. And as such I would protect any member of it with my

15

life. For you to suggest otherwise is incredibly insulting, to say the least."

Never one to know when to be quiet, Jared blurted, "But Seb's not pack."

Seb flinched. That comment stung, but he wasn't exactly sure why, because Jared was right—he wasn't pack.

Nathan huffed, and Tim's lips twitched as if fighting a smile. "You told our alpha that Sebastian was like family to you. Or am I mistaken?"

Jared flushed and looked down at the floor. Seb grinned as warmth replaced the hurt of moments before. "Yeah," Jared said, so softly that Seb struggled to hear him.

"So as Nathan's mate, anyone you class as family is automatically under the Regent's Park pack's protection." Tim spoke slowly as though explaining to a child.

Seb's grin widened. Jared liked to think he knew everything about shifters now, but he obviously hadn't known that.

"Why didn't you tell me?" Jared glared at Nathan and hit him on the arm. "For fuck's sake."

Nathan glared back at him, not so much as flinching. "I thought it was obvious."

"Well, not to me."

Jared sighed and rubbed at his eyes. It made Seb feel tired suddenly, and he couldn't suppress the yawn that followed. Finally, Jared's shoulders sagged and he sat on the edge of the bed, carefully avoiding Seb's injured foot.

"I'm sorry, Tim. I didn't mean to imply that you weren't capable, and I know I overreacted, but I also have first-hand experience of what shifters can do to a human." He rubbed at his shoulder, and

Seb immediately felt guilty for forgetting. Of course, Jared would react that way. "The thought that one or more shifters from another pack are harassing Seb scares the shit out of me."

Tim's whole posture changed and he relaxed against the wall with a short nod. "I understand. But you can trust me to keep him safe."

Seb lay there feeling like a damsel in distress. A flare of irritation spiked in his chest. "And I repeat, *I am right here*, guys. I might not have any freaky shifter DNA in my blood, but you can't discuss me as though my opinion counts for fuck all. For once, this is all about me."

The sparkle in Tim's eyes as he met Seb's gaze shouldn't have been so appealing. Seb looked away quickly, concentrating on the bandage covering his wrist as Tim spoke.

"So, Seb… are you okay for me to take you to hospital, or do you want Jared and Nathan to come too?"

Without looking up, Seb said, "There's no point in everyone going." He did glance up then and give Jared the best smile he could manage. "Go home. I'll call you later."

"You'd better," Jared grumbled. "And don't think this discussion's finished by any means. I want to know everything—"

Seb held up his hand to interrupt. "Yeah, yeah, I get it. But not now, okay?"

"Right. Glad we got that sorted." Tim rubbed his hands together. Seb got the feeling he wanted to shoo Nathan and Jared out of the flat, but he didn't do that. Instead he pointed at Seb's bare legs. "Let's get some clothes on you, and then we can go."

# Chapter Two

"Here, let me help." Tim wrapped his arm around Seb's waist and hoisted him to his feet, startling a laugh out of him.

"I always forget just how strong you lot are."

Tim smiled and angled him towards the bedroom door. With Seb flush against his side like that, it was impossible not to breathe in his scent. Though heavily laced with the alcohol he'd drunk earlier, faint traces of Seb's underlying scent filtered through and Tim inhaled deeply. He knew better than to do it, of course. Jared had made it clear on many occasions that Seb wasn't interested in shifters—for reasons Tim wasn't privy to—but Tim couldn't help himself. Seb smelled good.

Jared and Nathan had finally left about five minutes before; otherwise Nathan would no doubt be giving him a warning glare right about now. Seb might not recognise that Tim was effectively scenting him, but Nathan would have. Probably Jared too. He turned his head away from Seb's neck and temptation, then guided him out of the bedroom.

They stopped at the top of the stairs. Seb leaned into him, his good arm slung a little awkwardly around Tim's shoulder and his ankle held off the ground. The staircase wasn't wide enough to easily accommodate two grown men walking side by side.

Tim sighed. "I could carry you down." He fully expected Seb to scoff and tell him where he could stick that suggestion, but it was met with silence. "Sebastian?"

"It looks such a bloody long way down, and my ankle is fucking killing…." The resigned huff that accompanied that statement sent warm air ghosting across the side of Tim's neck; he fought back a shiver.

Christ, he needed to get himself under control. Seb's injuries, combined with the fact he was considered pack—despite what Seb and Jared seemed to think—triggered Tim's protective instincts, and the idea of carrying him down the stairs was so appealing that he was seconds away from just scooping him up, whether Seb wanted him to or not. But he held still, waiting for Seb to agree.

"God, go on, then." Seb pointed down with his bandaged hand. "But can we not mention it to anyone. If Nathan finds out, I'll never hear the end of it."

*Neither would I.* "It'll be our secret."

Seb smiled at him, wide and sincere. "Thanks."

Tim smiled back and tried not to appear too eager when he bent to hook his other arm under Seb's knees. He lifted him easily, adjusting his hold until Seb was secure and had his arms around Tim's neck, holding on tight. Seb wore a slightly fearful expression, and Tim laughed softly. "I'm not going to drop you."

"I know, but this isn't something I do a lot of." Seb cast a pointed look down at Tim's hands on him. "It's weird and unnerving, and again I feel like the heroine in some bodice-ripper novel."

Tim laughed out loud at that and really wasn't thinking when he grinned and whispered, "Are you implying I want to have my wicked way with you?" He glanced at Seb as he spoke, and met raised eyebrows. Heat infused Tim's cheeks, but before he could make any attempt to backtrack, Seb nodded at his ankle and said, "Nah, I'm in too much pain for any shenanigans."

Awkwardness clung to the conversation like a wet blanket, but Tim soldiered on, determined to get them back to the easy-going conversation of a couple of minutes ago. "Lucky for you I know a man who can fix that."

They reached the bottom of the stairs, and reluctantly, Tim set Seb on his good foot but kept an arm around his waist for support.

"Your brother, yes?"

Tim nodded. "Yeah, David." He was about to add a bit more about David when he noticed a black bucket next to the front door. "How're you feeling now?" He poked it with his foot. "Think you'll need that in the car?"

Seb looked conflicted. "I really don't fancy throwing up in a bucket in front of you." Then he ran a hand over his belly and his shoulders sagged. "But I still feel a bit shit, and I don't think throwing up on your seats is the better option."

The next sentence was quiet as Seb focused on his feet. "Yeah, we probably should bring it."

Tim sympathised and tried not to make a big deal of it, simply picked up the bucket and handed it to Seb. "Can you hold it while I get the door?"

Seb took it and then glanced at the door uncertainly.

It took Tim a couple of seconds to catch on. "There are no shifters nearby, I promise." Taking Seb's chin between his fingers, he tilted his head until their gazes met. "I meant what I said earlier. I'll keep you safe."

21

Being this close was playing havoc with Tim's senses. Even in the dark entranceway, Seb's eyes were the blue-green of the sea, and so focused on Tim, it made his breath catch. Seb's scent wrapped around him as if he'd bathed in it. It would be so easy to lean forward and just—*Jesus*.

Snapping his eyes shut, Tim let go of Seb and gritted his teeth. "Come on."

Tim's car, an older model Honda CRV, was only a little way down the street, but Seb was shivering by the time they reached it.

"Shit, sorry," Tim apologised. "I never thought to bring your coat."

Being a shifter, the cold barely affected him, and he'd forgotten to suggest the coat with his mind occupied by things other than Seb's well-being. He was a doctor, to both humans and shifters; he was better than this.

Seb shrugged as he manoeuvred himself into the car. "It's not your fault. Who would have thought I'd need one in bloody September. I'll live."

Tim shut the car door and hurried round to the driver's side, eager to get the car started and warmed up. Glancing over at Seb, he saw he had the bucket positioned on his lap. Ready.

Seb caught him looking and grimaced. "Thought I'd better have it handy, just in case." As though embarrassed by the whole thing, he turned and looked out the window, and Tim pulled the car out into the street.

The hospital was about a twenty-minute drive at this time of the morning. Ten minutes into the journey, Seb groaned and rested his head against the seat back.

"You feeling okay?" Tim spared him a glance and noted the paleness of his skin and the sheen of sweat across his forehead.

"Not really," Seb replied through gritted teeth. His fingers curled around the edge of the bucket and held on. "Can you put some music on, or talk, or—" He breathed through his mouth and his knuckles turned white. "Just so you don't have to—" and then he promptly leaned over the bucket and threw up.

Tim turned the radio on loud and concentrated on the road. Seb would no doubt be embarrassed enough without him watching. He was no stranger to people being ill, obviously, but he didn't think he'd ever get used to the smell of sick. He cracked the front windows on both sides, just an inch or so to let in some fresh air.

Seb groaned again, but thankfully slumped back in his seat, finished. "Fuck. I'm so sorry."

Out of the corner of his eye, Tim watched him. Some colour had returned to his cheeks, but it was hard to tell if that was him feeling better or just being embarrassed. *Probably a bit of both.* Seb turned his head to the slightly open window and sighed.

"How're you feeling now?" Tim took a right turn and spotted the tall hospital building up ahead. "Better?"

"So much better. You have no idea." Seb fidgeted in his seat. "Sorry about the smell, though. You can open the windows more if you want. I'll take cold air over the smell of sick any day."

Tim lowered the windows another few inches, the fresh air a welcome relief. "We're almost there, anyway."

23

Seb perked up a bit at that and wiped his face on his sleeve. "Don't suppose you've anything to drink. Water or Coke, or something? My mouth tastes awful."

"Try the glove box. I think there might be a bottle of water in there. I might've already drunk some of it, but you're welcome to the rest if it doesn't bother you."

Seb snorted a laugh. "It doesn't bother me." He rifled through the glove box and held up a half-full water and a pack of Polos. "Jackpot." After downing the water, he popped a couple of Polos in his mouth and offered one to Tim. "Hopefully I won't smell too bad when we meet your brother." He shoved the bucket onto the floor between his feet. "The sooner we can get rid of this the better, though. Again, I'm really sorry."

Tim shrugged. "It's fine, honestly." He'd seen far, far worse than that. Being the doctor for a shifter pack wasn't for the faint-hearted. "And don't worry about David, he's an A&E nurse." After pulling in to the hospital car park, he turned off the engine and smiled. "His Friday nights are filled with drunk idiots throwing up everywhere."

Seb's mouth fell open, and Tim smiled wider as Seb's eyes narrowed. "Oh, fuck off," Seb said with a laugh. "In my defence, when I was happily drinking those beers, I thought I'd be safely tucked up in bed right now, sleeping off my hangover, not still awake and driving around London."

"Well, we're here now." Tim reached for his phone and sent a quick text to let David know they were outside. "Come on."

Tim got out and walked quickly around the back of the car to help Seb, and with a hand around

24

his waist, managed to him out without too much jostling.

Seb leaned into him slightly and breathed deep. "God, that fresh air smells good."

Tim hummed in agreement, his nose so close to Seb's neck that all he smelled was his skin.

"Is it far to A&E?" He glanced around looking for a signpost.

"Reception is around the front of that building over there, but I'm just waiting for—" Tim pointed at the double doors to their left. "—that."

His brother, dressed in nurse's scrubs, walked through the doors, pushing a wheelchair in front of him. He grinned when he looked up and saw Tim. "What've you got for me this time?"

"This is Sebastian Calloway, human member of the Regent's Park pack." Tim then turned to Seb again. "Seb, this is my brother, David."

David nodded in understanding. "Human member, eh? Employee or partner?"

Seb glanced at Tim, confused.

Tim explained. "Usually human members either work for one of the pack businesses or are involved with a pack member."

"Which one are you?" David asked, parking the wheelchair in front of Seb. "I'm guessing this is for you?"

"Yeah." Seb shuffled forward, grabbed onto one of the armrests, then lowered himself into the chair. "And I'm neither."

"Oh?" David raised an eyebrow, so Tim jumped in to clarify.

"Seb is Jared's best friend." Would David make the connection? He hoped not, but—

David started to smile again and shot a quick look Tim's way. "Are you the one who's living in Jared's old apartment?" When Seb nodded, David's smile widened. "Ahh, so you're *that* friend."

"Um… maybe?" Seb sent Tim a questioning look, and Tim tried not to blush.

*Fucking David.*

Before David could say anything more, Tim fished the bucket out of the passenger side of his car and thrust it at him. "Here, do something with that for me, would you?" He smiled with all his teeth and hoped David got the message to *shut the fuck up already*. Why had he thought telling his brother anything about Seb was a good idea?

*Because I never thought they'd actually have cause to meet. That's why.*

David took the bucket but growled softly, startling Seb, who jumped a little. "Since you asked so nicely," David snipped. His tone softened considerably when he saw Seb's reaction and realised what he'd done. "Fuck, sorry. Didn't mean to make you jump. I forgot how tetchy my brother gets when he's tired."

With that, David gestured for Tim to push the wheelchair and started back towards the double doors. "Come on, it's cold out here, and Seb's starting to shiver."

*Shit*, Tim had totally forgotten Seb's lack of coat. Cursing himself under his breath, he grabbed hold of the chair and pushed at a brisk pace, catching up to David as the doors opened automatically.

Instead of following the signs for A&E, David led them down another corridor.

"Where are we going?" Seb half turned in his chair to catch Tim's eye. "It said Reception was back that way." He hooked his thumb over his shoulder.

"Shifters have a special wing in this hospital." Tim slowed down and let David get a little ahead. Tim knew the way himself after being here so many times.

Seb frowned. "I didn't think they got sick? And in case it's slipped your memory, I'm not a shifter."

"But you're pack." He smiled at a couple of nurses who passed and said hello to him. "And they don't, generally. But it's a maternity hospital too, and now and again something crops up that takes longer to heal, or they need a little help."

"Like Nathan did after that fight with the rogue pack?"

"Yeah, just like that." Tim spied David leaning against the doorframe of a room at the end of the hall. "And they treat human pack members here as well."

"Do they get preferential treatment, then? Seen quicker than us mere regular humans?"

Tim huffed out a laugh and leaned down to whisper in his ear. "You can try and ignore it all you like, but the fact remains you're seen as pack now. Maybe act like that's a good thing, at least while we're here."

David raised an eyebrow as they stopped in front of him. He'd probably heard every word, but hopefully no one else had. People gossiped, and Seb's lack of enthusiasm about belonging to their pack wouldn't be the best thing to find its way back to Cam, the Regent's Park pack alpha.

David motioned for Tim to wheel Seb into the room first. "We have a special wing so that anyone who comes here knows they'll be treated by someone sensitive to their needs, whether human or shifter, and that they're safe."

"Safe?" Seb glanced from Tim to David and then back again.

David sighed. "I'm sure you're well aware that not everyone likes shifters or human members of shifter packs. Would you want to risk being treated by someone like that?"

Seb shrugged. "I suppose not."

"Anyway." David pointed to the corner of the room where Seb's bucket sat—now clean, thank God. "If you still feel ill, there's that, or these." He lifted a pile of cardboard sick-bowl things and waved them under Seb's nose.

"Yeah, I'm good, thanks."

Laughing at the sudden flush on Seb's cheeks, David held his hands up. "Well, it's all there in case. Someone'll be along in a few minutes, but I've got to nip and check on something. Be back in a sec."

He slipped out the door with a wave, leaving Tim alone with Seb.

Without the urgency of getting Seb to the hospital, Tim found himself uncomfortably aware of Seb's everything—his scent, his breathing, the way his gaze darted to him every few seconds.

"So," Tim started and then realised he had no idea what to follow it up with.

Seb snorted. "So?" He held Tim's gaze for a moment before settling back in his chair with a sigh and closing his eyes.

Tim glanced at the way Seb held his wrist in his lap, reminded of the reason they were there. "Those shifters outside your flat tonight, they were from P-Pack?"

Seb's lips curved up at the edges. "I think so." He tapped his nose. "Not so easy for me to tell, but I'm sure Nathan could tell you." Looking up at Tim, he added, "Didn't you recognise the scent?"

"No, but then I don't have much to do with the other packs like Nathan does. It was familiar, but I can't differentiate between packs as easily as Nathan and the other unit members can." And he hadn't lingered long enough in the hallway to try, too concerned with getting to Seb. "How long have P-Pack been doing that?"

"Tonight was the first time I've seen them through my front door. Usually I see a van with the P-Pack logo parked down the street, or sometimes they get out and lean against it where I can see them from my window." He stopped and drew his bottom lip between his teeth.

Tim leaned forward a little. "Is that all?"

Seb studied him for a second as though debating whether to say more. Then he added quietly, "I can't be certain, but a couple of times I've had the feeling that someone's watching me. Maybe. Fuck, I don't know. I could be imagining it!" He scrubbed his good hand over his eyes and then yawned, making Tim do the same.

*Christ, I'm tired.* A quick check of his phone told him why: 5.00 a.m. "Have you told Jared or Nathan?"

Seb shook his head.

"Why not?"

"You know why not." Another sigh. "Jared worries enough as it is since all that shit with the rogue pack. You saw him earlier."

29

"Yeah, I did."

Personally, Tim thought Jared had every reason to worry. Relations with the Primrose Hill pack were strained these days, to say the least. The majority of the ill feeling stemmed from Nathan being alive and still with his pack after biting Jared and keeping it secret. Members of both packs had witnessed Alpha Newell's disapproval and his consequent efforts to get rid of Nathan. The fact that Nathan survived and wasn't punished further hadn't sat well with Newell, but he couldn't go to the authorities or make any further demands from Cam as he'd given his word as Alpha. That didn't mean he had to be happy about it, though.

As much as Tim wanted to share all that with Seb, get him to understand that the situation was more serious than he gave it credit for, it wasn't Tim's place. Although Seb was considered pack as far as protecting him went, that didn't extend to pack business.

But he had to say something....

Tim wasn't privy to what had gone on at the meetings between Cam and his betas, but Alec had hinted enough to imply things weren't good between the two packs. "If some of the P-Pack shifters are harassing you, Seb, I think Jared's right to be concerned. Don't you?"

"I'd hardly call it harassment."

"No?"

The door opened, stopping their conversation, and David came in, followed by the doctor.

Tim smiled and stood. "John, good to see you again."

Dr John Cordon was in his early fifties, tall, silver-haired, and hot. He'd worked at the hospital for as long as Tim could remember, and Tim used to have the biggest crush on him. Even now, the way his eyes lit up as he smiled sent a little shiver down Tim's spine.

"You too," John replied, smiling back at him.

They shook hands, and then Tim stood back out of the way to let him do his work.

# Chapter Three

Two hours later, Seb had been X-rayed, poked at, and prodded, and fitted with a temporary cast for his ankle. They'd also given him some strong painkillers—thank God—and a crutch. Just the one, since he'd damaged his wrist, too. The doctor had explained that normally they'd recommend he use it under his right arm, but since he'd injured that one, the left would have to do.

*Whatever.* Seb had nodded and thanked him anyway.

Declared concussion-free, the doctor allowed him to go home and rest without needing supervision. *Thank God.* He was so tired, he could probably sleep in the wheelchair as Tim pushed him out to the car.

David had given him a blanket, and Seb pulled it up to his chin against the chill. "So, is David younger or older than you?" It hadn't come up while they were in the hospital, and Seb was curious.

"Older by three years."

"I liked him. He seems like a nice guy."

"He is." There was a slight edge to Tim's voice.

Seb smirked, pretty sure Tim was a little jealous.

They reached the car, and Tim pulled them to a stop with more force than Seb thought necessary. "Do you need any help getting in?"

"No, I think I can manage, thanks."

Tim still insisted on hovering while Seb manoeuvred himself into the passenger seat, but Seb let it go. It was quite nice having someone fuss over him.

Tim got in to start the engine and get the heat going, then got out to return the wheelchair to the ward. He pushed it with quick, determined steps and Seb unashamedly watched his arse the whole time.

Once they were on their way, the warm air washed over him and Seb relaxed into the seat with a sigh.

Tim glanced at him. "Want me to take you home or back to Jared and Nathan's?"

"What for?" Tiredness amplified Seb's irritation; he was sick of shifters treating him as if he was made of glass. His social circle might now include an ever-increasing number of shifters, but he'd managed just fine before they came along.

Obviously sensing his mood swing, Tim hesitated before replying. He tapped his fingers on the steering wheel and Seb waited, watching him all the while.

Tim cleared his throat. "Jared texted me while we were in the hospital. He said you weren't answering."

"Left my phone back at the flat." Which probably wasn't the best idea, but he'd been distracted with the pain. "What did he say?"

"He wants you to stay at their place for a couple of days. Until—"

"No! I don't want to—"

"Seb." Tim reached over and put his hand on Seb's thigh. That, more than Tim saying his name, stopped Seb midsentence. "They're worried. I actually think it's a good idea. At least until we can confirm who was outside your flat and what the fuck they were doing there."

Tim's voice turned gravelly on the last few words, and when Seb glanced over, he saw a hint of sharp teeth before Tim snapped his mouth shut.

Was he being unreasonably stubborn about this? It wouldn't be the first time. As hard as it was for Seb to accept, perhaps the others had a point. He wasn't au fait with shifter politics. Jared was far more interested in that sort of stuff, especially now. For all Seb knew, he could unwittingly have become some sort of pawn in the whole inter-pack rivalry thing.

"Fine." Seb stared straight ahead, not wanting to see Tim's face in case he looked smug. That would just piss him off and make him want to change his mind on principle.

But Tim just let out a deep breath. Out of the corner of his eye, Seb saw his shoulders relax. "Thank fuck for that." He seemed far more relieved than Seb thought the situation warranted.

Seb slowly turned in his seat, careful not to bang his sore ankle or wrist. "Has Jared been giving you a hard time?"

Tim's smile was wry when he met Seb's gaze. "Let's just say he's finding it hard being out of the loop where you're concerned."

"Yeah, I can imagine. I know he didn't turn when Nathan bit him, but ever since then he's a lot more…." Seb struggled to find the right word.

"Overprotective?"

"Yes."

Tim laughed. "I'm afraid that does seem to be a trait that Jared's retained. Nathan is far worse with it than a lot of shifters, so I guess it's no wonder. Both Jared and Nathan just want you safe. Is it so bad to have people concerned over your safety?"

34

God, now he was making Seb feel bad. *I'm the injured party here, for fuck's sake.* "No. But I like being human. I like living my human life, and I've absolutely no wish to get involved with all this pack crap." He sat up a little straighter. "I mean, I'm happy for Jared—he and Nathan are obviously meant for each other—and I like Nathan, but I don't want what they have. Ever since Jared met Nathan, his life hasn't been the same. Everything is 'pack this' or 'pack that.' It's like he's part of a whole and not just Jared anymore."

"And you don't want that?"

Tim's voice was quiet after Seb's rant, but Seb didn't pause to think why. "Fuck no." He suddenly realised how ungrateful that sounded after all the preferential treatment he'd just received at the hospital. "Shit, sorry. I know being Jared's best friend comes with a whole lot of extra perks these days, and I'm thankful for getting these treated so fast." He held up his wrist. "But the whole *mates* thing creeps me the fuck out, and the thought of having everybody involved in my business makes me want to run a mile. Do you know what I mean?"

When they stopped at traffic lights, he looked up and found Tim watching him.

"No, not really." Tim's gaze lingered on Seb's for a second, and then the lights changed and he focused back on the road without another word.

*Bollocks.* For a moment there, Seb had forgotten who he was talking to, too busy letting out some of the feelings that he kept buried around Jared these days. "Sorry," he muttered again, feeling incredibly guilty all of a sudden and not quite sure why. All of what he'd said had been the truth.

35

"It's okay." Tim didn't glance Seb's way, and that tight set to his shoulders was back. "I know pack life can seem… a bit overwhelming from the outside. But they're my family, and I wouldn't want it any other way."

They lapsed into silence, and Seb sat facing out the window. The atmosphere wasn't uncomfortable, but it was nothing like the easy back and forth they'd enjoyed earlier. Maybe that was for the best. Seb had started to really enjoy Tim's company, but he didn't want him to get the wrong idea. Jared had not so subtly hinted that Tim liked him, and hot doctor or not, Seb just wasn't going there.

Five minutes later, Seb recognised Nathan's pack building as Tim pulled to a stop in front of it and turned off the engine. Almost immediately the front door opened and Jared walked out, followed by Gareth.

*Oh lovely. A welcoming committee.*

Seb had met the rest of Nathan's pack once before, and although they'd all been nice enough, something about Gareth put him on edge. Probably because he was stronger than Nathan, and Nathan was terrifying enough when he wanted to be.

Jared practically bounded down the steps and towards the car. Seb had about ten seconds before Jared had the door open. He quickly turned to Tim and smiled. "Thank you for tonight. Despite what you might think, I do appreciate everything you and your brother have done for me."

Tim smiled back, but it seemed duller than usual. *Or maybe I'm imagining it.* "You're welcome. If you ever need me—" He stopped and cleared his throat, motioning to Seb's injuries. "If they start bothering you, get Jared to give me a call."

Seb's words spilled out of their own accord. "If you give me your number, I could call you myself."
*Why did I say that?*

Tim held his gaze for a long moment, and just as he started to speak, Jared wrenched the passenger-side door open. He leaned in and wrapped Seb in a careful hug. "Thanks for coming back here," he whispered. "I know it probably pissed you off no end, but thanks. I felt all weird, and just needed to see that you're safe."

"Yeah, I know." Seb patted Jared on the shoulder as he pulled back and then stood. "You and your freaky shifter habits."

He sensed Tim still beside him, but Jared was fussing over him, drawing his attention.

"Do you need a hand getting out?" Jared looked so desperate to help that Seb took pity on him.

"Yeah, please." Aware that things felt unfinished between himself and Tim, but not knowing how to fix that with Jared hovering by the open door, Seb put his hand on Tim's arm. "Thanks again. I guess I'll see you around."

Tim nodded, his smile barely there this time. "Take care, Seb."

As soon as Jared helped him out of the car and shut the door, Tim drove off. Seb watched him go until he turned the corner and disappeared.

"Everything okay?" Jared slipped an arm around Seb's waist, taking nearly all his weight and holding Seb's crutch in his other hand.

Jared's increased strength wasn't anywhere like that of a shifter, but it was a substantial difference compared to Seb's own, and it still surprised him sometimes.

37

"Yeah. Let's get inside. Looks like rain."

Jared let Seb sleep until twelve o'clock before coming in with a cup of tea. "Fancy getting up? There's a couple of people who'd like to talk to you."

Seb eyed the mug Jared set down on the bedside table. He yawned widely. "A bacon sarnie would have worked better."

"Nathan's cooking you one."

Jared looked all smug about that, and Seb rolled his eyes.

"And by *people*, do you mean *actual* people, or shifters?"

Jared cast a glance back through the open door out to the hallway, where Nathan—and whoever else was out there—could no doubt hear them, and then he walked over and closed the door. "Can you not?"

"What?" Seb inched himself upright with his good hand, shoving away Jared's efforts to help.

"Shifters are people."

God, it was too early to deal with Jared's protectiveness, especially when it wasn't aimed at him. Before Nathan had stumbled onto the scene, Jared wouldn't have batted an eye at comments like that. Seb missed those days sometimes. "You know what I mean."

"Nathan's out there with Gareth and Alec."

Seb sat up a little straighter at that bit of information. "I thought Alec and Nathan hated each other?"

He'd listened to some of what Jared told him about the pack. Just not everything. An in-pack feud tended to stick in the memory.

Jared shrugged. "I think *hate* is a little strong." He glanced back to the door as if imagining what was on the other side. "'Intensely dislike' might be more accurate." Seb laughed. "Which is all the more reason for us to get out there. The atmosphere was a little… frosty." He grinned and Seb found himself grinning back. There was the old Jared he knew and loved.

"Yeah, okay." Seb took a sip of his tea, savouring the warmth as he swallowed it down. "Give me five minutes to get dressed, and I'll be out to give my statement."

"They're not going to interrogate you."

"Mm-hmm. They just want to ask me some questions, right?"

Jared rolled his eyes, but he stood and headed towards the door. "Five minutes. The sooner we get Alec out of Nathan's space the better."

He put a finger to his lips before pulling the door open, and Seb nodded to show he understood. *Damn shifters and their fucking super senses.*

Dressed in a pair of Jared's pyjama bottoms and a T-shirt, Seb grabbed his crutch and followed Jared down the hallway to the living room.

From the way Jared spoke about Nathan and Alec's relationship, Seb had expected to walk into some sort of standoff, but everyone was sitting down and looking fairly amiable when he and Jared entered the room. It wasn't until he caught a glimpse of the tight set to Nathan's mouth and eyes that he realised there was any tension at all.

Jared put his hand on the small of Seb's back and guided him to the armchair in the corner, making introductions as he went. "Gareth, you and Seb already know each other. Alec, this is my best friend Sebastian Calloway. He's been renting my old flat since I moved in here with Nathan."

Seb held in his huff. *Renting* was a bit of a stretch. Jared had bought that flat outright with inheritance money and refused to let Seb pay for anything other than bills and food. Not that he wasn't incredibly grateful—his last place hadn't been anywhere near as nice, and now he had privacy—but it still made him feel as though he was taking advantage.

Jared waited for Seb to settle himself in the chair. "Seb, this is Alec Knight, also a Regent's Park pack beta."

The guy sitting on the far end of the sofa was huge: broad shoulders that seemed to take up a full sofa cushion and legs that stretched out a long way in front of him. He had dark hair, with maybe the odd fleck of silver in it, although Seb wasn't sure if that was a trick of the light or not.

"It's good to finally meet you." Alec smiled, warm and welcoming.

It caught Seb off guard and he smiled back. Jared had painted Alec as the typical arrogant shifter—cold and uncaring, especially where humans were concerned. But Alec now regarded Seb with an expression that, if anything, he'd class as concerned.

Alec's forehead creased into a frown when his gaze landed on Seb's wrapped ankle. "Is that a result of last night?" he asked, gesturing to Seb's wrist too.

Casting a quick glance at Jared, who gave him a small nod of encouragement, Seb replied. "Yeah. I fell down the stairs." He shrugged, a bit embarrassed about the whole thing now. Did it really warrant all this concern?

Alec hummed and let his gaze wander back down over Seb's injuries. "I'm sorry you were hurt. But I understand you were in Tim's capable hands?"

Seb felt his cheeks heat a little. *Why am I blushing at that?*

An image of Tim getting all growly at Jared flashed in his head. Yeah, maybe that was why. He might not want to get involved with one, but there was no denying he found shifters hot.

"Yes," he said, having to clear his throat to get rid of the sleep huskiness. "Him and his brother, David." Despite wanting to squirm under Alec's intense scrutiny, Seb sat perfectly still, not quite sure what was going on. As far as interrogations went, they'd not asked him much, really.

Seemingly satisfied with checking out Seb's injuries, Alec turned his focus to Nathan, and his whole demeanour changed. The warmth in his eyes vanished, and when he spoke his tone was curt, businesslike. "I shouldn't have to remind you that Sebastian's safety is your responsibility."

Nathan sat rigid in his chair. "I know that."

Alec waved a hand at Seb's ankle. "And yet here he sits, injured and afraid. If you need assistance, you should ask for it."

"It's not Nathan's fault," Seb protested. "I was drunk, and I fell down the stairs because I was startled," he added, because injured, yes, but he wasn't afraid now.

41

Alec met his gaze, and that warm smile was back. "Jared thinks of you as family," he explained patiently. "This affords you the same protection as him. As Jared's mate, Nathan is responsible for ensuring that both Jared and you are safe. As I understand it, this isn't your first interaction with P-Pack shifters. Nathan should have informed Gareth before things escalated to this."

Again his gaze dropped to Seb's ankle. Seb was beginning to wish he could hide it from view. He fully expected Jared to jump in about now as usually he wasn't one to hold his tongue, but Jared didn't say a word. Clearly there were some shifter hierarchy rules at play that Seb didn't understand.

Gareth sat forward, his elbows on his knees. "Calm down, Alec. We can't be certain that every instance was down to shifters from the Primrose Hill pack. And besides, from what *I* understand, neither Nathan nor Jared knew about any of it until last night." He looked over at Seb. "That's right, isn't it?"

Gareth had one eyebrow raised, and Seb felt like he was being chastised for doing something stupid. "Yeah. I didn't think it was important, so I didn't say anything."

Four sets of eyes focused on him with varying degrees of incredulity. Seb chose to look at Jared, the safest bet, in his opinion, and he almost laughed at the "are you fucking stupid?" expression on his best friend's face. "Look," he added quickly before anyone could start shouting. "I'm not a shifter, so I can't be certain exactly who's been lurking around the area, but I've seen a couple of suspicious-looking *people* with a P-Pack van. Whether or not it's theirs or—" *God, I'm rambling, but having three huge*

42

*shifters in the room is kind of intimidating.* He shrugged. "No one's actually growled outside the flat until last night."

No way was he mentioning his suspicions about being followed. Tim didn't appear to have told anyone, so it can't have been that important. Seb still thought they were taking this far too seriously. Everyone in this room knew that if members of P-Pack wanted to hurt him, then they could easily have done so. The fact that he was sporting a broken ankle and a sprained wrist was his own fault for being drunk and clumsy.

Maybe he needed to spell that out. "If they wanted to hurt me, there's nothing I could have done to stop them."

"That's very true." Gareth turned to Alec. "What d'you reckon? We've got to report to Cam in an hour. He'll want answers."

Alec sighed and ran a hand through his hair. He turned to Nathan, and that same curt tone was back again. "You sure it was P-Pack last night?"

Seb was desperate to know what the story was between those two.

Nathan nodded. "Positive. And it might've been the first time they made their presence known, but I think they've been to his front door more than once. Their scent seemed days old in places."

That thought made Seb shift uneasily in his seat. Before this, he'd imagined they'd scraped their claws or whatever over his door and then run off. Kind of like a shifter version of "knock-a-door-run." Had they been down there while he slept, listening at his door like the creepers they were? He thought back to what else he got up to in bed and swallowed. *Fuck.*

The thought of them hearing him jack off made his skin crawl.

Alec stood and walked over to stare out the window, as if the view outside held all the answers. "What the hell is Newell up to?"

"Newell?" With the way they threw names around, Seb could do with a who's-who wall planner or something.

Alec turned to face him and his features softened a bit. When he wasn't glaring at Nathan, Alec was seriously hot for an older guy. Shifters seemed to luck out in the gene pool, and being around so many of them was undermining Seb's no-shifter rule.

Alec said, "Steven Newell is the alpha of the Primrose Hill pack."

Seb perked up. He knew all about what had gone down with the rogue pack and how the P-Pack alpha suggested they should use Nathan as bait. Jared had been quite vocal with how he felt about it all. "Oh, you mean the wanker who wanted Nathan dead?"

"Alpha Newell is a well-respected alpha and should be treated as such." Alec's steady gaze seemed to bore right through Seb, and for a second he feared he'd overstepped. Until Alec smirked. "But yes, he's the wanker who wanted Nathan dead."

Alec's gaze flicked to Nathan, and for the first time that afternoon, his expression showed something other than annoyance. Seb couldn't place it, but whatever it was disappeared as quickly as it came.

Alec admitted, "Alpha Newell wasn't happy with the way that turned out, and relations between our two packs are somewhat strained."

Jared visibly paled at the reminder, and Seb remembered in unfortunate detail what Jared had told him about Nathan's injuries from that night. No one needed to see their partner's bones first-hand. If Seb was in Jared's position, he'd probably feel ill at the reminder too.

Nathan looked to Gareth. "What now? Can we go to the police, since Seb's human?"

Gareth sighed and stood to join Alec. "No. They haven't done anything for us to formally complain about." His gaze landed on Seb and he offered him an apologetic smile. "I know you probably think otherwise, but unless they were the ones to actually cause you bodily harm, then we have no proof that the police can act on. They won't take our word for it against another pack."

Nathan directed his question to Gareth. "What about between our packs? They'll know I caught their scent because they made absolutely no attempt to hide it."

God, Seb was almost bursting to know what was up between him and Alec. Jared had to know, and Seb was going to ask him as soon as this little gathering was over.

Gareth answered Nathan. "I'm sure Newell's *irritation* with you has filtered down through his ranks." Alec scoffed at the word *irritation*, but Gareth ignored him and carried on. "It could just be a few idiots wanting to impress their alpha, or it could be something else. We'll go and talk to Cam and see how he wants to handle this. But for now, I suggest you keep Seb here."

"What?" Seb had been quite happy to sit back and watch as they discussed their shifter politics, since inter-pack fighting had nothing to do with him, but this…. "I'm not staying here. I have a home and a job. Besides which, I have no wish to be the third wheel with these two."

Jared overshared about his sex life with Nathan, which was fine; Seb didn't give a shit about that. But he didn't want to be around the pair of them 24/7, knowing how much time they spent having sex. That would be awkward and—since Seb wasn't getting laid anytime soon considering the state of him—frustrating.

Jared gestured to Seb's foot and frowned. "Will they let you work with a cast on?"

"I work at a desk. It's not like I have a lot of walking to do."

"I'm sure there's health and safety issues, though."

"I very much doubt it." Seb rolled his eyes. He so wasn't staying with Jared and Nathan. "I'll call them first thing Monday morning and see. But I can always work at home for a bit. There's a couple of people I know who did that last month, so I'll—" He caught Jared's grin and sighed. "—work from my home, not yours."

Before Jared could protest further, Alec spoke. He had the kind of authority that made everyone stop and listen. "Sebastian. While we all understand that you're eager to get back home, would you please consider remaining under our close protection until we've had chance to talk to Cam?"

Seb found himself wanting to agree, but he stubbornly kept quiet.

Alec sighed. "If you don't want to stay here with Jared and Nathan, Tim has a flat in my building. I'm sure he has a spare room that you could use."

Alec's lips twitched, and Seb felt warmth spread across his cheeks. The thought of sharing with Tim made him all kinds of uncomfortable, and he wasn't really thinking when he replied. "I can stay here. It's fine."

*Shit.*

Both Jared and Nathan had a smug look about them, and Seb gave Jared the finger, just to be petty.

Gareth said, "Okay, now that's settled, we'll leave you to it." He gestured for Alec to go first.

Alec hesitated. "I'd appreciate you letting us know immediately of anything remotely suspicious from now on."

Seb nodded. He wasn't stupid. "Sure."

"Good." Without bothering to say anything further, Alec turned on his heel and left the room.

Gareth rolled his eyes at Alec's departure. "I'll see you guys later, let you know what Cam said." He gave Nathan a one-armed hug and then hurried after Alec.

As soon as the front door opened and closed, Seb turned to Jared. "What's with—"

Jared shook his head sharply and gestured towards his bedroom.

*Ugh.* This was why he'd never get involved with a shifter—no fucking privacy.

"Fine." Seb reached for his crutch, then promptly realised the chair was way too low for him to get out of easily, especially with a busted wrist too. With a sigh, he motioned for Jared. "Come and help me up?"

With Jared's aid, Seb hobbled into the bedroom and made himself comfortable on the massive bed. Once the door was firmly shut, he glanced at Jared. "What's the story with Nathan and Alec, then?"

# Chapter Four

Tim woke late on Sunday morning. Staying up all night on Friday had caught up with him, and he'd collapsed in bed about ten o'clock the night before, knackered.

His first thought was Seb—his ankle was due to be cast properly today, and Tim really wanted to take him back to the hospital, just to make sure everything went okay. Well, that was the reason he was telling himself, anyway. Seb was his patient; it was good practice to follow through on his treatment.

His phone sat on the bedside table next to him, and as he reached for it, he noticed a message already on the screen. From Alec.

*Fyi Seb staying with Nate & J.*

He knew he'd talked about Seb too much in front of Alec. Of course he'd noticed. He replied with *Thanks*, then set his phone back down.

To a lot of people outside his unit, Alec appeared cold and unapproachable. He'd been that way with Tim when he'd first met him. But after Tim's parents died, Alec had stepped in and helped him pick up the pieces. At first because Cam asked him to, but later he and Alec had become friends. As pack doctor, Tim wasn't part of any one unit, but when Cam asked him if he wanted to choose a beta to report to, he didn't hesitate to say yes. And he'd chosen Alec.

He stared up at the ceiling, debating what to do. Jared would want to take Seb to the hospital, obviously, but that didn't stop Tim from grabbing

his phone again and searching for Seb's number—
*Shit.* He never actually got it from him.

And Seb didn't have his either.

Seb wasn't due at the hospital until three o'clock, and it was only eleven now. Maybe he could make a house call? That was what he'd do for any of the pack, so why not Seb?


Two hours later, Tim was showered, fed, and waiting on the doorstep of Nathan's building. He'd texted Gareth to let him know he was coming— pack courtesy—and waited for whoever was on patrol to come and let him in. He should really have texted Nathan too, but he hadn't.

When the familiar figure appeared in the hallway, Tim groaned. *Just my fucking luck.*

"Hey." Nathan opened the front door and stood back to let him pass. His expression gave nothing away. "Thought we might see you today."

Tim shrugged and smiled, relaxing a little when Nathan returned it. "Just checking on my patient."

Nathan's raised eyebrow let Tim know he saw right through him. It wasn't as though Tim could hide his attraction to Seb, especially not from Nathan. "Is that so?"

Tim sighed as he walked inside and Nathan shut and bolted the door behind him. "You're not the one on patrol, are you?"

"No. Luke is." He made no move towards the stairs, so Tim leaned against the wall and waited for whatever it was Nathan wanted to say. "I thought you might come today, so I asked him to let me know when you showed up."

"Fuck. Am I that obvious?"

Nathan laughed. "Well, you do look at Seb with this sort of hungry expression. Jared just thinks you want to fuck him."

"And you? What do you think?" Tim bit his lip as Nathan studied him. *He* didn't know what he wanted from Seb, so he didn't expect Nathan to have the answers.

"I think it's more than that. You got pretty defensive at his flat on Friday night."

Tim winced. He hadn't lost control like that in a long while. "I didn't mean to scare Jared, but—"

"He insulted you. I get it." Nathan stood to his full height and smirked. "Besides, he has me to protect him. He wasn't scared." Tim's huff of surprised laughter had them both grinning, and Nathan joined him leaning against the wall. "I know Jared's mouthy and doesn't care much for pack etiquette, but he didn't mean to insult you. He was just worried about Seb."

"Yeah, I know." Tim liked Jared, a lot. And he was well aware of Jared's thoughts on some of the pack rules and on shifters in general. Being bonded to Nathan had changed some of his opinions on shifters as a whole, and most of the time it made Tim laugh. "I don't know why I reacted that way."

"Don't give me that bollocks." Nathan gave him a pointed look. "I've been there, remember?"

Tim scoffed. "This is so not the same thing, Nate. I'm not bonded to Sebastian Calloway and he's not my mate. He's *human*."

"So is Jared," Nathan shot back.

"Yeah, but you bit him and then fucked him." Tim sighed. He was finished with this conversation. "I've done neither of those things."

Nathan leaned in close and whispered, "But you want to."

His words made Tim's jaw tingle with the need to shift and bare his teeth. His heart thudded.

Nathan added a bit more. "You want him to be yours. And that's why you reacted like that."

*Fuck.* The idea of sinking his teeth into Seb's neck, feeling that snap of the connection as it bound them together… it made his chest ache and his dick throb. "Seb doesn't want any of that. You know he doesn't."

"Neither did Jared," Nathan replied softly.

Tim snapped his gaze up. "I'm not going to force—"

"I didn't mean that, for fuck's sake." At least now Nathan looked as horrified as Tim felt. "I just meant that people can change their mind, that's all. Get to know him better. If his opinions of shifters are anything like Jared's were, then you need to show him that you're not like that."

"Like what, exactly?" Tim knew all about Nathan biting Jared and then essentially kidnapping him, but by the time he met them, the bond was well and truly in place.

"When I first met Jared, he hated all shifters on principle. Thought they were arrogant, selfish, with no regard for humans whatsoever." Nathan glanced up at the ceiling and smiled.

Tim sighed. "Nate, you and Jared *bonded*, for fuck's sake. You had a little help changing his mind. How am I supposed to convince Seb that we're not all like that, when his best friend was first put in the hospital by one and then bitten and kidnapped by another?" Nathan growled but Tim dismissed him with a wave. Too bad if he didn't like hearing the truth. "And anyway, Jared still thinks most shifters are arrogant arseholes."

Nathan was silent for several tense seconds, and Tim wondered if he was about to be asked to leave. It wasn't as though he had any official business here, after all. "I didn't say it would be easy." He glanced at Tim and smiled, small but honest. "But if there's any chance you could feel like I do, then you need to take it." Keeping his gaze locked with Tim's, Nathan ran a hand over his own chest. "Being with Jared now is worth all the shit we went through to get here."

Tim looked at him, unsure what to say to that. All he'd wanted to do was come and see how Seb was. Bonded? Did he want that? And if he did, did he want it with Seb? He shook his head at the thought. "Look, Nate, I'm happy that things worked out for you and Jared. But I can't imagine that Seb would want me to bite him, and we both know that's my best hope of creating a bond."

Nathan cocked his head to one side. "If you have no intention of pursuing this, then why are you here? Me and Jared can take him to hospital."

"I know that. I just—" *Just what?* "—wanted to check up on my patient."

"Uh-huh. Of course you did."

And yeah, Tim totally deserved the sceptical look Nathan aimed at him.

All this talk about Seb and bonding had set him on edge. The full moon was almost two weeks away, but he felt his wolf close to the surface, his body itching to shift. He shook out his shoulders in an effort to quell it. "Are you going to take me up, or are we going to stand here and chat all day?"

The roughness of Tim's voice had Nathan raising his eyebrows. "Calm down, doc. I'm not taking you up there like that."

Tim took a deep breath in and let it out slowly. "I'm fine." Thankfully he sounded back to normal, and he followed it up with what he hoped resembled a smile. "Really." Nathan continued to study him, subtly scenting the air, and Tim fought to regain his usual calm. "Honestly. I just want to check the swelling on his ankle and wrist."

Nathan pushed off the wall with a sigh. "Come on, then."

Jared met them in the hall after Nathan let them inside the flat. Jared's face was a picture of surprise when he saw Tim. "Oh hey, Tim."

"Hey."

"Wasn't expecting to see you so soon." Jared smiled and glanced down the hall to the bedrooms. "Come to check on Seb?"

Jared didn't seem to think it was odd, not like Nathan had, and Tim relaxed more. Maybe Nathan hadn't mentioned anything to him.

"Yeah." He lifted his medical bag a little for Jared to see. "How's he doing?" Jared laughed and made a seesaw motion with his hand. "That bad, huh?"

"Let's just say he's discovering how difficult it is to do things with an injured wrist and ankle, and he's not very impressed."

"Pissed off and grumpy as fuck," Nathan chimed in. "Unless he's perked up in the last fifteen minutes?"

"Not so much, no." Jared met Tim's gaze and narrowed his eyes slightly. "Seeing you might cheer him up. He was singing your praises last night."

Tim tried not to smile too widely at that, but he failed miserably. "Oh?"

Nathan laughed behind him and muttered "Told you people change their minds" just for Tim's ears.

"Yeah," Jared carried on, oblivious. "You and your brother made quite an impression."

*Bloody David.*

*I will not be jealous of my brother.* "I'm glad we could help."

All three of them now stood in the hall. Seb's scent was a subtle undertone to Jared's and Nathan's, teasing him. "Is he in his room or…?" He gestured to the living room.

"Oh, he's in the spare room. Dressed," Jared added, when Tim hesitated. "Apparently lying in bed is comfier than being on the sofa. Go on through." He moved aside to let Tim pass.

Tim was well acquainted with the master bedroom after treating an injured Nathan in there a few months back. The door to the bathroom stood wide open, so by default the one left had to be the guest room. It sounded quiet inside, just Seb's breathing interrupted by the soft tapping of keys on a phone or tablet. After knocking gently, Tim waited for Seb to answer.

"Come in."

The door creaked and Tim lingered in the doorway. "Hey."

"Oh, hey." Seb smiled widely and set his phone down on the bed next to him. "Are you here to check up on me, or…?"

"Something like that." Tim smiled back and moved farther into the room. He'd dressed casually in a grey long-sleeved T-shirt and black jeans. In hindsight, if he'd wanted to make this a professional visit, he should have dressed more appropriately. *Too late now.* "You're looking much better."

"Thanks. I feel it." Seb glanced down at his wrist, then his ankle. "Well, I don't have a headache, anyway. These still hurt, though."

Tim moved to sit on the edge of the bed, then hesitated. "May I?"

"Sure."

He sat down, careful not to jostle Seb. "Mind if I take a quick look at you?"

Seb gave him a curious look. "No. That's the reason you came, right?"

"Um, yeah." *So unprofessional.* He took hold of Seb's wrist and carefully inspected it. "How's the pain? Better, worse... about the same?"

Seb winced and Tim set his hand back down on the bed.

"About the same."

"Good. What about your ankle?" He shuffled around to get a better look at it, but didn't touch it. They'd check it soon enough in the fracture clinic. "How's that feeling?"

"Hurts like a bitch."

"Yeah, I bet." Tim chuckled and Seb glared at him. "Sorry. It'll feel better with a proper cast on it. Give it more support."

They lapsed into silence.

Tim struggled to think of something to say that sounded even remotely related to Seb's injuries. "Any other aches and pains?"

"Nope. Just a bit knackered still." Seb fiddled with the edge of the quilt cover, then shot a quick glance at the door. "Can you close that for a sec?"

Tim immediately wondered what Seb wanted the privacy for, but he refused to let his thoughts get carried away.

Seb waited for him to sit back down on the bed. "Look, thanks for not telling anyone about what I said to you at the hospital."

"Which bit?" As required, Tim had given Alec a brief rundown when he'd spoken to him, but he'd been reluctant to share all of what Seb said. It felt wrong to do so without asking him first, even though Seb was probably aware there were very few secrets in a shifter pack. So Tim had withheld some of it.

"About my suspicions that someone was following me."

"Ahh." Yeah, Alec would be pissed off at him if he found out about that titbit of information, but it wasn't as though Seb had proof. It was just a feeling at this point. "Did you tell Jared about it?"

Seb's gaze darted away, now fixing on the very interesting bandage wrapped around his wrist. "Um…."

"I'm guessing that's a no."

"I could be imagining it. I mean, it's not like I can smell them nearby or anything."

Seb sighed and ran a hand through his hair, the movement capturing Tim's attention. Unlike Jared's bright blond—Tim knew he dyed it—Seb's hair looked a natural dark blond, was shaved at the sides and long on top. Tim idly wondered what the shaved bits would feel like under his fingers.

"Still worth mentioning, though." As he sat and watched Seb playing with the long strands of hair that fell into his face, the more he thought Seb should mention it. Jared had Nathan watching out for him if any other shifters looked his way, but who did Seb have? Tim pushed away the small voice in his head that whispered *me*. "Better to be on the safe side."

"You're probably right." Seb picked up his phone from off the bed. "After I get back from the hospital, though. If I start that conversation now, I'll never make my appointment."

"About that…." Tim debated whether to take the turn in conversation for the opportunity it was. Kind of. "I'm headed there anyway this afternoon, and I wondered if you wanted to come with me?"

Seb glanced at the closed door, then back at him. "You sure?"

He looked torn, and Tim wished he knew what was going through his mind. "Yes. It'll save Jared a trip out."

"Well, in that case, that'd be great."

Seb smiled, his blue-green eyes crinkling at the corners, and Tim's heart gave a traitorous flutter. Maybe coming here was a bad idea, after all. The more time he spent with Seb, the more he wanted him. The fact Seb was hurt and needed taking care of called to both the doctor part of him and the wolf inside. *I'm so fucked.*

Unless Nathan was right? Could he get to know Seb better and show him that some shifters were worth the effort? Whatever the outcome, he had to try. "You about ready? We should probably get going soon. I'm not sure what the traffic'll be like on a Sunday afternoon."

"Shitty, I'm sure. Like every other day." Seb carefully swung his legs off the bed and put his good foot on the floor. "And yeah, I'm ready to go. Might as well head out now." His crutch leaned against the wall next to the bed and he reached for it, pushing himself up. When he wobbled slightly, Tim stood without thinking and slid an arm around Seb's waist to steady him.

As his fingers settled on Seb's hip, he realised what he was doing and faltered. "Sorry, I—"

Seb's eyes met Tim's for the briefest of moments, and Tim's breath caught. It would take nothing to pull him closer, angle his body so they faced each other, and—

"Thanks." Seb leaned on his crutch and adjusted his weight. "Still getting used to it."

"No problem," Tim husked. Reluctantly he let go and took a couple of steps back. "After you."

He followed as Seb made his way towards the kitchen, where Jared's voice filtered out.

Watching him hobble through the hallway was tough. Every few steps, Seb muttered about his palm being sore and couldn't they make crutches with better grips? Whether he knew Tim could hear or not, it still made him want to knock that damn crutch out of the way and take its place. He kept his hands fisted by his side so that he wasn't tempted to do it.

Jared and Nathan were leaning against the kitchen worktop; they looked up as Seb entered.

"Fuck me," Seb groused, propping the crutch beside Jared and rubbing his hand. "Why couldn't I have hurt my left hand? It's so fucking awkward like this."

Jared snorted. "Yeah, must be hard. I know how much you use that right hand."

Nathan laughed and high-fived him. Seb gave him them both the finger, and Tim prayed the flare of arousal that comment had caused wasn't strong enough for Nathan to notice.

"Do you want to leave now?" Jared asked, fishing his car keys out of his jeans pocket.

"I do, but Tim's offered to take me." Seb glanced at Tim as he spoke, a small smile in place.

Jared looked from Tim to Seb and back again, his expression far less friendly. "Has he, now?"

The edge to Jared's voice took Tim by surprise. He liked Jared, considered the pair of them friends, and the only time he'd had that tone directed at him was when Nathan had lain beaten and bloody on their bed. A prickle of unease started at the base of his spine and he stood a little straighter. "Is there a problem with that?"

Jared sighed. "No, sorry." The edge was gone, but Tim still got the feeling he wasn't happy about something. "It's just…." Jared's gaze flicked back to Seb, brow furrowed. "Look, I know it's none of my business, and I like you, Tim, but—"

"*Jared*," Seb hissed, his gaze boring holes into the side of Jared's head.

Jared turned to face him. "What? I know what shifters are like, okay? And I know he's interested in way more than—"

"For fuck's sake, J." Seb grabbed his crutch, shoved it under his arm, and aimed an angry glare Jared's way. "I'm twenty-six, not sixteen. And you're right, this is none of your business."

Nathan looked annoyed too, and Tim got the feeling they'd be having words after he and Seb left.

Not wanting whatever this was to escalate, Tim cleared his throat to get everyone's attention. "I'm not sure what your issue is, Jared, but I promise you he's in good hands. I'm going to the hospital anyway to see David." *Well, I am now.* "So I offered to take Seb. I thought it made sense, that's all."

"It makes perfect sense. Ignore J." Seb shooed Tim forward with the end of his crutch. "I'll see you two later. And we're going to have a nice long chat about me going back home."

"Seb—"

"Bye, J." Seb walked out of the kitchen, and Tim nodded at Nathan and Jared before going after him.

As they opened the front door, Tim heard Nathan say a little pissily, "So, what *are* shifters like, exactly?" Tim snorted as he pulled the door shut after them. He had a feeling he knew what Jared had been getting at, and while Tim appreciated him being concerned for his friend, he didn't like what he'd implied. As if he would ever force Seb into anything. The very idea of anyone doing that made his hackles rise.

"What's so funny?" Seb eyed him suspiciously as they walked towards the stairwell.

"Didn't you hear Nathan just then?" Tim hadn't realised it'd been too quiet for Seb, but Seb shook his head. Tim filled him in.

"Ouch." He grinned, though. "Serves him right for being so bloody...." Seb's smile dimmed, and when he met Tim's gaze, he seemed sheepish.

God, this really wasn't a conversation Tim wanted to have. "Jared's opinion of shifters hasn't changed all that much, has it?" he asked, letting Seb lead the way towards the stairwell. "I thought with him and Nathan bonded, he'd realise...." He sighed and scrubbed at his forehead. "He appears to be under the impression that I'm going to take advantage of you and somehow coerce you into having sex with me."

Seb stumbled before righting himself and slowly turned to face Tim. "He actually said that?"

"Not in so many words, but the implication was there. Apparently he still sees shifters in a less than favourable light, and Nathan isn't too pleased with him." Though knowing the way those two were with each other, Tim guessed it would last all of five minutes before that changed and they were all over each other again. Newly mated couples had a hard time keeping their hands off each other, and Jared and Nathan took that to another level entirely—not that he was jealous. Much.

Seb glanced back down the hallway before meeting Tim's gaze. "The thing with Jared is…." He paused, looking conflicted.

"I know about his shifter boyfriend before Nathan, and what he did to Jared."

"Oh."

"I wanted his medical history before the first full moon, so we knew what we were dealing with." Tim totally understood Jared's wariness around shifters then, but that was almost three months ago. Didn't he know them all well enough by now to see that the Regent's Park pack weren't like that? That *he* wasn't like that?

As if reading his mind, Seb reached out with his injured wrist and rested his fingers gently on Tim's arm. "It was a fucking awful time for him, and it's probably going to take a while yet for him to fully trust that not every shifter is an arsehole. It's nothing personal."

Tim scoffed. "It certainly felt like it."

62

"Believe me when I say that Jared likes you. A lot." Seb grinned, and even though Tim still smarted from Jared's comments, he couldn't help but smile back.

"Hmm." He remained unconvinced—he used to think so too until Seb got injured.

"He does. But me getting hurt—albeit indirectly—because of shifters brings back a lot of painful memories for him."

Tim's shoulders slumped as he let that sink in. Having been a shifter all his life, he had no appreciation of what it was like to feel that vulnerable, to know that no matter how physically strong you were, the person you were with could snap you like a twig. Jared had trusted a shifter not to use his advantage against him, and it had ended badly. And now Seb was hurt, indirectly because of shifter activity. No wonder Jared was a little tetchy.

"Fuck, I didn't think." He made to take a step back towards Nathan and Jared's flat, but Seb caught the edge of his sleeve.

"Where are you going?"

"Back to apologise."

"To Jared?" When Tim nodded, Seb raised his eyebrows. "I never said he wasn't being a dick, just that he had his reasons. I wanted you to understand where he was coming from, but that doesn't mean he has a right to talk to you like that."

Tim opened his mouth and then closed it, not sure what to say.

Seb gestured down the hallway. "Can anyone hear what we're saying? I forget what's soundproofed and what isn't."

"I doubt it. I suspect the pair of them are otherwise occupied by now, anyway."

Seb laughed loudly. "Yeah, you're probably right. Come on." He faced forward again and walked the few steps to the door to the stairs, but stopped once they walked through. "Shit, I forgot about these." His cheeks flushed with colour and he glanced up at the ceiling with a sigh, adding in a small voice, "I could probably make it down easily enough, but not being able to grab onto the handrail makes me kind of nervous."

He looked anywhere but at Tim, embarrassment clear in his expression. Before the moment could get awkward—and giving Seb no chance to object—Tim scooped him up, bridal style, and started down the stairs.

Letting out a startled laugh, Seb clung tight to his crutch so it didn't slip out of his hands. "Twice in one weekend. You're going to give me a complex."

Tim bit the inside of his cheek. If Seb knew how much he liked being able to take care of him, how much his *wolf* liked it, he wouldn't find it half as amusing or embarrassing. Clearing his throat, he hitched him a little higher, then started down the stairs. "It's just quicker this way, and I don't want to make you late for your appointment. We're running a little behind."

"Fair enough."

Not daring to meet Seb's eyes—their faces were so close together, he didn't like his chances of not doing something stupid like kissing him—Tim quickly made his way down the steps. But there was a question on the tip of his tongue that he couldn't suppress. As he set Seb on his feet again, he asked, "What about you?"

"Hmm?"

"How do you feel about getting involved with shifters?" He knew Seb's thoughts on being part of the pack, but what about shifters themselves? Although Jared had made it clear what Seb's views were, Tim wanted to hear it for himself. Maybe then he could stop kidding himself that he had a chance with Seb.

Seb held his gaze for several seconds before gesturing to the front doors. "Let's talk in the car."

Tim couldn't decide whether that sounded ominous or not.

# Chapter Five

*"How do you feel about getting involved with shifters?"*
Well, wasn't that the million-dollar question? And
not one Seb felt prepared to answer. Before he
could open the front door to Nathan's building,
Tim stopped him and slipped in front of him.

"Let me go first." He opened it a few inches
and took a deep breath.

Seb never ceased to find it odd and sometimes
a little funny when shifters did that. But knowing
why Tim had his nose in the air this time only made
him tense. Did Tim really think some rival pack
member might be waiting for them? Seb wasn't
important enough to warrant that sort of attention.
Okay, so they'd messed with him a bit at the flat,
but he mostly thought that was because it was
Jared's old place and right on their doorstep. But
would they take the trouble to venture into another
pack's territory? From everything he'd read, Seb
thought it highly unlikely. But then, what did he
really know? "I told you I probably imagined being
followed, and I seriously doubt anyone would
follow me here, of all places."

Tim glanced over his shoulder. "We don't
know why they were at your flat the other night,
and I'm not taking any chances with your safety."

His low, serious tone sent a shiver down Seb's
spine. Having someone look out for him like this
was addictive. Especially when that someone was
tall, dark-haired, and sexy as hell… and would have
no trouble picking him up and fucking him against
a wall. Seb didn't want to find the whole protective
thing hot, but he couldn't help it. Tim's strength lay

hidden inside his toned but relatively slim build, not openly on display like a lot of the hugely muscled shifters Seb had seen before. If anything, that made him more curious to—*No*. No. No matter how hot the doctor was, a relationship with a shifter wasn't something Seb was after anytime soon. Or ever. And he had the feeling Tim wasn't a one-night stand kind of guy. "Anything?" he asked, stepping up close behind him and trying to peer over his shoulder.

Tim smelled like spicy citrus shower gel and something else Seb couldn't identify, just really fucking good, and Seb immediately took a step back.

"No. We're good to go." Tim opened the door wider and held it for Seb to hobble through.

"Thanks."

As soon as they were settled in the car with their seat belts fastened, Tim started the engine. "Are you going to answer my question?"

His head was turned away as he concentrated on pulling out into traffic, and Seb couldn't get a good look at his expression.

"Yeah." He leaned his head against the headrest and closed his eyes. The dull throb of his wrist and ankle gave him something to focus on while he searched for the right words. "I've been with shifters before. Not many," he added when Tim's hands tightened on the steering wheel. *Fuck, I don't have to reassure him.* "Anyway, I never had a problem with them, even after what happened to Jared. I mean, don't get me wrong, I hated that fucker and anyone who acted as entitled as he did, but I never hated *all* shifters. Not like Jared did. He had every reason to, and I supported him, but I figured not all of you had to be that bad."

Tim snorted. "How generous of you."

"I thought so."

A few beats of silence, and then Tim said softly, "I'm sure you know that I like you."

Seb didn't want to have all this out in the open. He liked spending time with Tim and selfishly wanted to keep doing it, but he couldn't string him along. "Yeah, I know."

"And forgive me for saying this, but I can't help my senses, and I get the impression you like me too."

"It's not that simple."

Tim sighed and waited for the traffic lights to turn green before speaking. "Why isn't it? You said yourself you don't feel as strongly as Jared, so—"

"That was before he and Nathan bonded." He covered his face with his good hand and let out a harsh breath. *Why did I choose to have this conversation in the car, where there's no fucking escape?*

As they turned the next corner, the hospital loomed up ahead, and Seb had never been so pleased to see the place.

"I don't understand? Jared loves Nathan. They're happy."

Seb waited for Tim to pull into the car park and find a space. "I'm telling you this because you deserve to know why I don't want to pursue anything with you." Tim flinched and Seb felt a stab of guilt, but he just couldn't do that. "It goes no farther than this car."

Tim glanced around the car park, then nodded. "Okay."

68

Shit, Seb hadn't even considered other shifters being able to hear them. He really needed to talk to Jared about their range of hearing and any other shit to watch out for. "I know Jared loves Nathan, and I know he's happy. I'm happy for him. But honestly? The whole way that happened scares the shit out of me. And it's as creepy as fuck."

"Oh."

Tim looked offended, but Seb was on a roll. He'd had this bottled up inside for months with no one to talk to—God knew he didn't want Jared to ever realise he felt that way—and unfortunately, Tim was about to get the full force of it.

"If you'd seen Jared before Nathan bit him, you'd know how hard it was to watch my best friend go from hating all shifters with a fiery passion to telling me 'Hey, I changed my mind. This one's not so bad.' At first I thought Nathan was forcing him to say that shit, that Jared was there against his will, and I was so close to reporting it to the police."

"Why didn't you?"

Seb laughed. "Good question." He unclipped his seat belt, just for something to do. "I suppose because he's my best friend and he asked me to trust him."

Tim sat staring through the windshield. "Do you wish you'd told the police?"

"No, of course not." Although a tiny part of him wondered whether Jared would've been better off if he had. He squashed it down quickly. "Whether I approve or not, Jared's the happiest I've seen him, and I'd never want to take that away from him. But it's not something I want."

"To be happy?"

Seb frowned and turned his head to find Tim watching him. "You know that's not what I meant. I don't want to have some magical shifter bollocks decide who I fall in love with. I can do that all on my own, thanks."

"Jared and Nathan were a special case. A bond is incredibly rare between a human and a shifter. You must know that?"

"Yes, but accidents happen. I know enough shifter lore to understand that if we're fucking and you get carried away and bite me, then it's bam! Instant bond."

Tim's mouth fell open in shock, and it took him a moment to answer. "I would never bite you against your will, Seb. *Never.*" He seemed so horrified by the idea of it that Seb felt a stab of guilt.

He softened his voice when he replied with "I'm sure that's what Nathan used to say too."

"That was different, for fuck's sake! He was in the middle of a fight, and Jared was in the wrong place at the wrong time."

"*But he still did it.*" Seb reached up to rub at his temples. All this arguing had given him a headache. "I'm just trying to explain how I feel." He met Tim's unhappy gaze and offered him a small smile. "I like you, Tim, I really do. But the thought of having my free will stripped away like that terrifies me. I'm sorry."

His words settled between them like a wall, and Seb immediately missed the ease of before. But he couldn't have it both ways.

Tim pulled his phone out of his pocket, and tapped at the screen. "I've asked my brother to meet us with a wheelchair."

Seb didn't protest. "Thank you."

A few minutes later, David walked out of the hospital entrance, not from A&E this time.

"No problem. He's not strictly supposed to be working in the fracture clinic, but pack is pack."

A couple of hours after a very chatty David wheeled him inside, Seb had a bright blue cast on his ankle and a new dressing on his wrist.

Unfortunately, David had been called back to A&E just before Seb was finished, so Tim pushed him back to the car with considerably less cheer than his brother. And that was all Seb's doing, which sucked because he'd only been honest.

Whatever was on Tim's mind had him frowning as he unlocked the car and opened Seb's door. Odds were it was something to do with their previous conversation, so Seb didn't pry. That left an awkward silence between them, and Seb sighed heavily as he dropped into the passenger seat. The journey home was going to be such fun.

About two miles from the hospital, they met traffic. Seb barely stifled a groan. Excellent, an extended journey time—just what they needed. They inched along at a snail's pace.

Eventually, Seb spotted the flashing blue lights of a police car. "Must've been an accident."

"Hmm."

Out of the corner of his eye, Seb saw Tim biting at his bottom lip. He had the look of a man warring with whether to speak or not, and Seb waited to see which he decided.

The car crept ever closer to the accident, which appeared to be a rear-end shunt blocking the inside lane, and just as Seb relaxed as it looked as though no one was injured, Tim spoke.

"We could just be friends."

Seb snapped his head back round to stare at him. "Friends?"

"Yeah."

He couldn't help it; he laughed. "I don't think that would work." *Friends? Jesus.*

"Why not?"

*Where to start?* "Because I don't think I could spend time with you and not want more."

Tim's brow crinkled in confusion. "Then I don't understand what the problem—"

"Liking you isn't the problem, I already told you that. If we spend time together, I'm going to want more. We're both going to want more. It's hard enough saying no to you now, so it'll be twice as hard to say it further down the line, and I can't risk being in that position. Even with you."

The hurt in Tim's eyes made it difficult to meet his gaze, but Seb forced himself not to look away. "You can trust me," Tim said. "I promise."

His mind spun with all the things Jared had told him. How out of control he'd felt at times, the pull between himself and Nathan too strong to fight. Seb shook his head. He didn't want that. "I'm sorry. I just can't."

Tim parked outside of Nathan's building but didn't turn off the engine. He slipped his phone out of his pocket and made a call. "We're back." Then he listened for a few seconds. "Yeah, please. See you in a sec." Turning to Seb, he smiled, but it was nothing like the smiles from that morning. "They're on their way down."

"Both of them?" Seb rolled his eyes. He didn't need a welcoming committee, just a hand up the stairs.

"Yep."

Tim sat stiffly in his seat, and Seb had the urge to reach out and rub the tension out of his shoulders, but he refrained. "You not coming up, then?"

"No. I've got a few things to do before I head home."

*I bet he'd have given a different answer if I'd agreed to be just friends.* "Okay. Well, thanks for taking me today. I really appreciate it."

The smile he got this time was a lot more genuine. Warmer. "You're welcome." He nodded to the cast. "And if you need anything, you can call me anytime." He looked up, dark blue eyes fixed on him in a way that made Seb's heart thud. "I mean it."

"Thank you."

Tim glanced up, and when Seb followed his gaze, he saw Nathan opening the front door, with Jared hot on his heels. Nathan paused, a hand on Jared's chest to keep him back before continuing down the steps. *Ever vigilant.* Seb wondered if they were always on such high alert or if this was all for his benefit. They'd be at the car soon, and then Tim would leave. He'd probably not return for a while if his hurt expression was anything to go by.

Seb slumped in his seat. *Why does doing the right thing seem to suck so much lately?*

Being bonded to someone wasn't something he wanted. The thought alone terrified him, so why

73

didn't he feel better about telling Tim no? He'd stuck by his principles, been strong. That should feel good, right? "I still don't have your number." The words fell out without his permission.

Tim frowned, so Seb added, "In case I need anything. Hey, you offered. You can't throw that out there and then leave me with no way to contact you."

*What the hell am I doing?*

"Jared's got it. Nathan too. I told you that." Tim narrowed his eyes a little, as if trying to decide what Seb's angle was.

Maybe when he found out, he could let Seb know, because all Seb could think of was not wanting to leave without having a way to get in touch with Tim. It felt wrong. "But what if they're not around? It could be an emergency, and—"

"*Sebastian.*"

It rolled off Tim's tongue, slow and seductive like a soft purr. Seb wanted to hear his full name all the time if it sounded like that. Fuck it, he needed to get out of the car and stop giving the poor guy mixed messages. *Why does he have to be so hot, and so nice, and just about everything I want in a guy? Why does he have to be a shifter?* "Sorry. You're right. I'll get it from Jared if I need it."

Nathan and Jared stood a few steps away from the car. Seb reluctantly undid his seat belt and reached for the door handle. "Goodbye, Tim."

"Wait."

Seb glanced back to see Tim thumbing through his wallet; he dug out a dog-eared business card and thrust it at him. Without a word, Seb took it, slipped it into his pocket, and got out of the car. Jared hung back, giving him space, and Seb hobbled over to him. Nathan ducked his head inside the car to talk to Tim.

"Nice." Jared nodded at his cast and Seb smiled. "How's it feeling?"

"Hurts, but I have painkillers, and it's not as bad as it was." He shrugged. "But it'll be about six weeks before I get the cast off."

"Sucks." Jared grimaced in sympathy. "What about your wrist?"

The new compression bandage poked out from under Seb's jacket. He flexed his fingers a little. "Fortunately that's only a mild sprain and should heal nicely all on its own. Apparently I need to start gentle exercises soon so that it doesn't stiffen up."

Jared smiled, albeit a little tightly, and rocked back on his heels. "Well, that's good news at least."

"Yeah."

"Look, Seb." Jared fidgeted under Seb's stare. "I'm really sorry about—"

*Fuck no, not again.* "Stop. We've been through this already. It's not your fault, or Nathan's. I don't blame either of you, and I'm not angry, so can we please just drop it?"

Jared's smile widened. "Yeah, okay."

"Good."

Nathan came up behind him then and slipped his arm around Jared's waist. He ducked his head and nuzzled at Jared's neck with a small contented sound. Seb looked away from them, just in time to see Tim's car pull off from the kerb. The two things together set off a flare of irritation, and as quickly as he could manage, he spun around and headed for the door to Nathan's building.

Since he couldn't exactly speed away, Jared easily caught up to him. "Hey, what's up with you?"

75

"Nothing."

Jared fell into step beside him, with Nathan on his other side. "You sure about that?"

"Yep."

Of course Nathan couldn't keep out of it. Of course. "Tim didn't look too happy either, and the inside of his car reeked of unresolved sexual tension."

Seb stopped, leaned on his crutch, and stared at Nathan. "You can't fucking smell that." He turned to Jared for clarification. "Can he? Is that a thing that has a… a… scent?" *Fucking ridiculous.* And even if it did have, there was absolutely none of that going on in Tim's car. *Liar, liar, pants on fire.* To his utter mortification, Seb felt his face heat.

Nathan laughed. "Fine, it doesn't. But other things do, and someone in that car was thinking about sex." He didn't add "And I bet it was you," but he gave Seb a look that spoke for him.

"Whatever. Can we just get inside? My leg hurts and I need to elevate it for a bit." He set off for the door again, and once they were inside, Nathan scooped him up without bothering to ask first and carried him up the stairs.

Seb couldn't find the energy to be pissed off at him, and if he was honest, it was a relief not to have to navigate his own way up. He hadn't lied to them; his ankle throbbed in earnest now and his bed called to him. In fact, Nathan might just as well carry him all the way into the guest bedroom, because a nap sounded pretty fucking appealing right about then.

When Seb suggested this he got the expected sarcastic reply, but his yawn clearly swayed Nathan, because he didn't set him down until they were next to his bed.

"Thanks," Seb mumbled through another yawn.

Nathan rolled his eyes. "Lazy bastard." The playful tone took the sting out of it, and he turned to leave Seb to it.

Jared lingered just inside the doorway. "You okay? I mean, apart from the obvious."

Seb sighed. *Am I that transparent?* Sometimes he hated how well he and Jared knew each other. "No. Maybe…. I don't know."

"Does it have anything to do with Tim and what I said earlier? Because Nathan already gave me shit for that." He looked a little sheepish, and Seb grinned up at him. "I know I was out of line, and I'm going to apologise to Tim. I just…. I'm worried about you."

"I know." Patting the bed next to him, Seb wondered how that conversation with Nathan had gone down. He'd bet good money it had ended with sex. Everything those two did ended with sex. "And you don't have to worry, you know. There's nothing going on between me and Tim."

Jared stared at him for a couple of seconds. "Really? Because I know he wants you, and according to Nathan, you want in the doctor's pants too."

"For fuck's sake, keep your nose out of my business," Seb hissed, facing the open door.

Nathan's laughter rang out from the kitchen and he shouted back, "Stop lusting after him, then."

Seb rolled his eyes and turned back to Jared to whisper, "I do *not* lust after him." He sighed. "And besides, there's no way I'm getting involved with a shifter. You know that."

"Is that my fault too?"

"What do you mean?"

Jared scooted back on the bed beside him and lay down with his hands behind his head. "You never used to feel like this. Before Nathan you were the one who thought not all of them were arrogant arseholes."

"That's not changed."

"But Tim—"

"Is a nice guy. I just don't want to get involved with him." Seb really hoped Jared would leave it at that. No way was he explaining that Jared and Nathan's bond was the main reason he didn't want to. "So," he said, shuffling back against the headboard until his foot rested comfortably on the bed. *God, that's better.* He lowered his voice again until it was barely a whisper. "You never did answer me about Nathan and Alec."

Jared turned his head to face him. "I said I didn't know."

"Yeah, but I thought you'd have asked him by now. Aren't you curious? I mean, even I could see that there's something going on with those two, and Tim swears Alec's a good guy." He smirked. "But he's not too keen on your boy, though, is he? And don't tell him I said anything."

Jared stared at him with an incredulous expression. "You do realise he can still hear you even when you whisper?"

"Even when it's that quiet?"

"Yep, even then." Nathan's voice at the doorway startled them both.

Seb glared at him. "Jesus, don't do that."

Nathan grinned back at him, all teeth. "Don't *whisper* about me, then."

He had a point. "Yeah, okay. Sorry." Nathan didn't make a move to leave again, so Seb figured he might as well ask. "Now that you're here, then, what's up with you and Alec? If you don't mind me asking," he added as an afterthought. Shifters got funny about pack stuff, and Seb would rather avoid pissing Nathan off if he could help it.

A dark look crossed Nathan's features, and for a second Seb assumed he was going to refuse, but then he glanced at the ceiling with a sigh. "I insulted him in front of the whole pack."

Seb frowned. "That's it?" The way Alec and Nathan interacted seemed far too hostile to be caused by a few words. "What the hell did you say?"

"It was more than enough, trust me." Nathan glanced at Jared briefly.

Seb got the feeling that he was about to tell them something that even Jared didn't know about. Was it wrong that he was getting a little excited at the prospect? Probably. But Nathan acted like this was a big reveal, so what did he expect?

Nathan's eyes locked with Seb's. "Both my parents were killed in the pack wars. You know about those, right?"

Seb nodded. He knew enough.

"Well, Alec was in my parents' unit. He was the youngest member." Nathan had trained his gaze on the far wall, but Seb wondered if he saw any of it. He looked miles away. "Six of them went out on patrol, and only Alec came back."

*Oh fuck.* Seb wished he'd never asked. He was expecting a bit of juicy gossip, maybe, but certainly not this. "Nathan, you don't have to—"

"It's okay." Nathan's small, sad smile made Seb feel even shittier. He couldn't even look at Jared. "You're both pack now. And if you're going to interact with Alec, which at the minute seems likely, then you should probably know why he acts so cold and unimpressed. Towards me, anyway."

Seb didn't really want to have to deal with any more of Nathan's pack, let alone any of the betas, but he kept quiet.

Nathan focused on Jared now, and whatever look Jared gave him in return seemed to strengthen his resolve because he stood a little straighter before continuing. "After they came back, there was a pack meeting to discuss what happened and plan our response to it. Killing almost a whole unit couldn't go unavenged. Our alpha at the time was… well, he wasn't Cam, and towards the end, the lives of his pack became less important than exacting immediate revenge." Nathan swallowed, and Seb found himself leaning forward a little, silently urging him to continue. "Cam was a family friend at the time. He warned me to stay away from the meeting—I was devastated about my parent's death, but also very angry at everyone, and as the sole survivor of the patrol, Alec took the brunt of it." The heavy sigh Nathan let out made his impressive shoulders sag. "I stormed into that room, accusing Alec of letting them die. How could he possibly have got away when no one else did? In front of the whole pack, I said he probably ran at the first sign of trouble. Cam pulled me out of there before I actually used the word *coward*, but I'd as good as called him it anyway."

"*Nathan*." Jared's tone was soft and comforting, and Seb figured from the way he immediately stood and went to wrap his arms around his mate, calling another shifter a coward was a big fucking deal. "What happened then?"

Although muffled against Jared's shoulder, Nathan was loud enough for Seb to hear. Just.

"Nothing. I should have been punished. By rights, Alec could have challenged me to a fight for what I said, but Cam intervened. Cam said I was young and grief-stricken, that my parents' death had made me act without thinking, and I couldn't be held responsible for my actions. I was let off with a warning. Our alpha told Cam to take me home and talk some sense into me, warn me how lucky I'd been, and above all to keep me away from any future pack meetings."

Seb waited for Jared to step back a bit. Then he said, "If your alpha accepted you'd said all that because you were too upset to think clearly, why didn't Alec?"

"I don't know. Maybe he would have if I'd ever apologised."

*Oh.*

Jared slipped his hand around Nathan's. "Why didn't you?"

Seb had been thinking the exact same thing, but knowing what he did of Nathan, he suspected he already knew the answer.

Nathan tugged Jared close again and wrapped him in his arms. "Because for a long time I wasn't sorry. And by the time I could look at the whole thing rationally—Alec was many things, but a coward wasn't one of them—it was too late." He buried his face in the crook of Jared's neck. The heavy exhale that followed sounded loud in the sudden quiet of the room. "And here we are ten years later, just about managing to be civil to each other."

At the risk of getting his head bitten off, Seb ventured, "You could always try apologising now, see if it makes a difference."

Nathan laughed but there was little humour in it. "I don't think Alec would believe me if I said it now."

Jared pulled back and looked him in the eye. "Do you even want to?"

"I don't know. He might not be a coward, but he can be an arrogant dick who's made it crystal clear what he thinks of me. I'm not sure if I could get the words out now, even if he'd listen."

Seb kept his thoughts to himself. It wasn't as though it really concerned him anyway; he'd been curious, that was all. He yawned, his body remembering how tired he'd been earlier before Nathan's story time.

Jared glanced over at him, then patted Nathan on the chest. "Come on. Let's leave Seb to catch up on his beauty sleep."

The heated look Nathan gave him in return made it obvious where they were going.

Seb sighed. "Shut the door on your way out, please."

As soon as they were gone and the door clicked shut, Seb shuffled down until his head hit the pillows. He idly wondered if the Nathan-Alec thing was common knowledge. It must be if Nathan had said what he did in front of the whole pack.

Seb's mind then wandered to Tim. Had he been in the pack then? Seb had no idea. In fact, he didn't know much about Tim at all.

*And now I'm not going to, either. Which is fine. Perfect.*

He closed his eyes and tried not to think of dark curly hair and blue eyes.

For all his fatigue, sleep was a long time coming.

# Chapter Six

As Tim climbed the stairs to his flat, a familiar scent greeted him. He didn't strictly need to live in Alec's building, since he wasn't part of his unit, but he'd chosen Alec as his beta, so it made sense. And it let him be closer to Cam in case—and he hoped it never came to it—anything ever happened to Cam that required Tim's services.

He opened the stairwell door to find Alec leaning against the wall next to Tim's flat. "Everything all right?" Tim unlocked the door and Alec followed him inside.

"I've just come from seeing Cam."

"Oh?" Tim walked through to the kitchen and set his keys on the worktop. Although he counted Alec as a close friend, it wasn't usual for Alec to discuss pack business unless it was common knowledge already. Alec wasn't a gossip, and whatever he and Cam discussed stayed between them. For him to bring it up, it must involve Tim somehow. "Drink?" he asked, turning to open the fridge.

"Coke, if you've got any?"

Tim fetched out two cans and passed one over.

"Thanks." Alec leaned against the worktop, tall and imposing, the sort of build people seemed to associate with shifters. With his short dark hair and intense brown eyes, he gave off that do-not-fuck-with-me vibe that a lot of shifters managed to project. Tim had long since accepted that he'd never be that way, and, considering he liked his human patients to feel at ease, was probably for the best. He still had the usual shifter strength; he just didn't look like he did.

Which came in handy sometimes. Fighting wasn't something Tim cared for, but he would do it in a heartbeat if any of his pack were in danger.

He took a drink from his can and then set it on the side. "Not that I don't enjoy seeing you, but haven't you got better things to be doing at seven o'clock on a Friday night?"

Tim didn't keep tabs on him or anything, but Alec wasn't one for staying in if he didn't have patrol.

Alec shrugged. "Maybe later. First I wanted to check in with you."

From the sounds of it, this wasn't going to be a quick conversation. Tim glanced from his bedroom to the living area. "Does this need to be private, or…?" The soundproofing in his flat as a whole was adequate, but if Alec definitely wanted to keep it from the rest of the building, then the bedroom was the best place to talk. For obvious reasons, all the bedrooms and bathrooms were fully soundproofed.

Alec shook his head. "Living room is fine."

"Okay."

They walked over to Tim's corner sofa and sat. Alec lounged in the corner, with one ankle propped on the opposite knee. "Are you involved with Seb Calloway?" He tilted his head a little and inhaled briefly, and Tim snorted.

"No, as you can tell." He hadn't seen Seb since Sunday; any trace of his scent on Tim had long since faded.

"Had to ask." Alec smirked and sat forward. "You wish you were, though, yes?"

Tim rolled his eyes. "Yes. And that's not news to you, either." He sighed, wondering where this could possibly end up. "What's going on?"

"Cam met with Alpha Newell three days ago, and again today."

Tim took another sip of his Coke, his mouth suddenly dry. A bad feeling settled in his gut; meetings with the P-Pack alpha rarely meant anything good these days. "And?"

"And according to Newell, they've been keeping an eye on Calloway. For his own safety, apparently."

"Really?" Tim frowned. "Is he supposed to be in danger?" The only danger Tim could see was from P-Pack themselves. "And if so, why not report it to Cam. Why take it upon themselves to protect him?"

"That's exactly what I said." Alec grinned, and for a second it softened his features. He was hot for an older guy—okay, so he was only ten years older than Tim, but he was so serious most of the time that he seemed older than that. But then his smile faded and the mask was back in place. "According to Cam, Newell believes that some of the rogue shifters have returned."

"Returned? How is that possible? I thought you killed them all at the warehouse."

"We did."

Now Tim was really confused. The aftermath of that fight had been brutal and bloody, fatal to some. But they'd eradicated the rogue pack. There should be no threat anymore. "Then how—"

"Newell suggested there was a chance that some of them got away." Alec sneered as he said it;

his teeth lengthened and a low growl filled the room.

If Tim didn't know him as well as he did, he might be a little bit terrified right then.

But Alec's control was impeccable. "He didn't come right out and say it, but the implication was that *we* let some of them escape. Not his pack."

A harsh laugh burst out before Tim could stop it, because Alec's unit were meticulous. If tasked with killing all the rogue pack, then Tim would bet everything on them completing that task. To suggest they'd let some of the rogue shifters slip through their fingers was naive at best, insulting at worst. Even if a few had managed to get away, they would have been tracked and hunted down. "That's bollocks."

Alec's smile was back in an instant. "That's also what I said. I fear I'm becoming a bad influence on you."

His smile stayed in place this time, and a surge of affection welled up in Tim's chest.

He was well aware of Alec's reputation in the pack: hard-edged, serious, private—but Tim never saw him like that. Moments like the one they were having now weren't one-offs. Alec laughed a lot. Tim wished he'd let more people see this side of him, but most of the pack saw the guarded side.

And then there was Nathan…. But that was a different story altogether.

Tim busied himself with drinking his Coke while he waited for Alec to get to the point of his visit.

"Cam doesn't believe Newell either, but he can't come out and say that without offending another alpha and risking the consequences."

An insult like that would give Newell all sorts of options that weren't good for the Regent's Park pack. "And I'm guessing he doesn't want that."

"No. Not so soon after all that shit with the rogue pack. Relations between our packs aren't the best, and Cam wants to avoid any more bloodshed if he can help it."

Tim sensed there was more to come. "That's not all, is it?"

"No. He's asked for Cam's help in searching for these supposed rogue shifters. And apparently they'll continue to keep an eye on Calloway too."

Tim's head snapped up. "What? Why? If he wants Cam's help, then why can't we watch him?"

Alec raised an eyebrow at Tim's outburst. "His flat is virtually on their doorstep, nearer to their pack building than it is to this one. It makes sense for them to keep an eye on him."

"Are those your words or theirs?"

"Does it matter? Cam's hands are tied, Tim. He has no reason, no proof to doubt Alpha Newell's claims. Asking him to stay away from Calloway's place—"

"God, call him Seb, please."

"...Would suggest a lack of trust in P-Pack and imply that Seb is of importance to our pack. Neither of which Cam wants to do at the minute."

Tim sat there with a hundred thoughts running through his head, until finally one broke through to the surface. "It's because of Nathan, isn't it?"

"It's one theory." Alec sighed and ran a hand over his mouth. His teeth were back to normal, but Tim half expected to see them again at the mention of Nathan's name. "Alpha Newell wasn't exactly thrilled that Nathan survived. I wouldn't be at all surprised if he's tempted by a little revenge. And if they know Callow—*Seb's* connection to Jared, then it makes him an easy target."

"But Newell can't do anything to him, can he?"

"No. Well, not if he wants to keep his pack afterwards. If he hurts either Seb or Jared, then the police will be involved. And if he—or any of his pack acting on Newell's orders—attacks Nathan unprovoked, then Cam is within his rights to ask the alpha council for the right to challenge him." Alec drained the rest of his can and set it on the floor. "I can't discuss any more of it with you, but…." He suddenly looked uncharacteristically sheepish.

"What?"

"As I said, we can't have any of the pack watching Seb. And I'd rather keep Nathan and Jared away from there if possible."

It took Tim a couple of seconds to understand. "He's going back home? I thought he was stopping with Jared for a while."

"Ideal as that would be, you know how stubborn some humans are. As soon as I informed him that P-Pack had owned up to watching his flat and that they posed no discernible threat," he said through gritted teeth, "Seb insisted on going home."

"Can't you make him stay?"

Alec actually laughed. "And how do you suggest I do that? Kidnap him? That's more Nathan's style than mine."

Tim ignored the jibe, his mind still sorting through what Alec had said earlier. "At least suggest he stay until his wrist's fully healed. I'd be more comfortable if he had only one damaged limb."

"That's an excellent idea. Maybe someone in the medical profession could suggest that to him?"

Tim's resigned sigh made Alec laugh some more.

"Yes, because obviously he's going to listen to me. He'll think—" *No.* He did not want to go there with Alec.

*Too late.* Alec stared at him, eyes narrowing. "Something I should know?"

"Nope. Not sure I'm the right person to try to get him to stay, that's all." He could already picture the conversation in all of its awkward glory.

"Why not? As his doctor, surely you can deliver a persuasive argument?"

Tim groaned and buried his head in his hands. "And if I can't?"

"Then, as his doctor, you can do home visits. Surely a broken ankle needs constant monitoring?" He didn't wait for Tim's reply. "And if that fails, then you can date him, or pretend to. Whichever works to keep you near that flat as much as possible."

"Alec," Tim growled a warning.

"Tim. I don't think you're grasping the seriousness of the situation we're in. Seb is as good as family in Jared's eyes, therefore pack by default. Any threat to Seb will worry Jared, and as Jared's bonded mate, Nathan will feel it and his protective instincts will be triggered. If anything should happen to Seb and Nathan reacts by attacking a member of P-Pack before we can prove it was Newell's doing, then he'll be in deep shit. Cam will be put in an impossible situation, and Newell will get exactly what he wants."

"Either Nathan punished or Cam in trouble with the alpha council."

"Exactly."

*Fucking hell.* "Fine. I'll see if I can get Seb to stay with Jared."

And that had better work, because the other option was pretend boyfriends, and no way was he having that talk with Seb. Even if Seb agreed to it, which he could never see happening, P-Pack had been fooled that way with Jared and Nathan. At the start, anyway. They wouldn't be so easy to fool a second time. *Pretending* just wouldn't work.

Alec stood and waited for Tim to do the same before drawing him close with a hand on the side of his neck. Tim relaxed against Alex's solid warmth, the comforting scent of beta wolf surrounding him and settling some of the anxiety inside.

Alec dropped his head to the base of Tim's throat, and gently rubbed his cheek against the skin there. "I know how you feel about him and how uncomfortable this makes you. I wouldn't ask if it weren't so important to the pack and for Seb's safety."

Eyes closed, Tim tried to let go of any remaining tension. "I know." When he felt calm again, back to his old self, Tim stepped back and met Alec's gaze. "I'll let you know how it goes."

"That would be appreciated."

He followed Alec to the front door, let him out, and watched him disappear into the stairwell before closing his own door and slumping against it.

*Shit.*

Saturday morning, Tim sat on the edge of his bed, phone in hand. He'd given Seb his number last weekend, but as Seb hadn't texted or called—which he was trying not to be disappointed by—he didn't have his number. Should he text Nathan or Jared? After their conversation last Sunday, Tim figured Nathan would be more sympathetic to his cause, and he went ahead and texted him.

*Spoke to Alec yesterday, he wants me to persuade Seb to stay with you guys.*

The reply was almost immediate.

*Well then you better hurry. He wants J to drop him home tomorrow.*

Bollocks.

*Okay to come round in about 30 mins?*

*Yep. I wont be here but J will.*

Tim stared at the screen. He wasn't Jared's favourite person at present, but he needed to get round there if he was to have any hope of persuading Seb not to leave.

*That's fine. Can you do me a favour and not tell Seb I'm coming?*

The response took a while to come this time, and he imagined Nathan debating how to reply. Not telling Seb would likely mean not telling Jared either, and asking Nathan to lie—well, to omit the truth—to his bonded mate wasn't the most ethical thing Tim had ever done.

*Please*, he sent. *I don't want Seb to bolt before I get there.*

*This is the only time you ask me to do this.*

*Of course. And thank you.*

When Nathan didn't respond after a couple of minutes, Tim figured their conversation was over.

Now he needed to get dressed and head over to see Seb before Nathan changed his mind.


Thirty-five minutes later, Luke let him in the front door to their building.

Tim smiled. "Hey, not seen you in a while. Everything okay?"

"Yeah, can't complain." Luke grinned back at him and stepped aside for Tim to enter. "What did you do to piss off Nathan? He was grumbling about 'love-struck doctors and stupid humans' when I saw him this morning."

Tim groaned. The last thing he wanted was for the rest of Nathan's unit to know how he felt about Seb. After that the whole pack would know soon enough, and he liked to keep his love life private-ish where possible. Especially when his feelings weren't reciprocated. "I might have asked him not to tell Jared something."

Luke winced and sucked in a breath. "That would do it. You know how those two are."

"I do."

Tim ignored the pang of longing that always tore through him when he thought of bonded pairs. It hadn't been so bad when it was all theoretical, but seeing Nathan and Jared together, after having watched them go through all they did to get there, made the feelings that much more acute. What he wouldn't give for someone of his own like that. "But I needed to talk to Seb before he goes back to his flat."

Luke hummed in response as they walked along the hallway to the stairs. "Gareth said P-Pack admitted to following Seb and watching his house."

"So I understand."

"He doesn't trust them. I don't think Cam or any of the other betas do either."

Tim's chat with Alec flashed through his mind. "I think you're probably right. But there's not a lot anyone can do about it yet."

Luke sighed. "No."

They climbed the stairs in silence after that, and with a wave, Luke carried on up to his flat while Tim exited at the first floor.

No sound came from inside Nathan's flat, no TV or music, no signs of life in general. Tim checked his watch: 10:15. Surely someone was up? Nathan would have mentioned if both Jared and Seb were still asleep, wouldn't he?

Tim knocked on the door, cringing at how loud it sounded against the silence of the hallway. Listening for the telltale footsteps of someone approaching the door, he waited patiently for a couple of minutes.

But no one came. With a sigh and a less than charitable thought about Nathan, he tried again, a little louder this time.

And waited.

Finally he heard the shuffling gait and tap of a crutch that announced Seb coming to answer the door. It opened slowly, and a waft of Seb's scent washed over Tim and took him by surprise.

*Fuck, I missed that.* Taking another deep breath, he tried not to appear too obvious and focused on Seb's face, which had scrunched up adorably in confusion, a couple of pillow creases on one cheek. His dark blond hair had that tousled appearance, and honestly, Tim didn't think he could have looked any more appealing if he'd put actual effort into it.

Seb looked warm and sleep-rumpled, and Tim would like nothing more than to march him back to his bedroom and slip in bed beside him. *Fuck.*

He cleared his throat and attempted to pull himself together. This would not go over well if all he could manage was to stand and leer at him. "Hey, I didn't get you up, did I?"

"Whatever gave you that idea?" Seb fixed him with an unimpressed stare, which Tim totally deserved for such a stupid statement. "You better come in now you're here."

Seb stepped back and opened the door wider, and only then did Tim glance down and see what he was wearing. Or rather, what he was not wearing. Dark purple boxer briefs clung to him like a second skin, and the white T-shirt looked a couple of sizes too big and hung loosely on his frame, revealing the top of one shoulder and part of his collarbone.

Swallowing was far more difficult than it should be, as was raising his gaze to Seb's face. When he eventually managed it, Seb's cheeks had flushed and he had one hand in his hair.

"Um…." Seb looked down at his bare legs and shrugged. "Pyjama bottoms don't fit over my cast, so…."

Tim cleared his throat. "Oh… um, yeah. I wasn't—"

Wasn't what? Staring, drooling, wishing he could run his hands over the fine blond hairs covering Seb's thighs? Probably best if he didn't finish that sentence.

Tim quickly stepped inside and moved past Seb so that he was no longer tempted to be totally unprofessional. "Is Jared still in bed?" He glanced towards the closed bedroom door at the end of the hallway.

"Yeah. He was working late, I think." Seb followed as Tim headed for the relative safety of the kitchen. "Let me just go and put on some shorts."

*Oh, please don't, not on my account.*

But Seb was already disappearing into his bedroom.

After setting his bag on the worktop, Tim turned to face Seb as he came into the kitchen a few minutes later, and he forced himself to keep his gaze head-height. "How are you feeling?"

"So, this isn't just a social call, then?"

"A bit of both, actually."

Seb smirked and set his crutch to one side, leaning against the worktop. "Well, in that case, Doctor, I'm feeling pretty good." He flexed his right wrist a couple of times and wiggled his fingers. "I iced it twice a day like you said, and I've been exercising it a little now the swelling's gone down. It feels loads better."

"That's good," Tim mumbled, his brain still stuck on the thought of Seb 'exercising' his wrist. "What about your ankle?"

The blue cast stood out next to the paleness of Seb's skin, but Tim managed not to let his gaze linger too long.

Seb's smile dimmed a little as he glanced down. "It's okay, I suppose. I'm stuck with it for another five weeks, so it's not like anything's going to change."

Tim sighed. He had no experience to draw on to offer any sympathy. If he broke anything, it would fully heal in a matter of hours, a day at the absolute most. In the end he just nodded.

An uncomfortable silence stretched between them. Tim was acutely aware of how their last conversation had ended. Essentially, Seb wanted nothing to do with him, yet here he was lingering in his kitchen, like a bad smell. "Can I make you a drink?" he offered, more for something to say. "You can go sit down and take the weight off that ankle."

Seb looked down at where his foot rested with only the heel on the floor. "I'm not putting any weight on it now."

"Just do as your doctor tells you, for once."

With a snort and a muttered "You're not my doctor, actually," Seb grabbed his crutch and headed over to the sofa, carefully lowering himself onto the cushions.

Tim flicked the kettle on to boil and searched through the cupboards until he found the mugs. "Tea or coffee?"

"Coffee, please."

When Tim walked over carrying the two steaming mugs of coffee, Seb had his head resting against the back of the sofa, his eyes closed. He looked so peaceful that Tim was loath to disturb him. Maybe he was having trouble sleeping?

As he set the mugs on the coffee table, Seb's eyes fluttered open. "Thanks." He waited for Tim to sit on the chair next to the sofa. "Now that the professional part of your visit's over, what else did you come here to talk about? I'm pretty sure we covered everything in the car last weekend."

He sounded more resigned than annoyed, and Tim took that as a good sign. He might be clutching at straws, but he would take what he could get. "I understand you're thinking about returning home."

Seb snorted. "Good news travels fast."

Tim had to be careful about how much he said. Alec hadn't asked him not to repeat what he'd told Tim, but it probably wasn't meant for general discussion. He'd like to avoid outright lying if possible, though. "Alec told me. He's concerned, and so is Cam."

"I was led to believe there's no longer a threat. Aren't the Primrose Hill pack supposed to be your allies?"

"Yes, but—"

"Then what's the problem?"

There was one aspect of it he could share. "The P-Pack alpha—" Seb sniggered. "What?"

"*P-Pack*. I just realised why Jared finds it funny."

Tim ignored him and carried on. "Their alpha suspects some of the rogue pack escaped the warehouse during the attack. Since you're now considered pack, it would be easier if you lived in a pack house."

"Easier for who?" Seb didn't wait for a reply. "'The pack,' I'm guessing, because it certainly wouldn't be easier for me." He took a drink of his coffee and set the mug back on the table. "Look, Tim, I'm not trying to make things difficult. I just want to go home to my own bed and my own things. I've got shifters watching over me. Does it really matter what pack they're from?"

*Yes!* Tim wanted to scream, *of course it matters. We don't trust them.* But that wasn't common knowledge, and no matter how much he might trust

Seb, he couldn't betray Alec's trust in him. He said, "At least wait until your wrist's fully healed."

"Why? It doesn't hurt all that much now, and I can get around just fine on my crutch. Honestly, Tim, I'm good."

With Seb intent on returning to his flat, Tim bit his bottom lip, wondering if he dare broach what Alec had suggested as the second plan. Seb would never go for it in a million years. Fuck, he really didn't want to bring it up… but Alec had asked him to try.

He ran a hand over his eyes and sighed.

Seb shook his head. "Whatever it is, just spit it out."

"What?"

Seb laughed. "You look as though you've got bad news to tell me but can't find the right words."

Tim's smile was wry. "That about sums it up." He held up a finger. "One sec."

He pulled out his phone and sent a quick text to Alec. *Not going well. Can I tell Seb everything?*

The reply was immediate. *Do you trust him?*

*Yes.*

*Then tell him if you think it'll help.*

Tim slipped his phone back in his pocket and looked up to find Seb watching him.

Seb fiddled with the seam of his shorts, then spoke before Tim had chance to. "Jared told me everything, you know."

*Everything?* "About what?"

"About Cam asking him and Nathan to be fake boyfriends." He waved a hand in the air. "Before everyone knew they'd bonded."

Seb obviously had a point to make, so Tim gestured for him to go on. "And?"

"Well, it's obvious you guys have no concept of boundaries, so whatever it is you're not telling me, I'm guessing it's probably something along those lines." Tim gaped at him. "Am I wrong?" Seb raised an eyebrow in challenge.

*Fuck.* "No. You're not." He sighed and put his hand up before Seb could say anything else. "Let me explain everything first, and then we can talk. Please?"

Seb stared at him for another second before giving him a small nod. "Fine. Explain away."

Tim started at the beginning. He told Seb about the volatile history the two packs shared, about how Nathan's escape from the rogue pack had pissed of Alpha Newell, and how Cam and his betas didn't trust P-Pack not to be out for revenge.

Seb listened intently, not offering a comment or asking questions until Tim finished speaking. "I don't understand why P-Pack are pissed off with Nathan, though?" He frowned. "Newell told Cam to make Nathan the car driver, and Nathan did it. What does it matter if he didn't die? Surely that's a good thing, no?"

Tim paused, trying to find the right words to explain. To a shifter the insult was obvious, but probably not to Seb. "For us, yes. But Newell expected him to die, wanted him to. He believed driving the van on a suicide mission, with no help from either pack, was a fitting punishment for Nathan lying and essentially putting both packs in danger by harbouring an illegally bitten human."

"Oh. So when Nathan escaped, he felt... what? Cheated?"

"Essentially, yes."

"That's bollocks."

"Unfortunately, it's shifter politics. Newell didn't actually come out and accuse Cam of helping Nathan, but he heavily implied it."

Seb covered his face with his hands and groaned. "Christ, you lot make everything so fucking complicated. Why can't Newell just suck it up and let it go? What's Nathan to him, anyway?"

Tim hated trying to explain pack etiquette to humans; it always came off as petty, ridiculous, or cruel. "For Newell, I believe it's a matter of pride."

"It's always pride with you lot."

*You lot.* That was the second time Seb had used that expression. Was he intentionally trying to reiterate their differences?

In this case he was mostly right. A lot of the problems within packs, or between them, came down to pride.

Tim cleared his throat to get Seb's attention. "In light of all that, Alec asked me either to get you to stay, or to pretend to be my boyfriend, so I'd have an excuse to keep an eye on you and avoid offending P-Pack."

"Ugh, you're making my head hurt." Seb left his hands over his face and spoke through his fingers. "Wasn't this already tried with Jared and Nathan? I'm sure P-Pack aren't stupid. If you suddenly start visiting and say "Hey, we're boyfriends now," they're not going to fall for it."

"That's what I said, but…." *But I really like you, and it wouldn't be pretending for me.*

"But?"

"Getting Nathan to react badly is probably top of their list at the minute. And if anything happens to you, then Jared will be devastated, and by default, Nathan too. If you aren't concerned about your

101

own safety, then think about Nathan's. If he so much as lays a finger on a member of P-Pack without provocation, he'll be in serious trouble."

One second stretched into two, then three. Tim counted the soft ticks on the clock in the kitchen. It took Seb ten long seconds to answer. "What exactly would we have to do? Because I really can't stay here any longer."

Tim swallowed past the sudden lump in his throat. Nervous excitement threatened to bubble out any moment, but somehow he managed not to let it show.

*This has the potential to go spectacularly wrong, but I can't wait to get started.*

# Chapter Seven

Seb let his hands fall into his lap, unable to believe what he'd just agreed to.

The small happy smile that Tim was trying desperately to hide wasn't helping either. He'd said his piece last weekend, and nothing had changed, really, but fuck it, Seb had missed him.

He'd spent the whole week going over that conversation in the car, wondering if he'd been too hasty. He liked Tim, and he knew Tim liked him back, so in theory a little friends-with-benefits action should have sounded appealing, but... Tim didn't come across as the kind of guy who could handle a relationship like that.

Not that Seb knew him all that well, but he seemed like a nice guy. Despite Jared's comments last weekend, Jared thought a lot of Tim, too, and Seb had caught the wistful looks Tim shot Nathan's way when he thought no one was looking. He might say otherwise, but it was apparent Tim wanted a bond like the one Nathan had with Jared, and Seb couldn't ever want that.

What was the point in leading him on? None. There was no point. But neither did he want anything to happen to Nathan. So there he sat, trying to sort out a commitment-free way to act as boyfriends while still fooling a pack of possibly dangerous shifters.

*Not how I imagined spending my Saturday afternoon.*

He appeared to have rendered Tim speechless, so he said, "Look, this was your idea, the least—"

"Never my idea."

"But you think we should do it?"

"I think the best outcome is for you to stay here. But if that's not an option, then yes, I think we should do it." Tim stood, eyeing the space next to Seb with uncertainty before moving to sit next to him.

Their shoulders brushed. Tim felt warm and solid next to him, and it was an effort for Seb not to lean into it.

Tim reached out and took his hand. Seb froze for a second before allowing him to tangle their fingers.

Tim said softly, "I know this is the opposite of what you want. But I can't handle the thought of you being so close to their pack territory, with no one there to keep an eye out for you." He ran his thumb over the back of Seb's hand, gently caressing each knuckle as he went. "Nathan can't do it, for obvious reasons. But if there's someone else other than me that you'd rather have, then say so. I—"

Tim glanced down at their joined hands for a moment, and Seb wondered how much saying that had cost him.

None of this was helping with his determination not to fall for him. *Fuck. Why does it have to be so difficult?*

Tim looked up and met Seb's gaze; beautiful blue eyes fixed on him, full of sincerity. Tim meant every word. He'd rather Seb say no to him and yes to someone else if it meant Seb was safe.

That more than anything made his mind up, and he squeezed Tim's hand without thinking. "I don't want anyone else." Tim's eyes widened, and the flash of hope in them hurt Seb's heart because nothing had really changed. He added, "To be my pretend boyfriend."

"Okay."

The smile seemed genuine enough, but it didn't reach Tim's eyes. This was going to end up hurting one or both of them. They needed ground rules. "Jared told me it's all about scents. That to be believable we need to smell like we're fucking."

"Um—" Tim coughed, looking surprised. "Well, that's a lot of it, yes."

"We're not doing that, though. I don't care how real your alpha wants it to be, I'm not budging on that."

Seb had fucked shifters before, and the realisation that any one of them could have accidentally bitten him and possibly bonded them—for life—made his stomach churn. Why wasn't that common knowledge, for fuck's sake? Oh, but was it just...? "Is it only actual penetration that does it, or any type of sex?" Tim blushed, which, despite the seriousness of the conversation, made Seb laugh. "You're a doctor. Shouldn't you be used to this kind of talk?"

"I'm not normally having it with someone I'm—" He faltered. Seb gave his hand another squeeze and then let go, feeling oddly self-conscious. "—someone I'm interested in. Besides, I thought you'd vetoed the idea of any kind of sex. At all. I seem to remember you being quite clear about that."

"So, we don't actually have to...?" Seb gestured at his crotch and then at Tim's.

"No. We don't have to do it together."

"Oh." Seb had no right to feel disappointed, but for some reason he did. "Then how do we make ourselves smell right?"

Tim glanced at the ceiling and gave a small sigh. "The most effective way would be to masturbate and then smear the ejaculate into each other's skin."

Seb stared at him, suddenly feeling like he was back in the sex education class at school. "Wow. You make it sound so much fun."

"You were the one who said you didn't want to have any kind of relationship with me. I'm just trying to be practical and make this as painless as possible. For both of us."

Second thoughts began to kick in. Could they really jack off, smear come on each other, and just go about their business as if nothing had happened?

The answer he kept coming up with was a big fucking *no way!* From what Seb knew about shifters, he couldn't possibly see how Tim would be able to do it either. No matter how clinical he tried to make it sound. "What about you?"

Tim startled as though he'd been lost in thought. The pink tinge to his cheeks made Seb wonder if their thoughts had been along a similar line. "What about me?"

Trying not to sound arrogant, Seb met his gaze. "Won't it affect you if we do that?"

"Affect me how?"

Seb eyed him, eyebrows furrowed in confusion. *Is he being deliberately obtuse?* "Won't it… um, trigger your possessive instincts, or something like that?" He felt silly saying that out loud. *Damn Jared and all his stories of Possessive Nathan.*

Two seconds away from telling Tim to forget he'd said anything, Tim spoke so quietly that Seb had to lean closer to catch it all.

"Yes." Tim turned away before Seb could read the look in his eye. "You'll smell like me. Like *mine.*

It won't be anywhere near as strong as if we were bonded… but the instinct to protect you will be there."

The atmosphere between them crackled, suddenly so thick with tension that Seb could almost taste it. Tim sat with his fists loosely clenched, and Seb was certain that if he uncurled them, he'd find claws. "That's not fair on you," he whispered. "They shouldn't ask you do it, when you feel—"

Tim offered a wry smile. "It's *why* they asked me."

In Seb's opinion that seemed really fucking cruel.

Tim added, "It'll make things more believable."

Seb frowned, wondering how an alpha who supposedly cared so much about his pack could use one of his shifter's feelings like that?

As if catching his train of thought, Tim nudged him with his knee. "It's for the good of the pack."

"Right."

"I know Jared thinks we have no self-control, but I promise you that if we do this, I won't try and pressure you for more. No matter what my instincts tell me to do. I can control myself. You're in no danger from me."

Sincerity rolled off him, and Seb got caught in his gaze again, warm and inviting and promising all sorts of security.

*Yeah, it isn't Tim I don't trust.*

The moment of silence stretched out, threatening to head towards uncomfortable territory.

Tim broke it. "Well?" He smiled, tentative. "What do you say?"

*No, no way.*

It was going to end badly, Seb just knew it. But faced with that open, hopeful expression, he could only smile. "Yes."

Tim's smile spread wide, his eyes crinkling at the corners. "Thank you."

"What for? Isn't this all supposedly for my benefit?" He was pretty sure Tim wouldn't be thanking him by the end of it. More likely cursing the day they'd ever met.

"Yes, but I meant 'thank you for trusting me.'"

"Oh," Seb mumbled, embarrassed but not sure why, exactly. He stood up quickly, needing to put some space between them, and headed into the kitchen.

"Where are you going?"

Half turning to face Tim, Seb's crutch slipped on the edge of the rug and out from under him, and he fell forward. "Shit!" With nothing to hang on to, he fully expected to face-plant onto the floor at any second…

But then Tim was there, catching him in strong, sure arms and pulling him against his chest.

"Fuck," Seb mumbled, his face now smooshed against Tim's shoulder.

With his arms wrapped around Tim's neck, his crutch hung limply from his hand, all his weight supported by Tim's body. Tim's very firm, lean, warm body, which Seb had no trouble feeling through the lightweight jumper Tim wore. He allowed himself a moment to indulge in being surrounded by all the strength and safety that Tim offered.

Since all that had happened with Jared and Nathan, Seb hadn't been out much; he'd still felt out of sorts that his best friend was now bonded to a fucking shifter. The weeks had kind of slipped by until he couldn't remember the last time he'd even kissed a guy, let alone have one hold him like Tim was. It felt good, reminded him of what he was missing out on, and when he breathed in deep, a sigh escaped him because Tim smelled good too.

Seb buried his face in the crook of Tim's neck, chasing the smell until he realised what he was doing and abruptly stopped.

Slowly he pulled back to put a little space between them, but Tim didn't let him go far. Seb's heart pounded hard against his ribcage, each beat seeming so loud inside his head. Surely Tim could hear it. Almost afraid of what he might find, Seb waited a moment before lifting his head to meet Tim's gaze.

He knew it was a mistake as soon as he did it. *Oh fuck.*

Dark blue eyes met his, boring into his soul with an intensity that made Seb's breath catch. When was the last time someone had looked at him like that? Quite possibly never. It sent a rush of heat to his groin, lighting up a trail inside him.

Neither of them moved, their faces so close together that if Seb leaned forward just a few centimetres, they'd be kissing.

"Sebastian?"

His full name, spoken so reverently in Tim's velvety soft voice, was all it took. It rolled off his tongue like a caress, and Seb felt himself inch closer until their lips brushed. "Yes," he whispered, and he closed his eyes, kissing Tim like he'd wanted to from the start but had tried so hard not to.

All his doubts melted away with each slide of Tim's tongue against his. Strong arms holding him tight kept his fears from surfacing, and each broken moan that escaped Tim as they kissed splintered Seb's carefully constructed defences. His cock hardened, pushing against the constricting material of his shorts, and he nudged forward to find Tim in a similar state.

Somewhere deep in the back of his mind, Seb knew he needed to stop, needed to put an end to this before they went too far, but that voice got fainter the longer they kissed, until it became a distant hum. He clung to Tim's shoulders, wanting everything in that moment.

When Tim eventually eased him back, both hands on his waist, still supporting him, Seb wasn't anywhere near ready for it, but judging by the way he was breathing hard, it was just as well Tim had done it.

He groaned. "Shit, I'm sorry."

Seb glanced up with a frown, met with a pained expression on Tim's face. "What's wrong?"

"I've been telling you how good my control is for the past hour or so, and then I kiss you the moment you get close even though I know you don't want this."

He moved to look away, but Seb grabbed his chin.

"Firstly, I kissed you." He slid his hand into Tim's hair, and for a second considered coaxing him into another kiss, but Tim's fingers wrapped around his wrist, effectively holding him in place.

"And second?"

"I thought we just agreed to play pretend boyfriends. Doesn't that involve kissing?"

Tim's brow furrowed. "Yes, but there's no one here we have to convince."

The words doused the heat burning inside Seb, and he closed his eyes with a sigh. "Yeah, you're right."

Of course Tim would be confused with all the mixed signals Seb threw his way.

"Hey." Tim squeezed his waist and gave him a tiny shake until Seb opened his eyes and looked at him. "I would be more than happy to kiss you whenever, you know that. But you said that wasn't an option for us."

"I know I did."

"Has that changed?"

"No. Yes… maybe?" Seb let his head fall forward, hiding his face in Tim's shoulder again. "I don't know, okay? It's a shit answer, and you don't deserve being messed around like this, but I really don't know how I feel at the minute." He breathed deep and let it out in a long sigh. "I'm not sure I can pretend to be with you and not fall in love with you for real."

God, that was so not what he'd intended to say, but now the words were out there, he couldn't say they weren't true. Liking Tim had never been the problem.

Tim held him close and let several seconds go by before he spoke. "Would that be such a bad thing?"

"It's not what I want." He felt awful for saying that as Tim went rigid in his arms, but it was the truth. Or at least it had been ten minutes ago. "I don't want to become a shifter, and I don't want to end up in a mate bond with… anyone. Nothing good can come from falling for you."

111

Whatever Seb expected Tim to do in response, it wasn't for him to press a soft kiss to the top of Seb's head and wrap his arms around his back. Tim offering comfort after everything Seb just said only made Seb feel worse; guilt coursed through him as he selfishly relaxed into Tim's embrace.

For the first time, he wished he wanted what Jared had with Nathan. He wished the mere thought of it didn't terrify him. It would all be so easy then.

"Would you like to stay here, after all?" Tim whispered, his warm breath tickling Seb's ear. "Or I can ask Alec to find someone else to—"

"No!" Seb dug his fingers into Tim's biceps.

"No to which part?"

Seb swallowed hard. "Both. I want to go home—I need to." He took a breath and looked up. "And I don't want to do this with anyone else. I know that's probably stupid and incredibly selfish of me, but—"

Tim covered Seb's mouth with his hand. "We'll take it slow. They might not be watching you that closely. We may only need to look the part, not... not *act* it."

*Not smear each other's jizz all over our skin.*

"Okay." Seb could do that. He just needed a little space and time away from Tim to get his head together.

All this talk of boyfriends and jerking off, no wonder he was riled up. Who wouldn't be? He took a step back, got his crutch in place, and nodded at Tim that he could let go of him. A quick glance down showed his T-shirt hid the outline of his semi. Tim must have felt it earlier, but there was nothing he could do about that. At least Tim hadn't brought it up. "We'll play it by ear, then?"

"Yeah. I think that's best." Tim's voice had a gravelly edge to it, and every time he breathed in, his fingers flexed at his sides.

Seb was about to ask if he was okay, but Tim's head snapped to the front door.

A second later it opened to Nathan's amused voice. "Is it safe to come in? I can smell you two from the hallway."

Tim closed his eyes, a small groan escaping. "Yeah, it's fine. Come on in."

Thank God Tim answered, because Seb was still reeling from the fact that Nathan could smell what they'd been up to. Christ, how had he forgotten? No wonder Tim was all rough-voiced and finger-flexy. Seb had probably smelled of arousal while he stood there saying that he didn't want to get involved.

"Sorry," he whispered, hoping it was quiet enough that Nathan wouldn't hear.

Tim reached for Seb's hand. "Don't be. I'm not."

Nathan appeared in the kitchen and glanced over to the living area. His gaze dropped to their joined hands and then back up. Eyebrows raised, he said, "Something you want to share?"

"No." Seb replied at the same as Tim offered, "Alec wants us to pretend to be together."

*For fuck's sake, can no one keep a secret in this pack?* Seb turned to glare at Tim. "Really?"

Tim shrugged and let go of his hand. "They should know what's going on."

Nathan's expression turned serious. He nodded. "Yes, we should." Seb groaned, but

113

Nathan had already turned away, walking towards his own bedroom door. He yanked it open. "Oh good, you're up."

A sheepish Jared wandered out, one hand running through his hair.

Seb narrowed his eyes. "How long have you been awake?" He glanced back at Tim, accusingly. Surely Tim would've said if he'd heard Jared up and about?

Tim raised his hands in front of himself. "Don't look at me like that. Bedrooms are soundproofed, remember?"

"Oh." Seb focused on Jared instead. "Well?"

Jared motioned over his shoulder with his thumb. "I saw Tim arrive on the monitor, and you two seemed okay, so I thought I'd give you some space."

Tim cleared his throat and motioned to the sofa behind them. "If we all sit down, I'll explain everything before I go."

"Go?" Seb met his gaze. "Where are you going?" For whatever reason, the thought of Tim leaving made him edgy. "Surely we've got more things to discuss?"

"I think we've pretty much covered everything, don't you?" Tim smiled.

It looked natural enough, but Seb wasn't convinced. He was aware of Nathan and Jared watching them with open curiosity and had no doubt he'd be in for a grilling as soon as Tim left. Another reason for him not to go. "I suppose," he said grudgingly.

Tim led the way back to the sofa and sat down on the edge of the seat. Seb took one of the chairs this time; Jared took the other one, leaving Nathan to sit next to Tim.

Tim began. "I suspect you're not going to like it, but please let me get it all out before you jump in."

After an okay from Jared and a reluctant nod from Nathan, Tim started at the beginning and told them everything he'd just told Seb.

Seb alternated between watching Nathan and then Jared for their reactions. Judging from Nathan's obvious lack of surprise, Seb assumed he'd already known at least some of it. Jared hadn't said a word, hadn't once tried to interrupt, and it made Seb uneasy.

As soon as he finished speaking, Tim looked up and sighed. "So that's where we are now."

Jared stared at him, then at Seb. "And you're okay with all this?" Seb nodded. Jared covered his face with his hands and then blew out a harsh breath through his fingers. "Look," he said, letting his hands drop, "I really am sorry for what I said to you last week, Tim. It was out of line, and being worried about Seb was no excuse."

Tim smiled. "Thank you."

Seb knew Jared well enough to know that there was more to come.

"Are you both sure about this?" Jared looked to Nathan for support. "Do you think this is the right thing to do?"

Nathan shrugged one shoulder. "Under the circumstances, I really don't think I'm in any position to pass comment."

"That was different, though." Jared scooted his chair closer to the sofa and reached for Nathan's hand.

"Was it?" Nathan linked their fingers, and for a moment, Seb felt he and Tim were intruding. "It was for the good of the pack when we were asked to do it, and it's for the good of the pack now." He glanced at Tim. "I saw Gareth this morning. He explained most of this already, and I know Alec and I don't often agree—" Tim snorted, and Nathan shot him a small smile. "—but in this instance, I think he's right." He met Seb's gaze. "If you're still set on going home, then having Tim around as much as possible is the best of a bad situation."

Jared's head shot up. "You don't actually think he's in danger, do you?" He didn't give Nathan a chance to answer. "Because if there's even a remote chance of that, then why the fuck are we letting him go home at all?"

"Jared—"

"I'm getting pretty sick of you talking about me like I'm not here." Seb really wanted to jump to his feet and pace angrily about the living room. *Stupid fucking foot.* He made do with jabbing the end of his crutch in Jared's direction. "What the hell is wrong with you lately?" He glanced down at where Jared still clung to Nathan's hand, shocked to see Jared's nails digging in hard enough to draw blood. "Jesus, Jared."

Jared immediately looked down to where Seb was staring and snatched his hand back. "Shit, I'm sorry. I don't—" He shoved himself farther back into the chair and clasped his hands together in his lap.

Already in doctor mode, Tim kneeled in front of him and slowly reached out to tip Jared's chin up. "It's okay, Jared. We talked about this, remember?"

"Fuck." Jared cast a quick glance out the window. "The moon? But it's still ages away."

Tim shook his head. "We can lose control over things other than the pull of the moon. Seb is in danger, and you want to keep him safe. There's no strict rule for this, and you're a special case. It's all still relatively new, and I'd expect things to vary greatly for the first year while your body gets used to the changes. That includes your emotional responses as well as the physical ones."

Seb frowned. "But he's not a shifter."

"No, but the way he was bitten, and then—" Tim coughed, his cheeks tinged pink as apparently he struggled to find the right word.

Nathan grinned. "Fucked."

"Yes, thanks, Nathan." Tim rolled his eyes. "The way it all happened left Jared with a few subtle shifter traits that are markedly more noticeable around the full moon and at times of high stress. And possessiveness, or the urge to protect, seems to be one of them." He met Seb's gaze and held it. "I know it seems like everyone's trying to run your life and that we don't think you're capable of looking after yourself, but believe me when I say this is all about us and not about you. We just want you to be safe, Sebastian."

A shiver ran through Seb, and he didn't miss the way Tim's lips twitched before he finished speaking. "As the full moon nears, the urge to protect you will only get worse."

Seb huffed, trying not to let Tim's words affect him, but the idea was far more appealing that it should be. Picturing Tim all possessive and being his big bad shifter bodyguard was… hot. And God, he so didn't need to be thinking that with Nathan there as well. Tim might ignore any embarrassing scents filling the room, but Nathan would call him out in a heartbeat.

Seb flexed his bandaged wrist, hoping the slight twinge would get his mind off that track. "So, we're sorted, then? I'll go back to my flat, and Tim can keep an eye on me. Easy." He looked around the room expectantly, but no one spoke. "Excellent. I'll go and pack."

Jared stood at the same time Seb did. "You want to go now?"

His tone, edged with hurt, made Seb pause midstep. "Um…." He glanced at Tim, then Nathan, wanting someone to help him out.

*Why not go now? It's as good a time as any, right?*

Nathan gave a tiny shake of his head and mouthed, "Tomorrow."

*I guess one more night won't hurt.* "No. I was thinking more of tomorrow afternoon. Thought I'd let you cook me one last tasty dinner before I go back to my shitty cooking."

Jared beamed at him. *Totally the right thing to say, then.* "So generous of you." He was already heading towards the kitchen, smiling. "You staying for dinner, Tim?"

"Thanks, but I can't. I need to check in with Alec"

At the mention of that name, Seb stiffened a little. "Reporting back?" He couldn't help the edge to his tone.

Tim sighed. "It's not like that. I need to let him know what's going on." He cast a quick, meaningful glance Nathan's way. "As I'm sure Nathan will be doing with Gareth."

Seb looked to Nathan for confirmation, and he nodded.

"Yeah. I should really go up there in a sec."

Tim met his gaze. "We can't afford to have any secrets, Sebastian. Not about things like this."

Seb hummed but didn't comment further. He supposed Tim had a point, but that didn't mean he had to like it. "I'll walk you out."

He went first, ignoring Jared's raised eyebrows as he mouthed "Sebastian?" at him and being extra careful not to slip this time. The memory of that kiss sent a shiver down his spine.

Fuck it all, this was the worst plan he'd ever agreed to.

# Chapter Eight

Tim watched the deliberate way Seb placed his crutch down as he walked out to the hallway. The urge to help him was almost impossible to quell, but he managed.

Nathan's whispered "Be careful with him" startled him, and Tim glanced back to see both Jared and Nathan watching him. Seb carried on, oblivious.

"I will," Tim whispered back, just as softly. The more time he spent with Seb, the more his well-being became a priority.

Seb stopped in front of the door and shuffled around until he could lean back against the wall. He sighed, and Tim's heart stuttered; he expected Seb to change his mind about the whole thing.

After a quick look towards the living area, Seb seemed to decide on something. "I'm assuming you want to drive me to my flat tomorrow?"

Tim nodded. "Yeah, I think that would be best."

Seb scratched at the back of his head and let out a half laugh, half sigh. "I still have no idea how we're supposed to do this. I mean, are we supposed to be starting out dating, or already a couple, or—?"

Confusion marred Seb's features, and Tim couldn't stop himself from reaching out to smooth the lines on his forehead. Seb swallowed, but didn't move or look away.

"I think the easiest and most believable would be to start at the beginning."

"So… dating, then."

Seb's smile was small but definitely there, and the spark of hope it caused in Tim's chest made him smile in return. "Yes. Dating."

"Okay."

They stood awkwardly in the small hallway. Tim wanted to pull him in for a kiss, but was unsure whether he should or not. He should have spoken to Nathan about what was expected in this sort of situation. Nathan was the expert, after all. Going into this as unprepared as he was could be dangerous for everyone. The P-Pack shifters weren't stupid. Some of them were wankers, but they wouldn't be easily fooled. Not again. For about the fiftieth time, Tim wondered what the hell he was doing.

He cleared his throat and reached for the door handle. "I'll pick you up tomorrow. What time?"

"Just after lunch? About two?"

Tim nodded. "See you tomorrow, then."

Seb opened his mouth and then shut it again. "What?"

"Nothing. I just—" He rubbed a hand over his eyes before meeting Tim's gaze again. "Shouldn't we… I don't know." He waved his free hand back and forth between them. "Kiss or something?"

Tim's eyes widened as he immediately focused on Seb's mouth… where he was licking his lips. *Fucking hell.* "I—"

"I mean we don't have to, but I just thought—"

"No, you're right." Tim wasn't sure what was more mortifying—the fact that Nathan could hear every word of this, or the fact that he'd suggested the whole thing in the first place and yet it was Seb taking the lead. He straightened his shoulders and

121

attempted to look like he knew what he was doing. "If that's okay with you?"

Seb licked his bottom lip again. The sight made Tim's wolf stir, restless under the surface. "Yeah. I mean, we should get some practice in, right? So it doesn't look forced if we have to do it for real."

Tim didn't know whether to laugh or bang his head against the wall. Instead he put a hand on Seb's hip and moved closer. "Exactly." He slid his other hand around Seb's neck, his thumb rubbing back and forth behind his ear. "We need to be able to look convincing."

"Yeah."

He should stop, back the hell away, and go home… but Seb's eyes were so dark, almost black, inviting him to take what he wanted. Resting his forehead against Seb's, he placed a soft but chaste kiss on his lips, lingering a second or two before slowly pulling back. The scent of Seb's arousal filled the air around them, their proximity making it worse. It took all of Tim's self-control to step back and take his hands off Seb's body, and the flash of disappointment on Seb's face wasn't helping in the slightest.

Seb raised an eyebrow as if to say "that all you got?" and Tim was so tempted to lean in and show him how he really wanted to kiss him.

But he couldn't. Their earlier conversation, still fresh in his head, wouldn't let him.

"See you tomorrow."

"Yep. See you." Seb stayed pressed against the wall. The bulge in his shorts was hard to miss.

Yeah, attraction definitely wasn't the problem. For the first time ever, Tim almost wished he wasn't a shifter. *Almost.*

With a nod, Tim opened the door and left before he did something stupid. It would be bad enough facing Nathan after all that, let alone adding to it with anything else. The last thing he wanted to do was go and rehash all this with Alec, but the sooner he got it out of the way, the sooner he could go home. The next few weeks were going to be—*interesting* wasn't a strong enough word. He needed to have his head together to come out the other side in one piece.

Alec answered the door before Tim even had time to knock. Not that it surprised him. Alec had an exceptional sense of smell, even by shifter standards, and probably saw him on one of the monitors in his bedroom or bathroom. Each flat had them installed.

He gave Tim a slow once-over, breathed deeply, and smirked. "I take it things went better than you were expecting?" Stepping to the side, he ushered Tim in.

"He doesn't want to stay with Nathan."

Alec snorted. "No, I didn't think he would. From the smell of you, I'm assuming he was open to being your boyfriend, though?"

"*Pretend* boyfriend," Tim muttered, but of course Alec heard him.

"Really?" He waved a hand that encompassed Tim from head to toe. "Because his scent is all over yo—"

"Really." Tim sighed, tired of talking about the whole thing. "It's complicated. But trust me when I say he's not interested in any kind of relationship with a shifter."

Alec led him through to his large living area and took a seat in one corner of the sofa. He studied Tim for a second. "You explained what the pair of you might need to do?" Tim nodded. "And he's willing to do that?" Another nod. A look of understanding crossed Alec's face. "But not *actually* do it, right?"

Tim gave up trying not to get embarrassed. His cheeks flamed red, but Alec wouldn't stop until he knew exactly what was going on. His job was to make sure the pack was safe, that any possible threat was being dealt with, and Tim supposed that now included Seb. "I told him what might be required, and he agreed, but he doesn't want to get involved for real—not boyfriends, and not friends with benefits. Not even sex for the sake of him smelling right. Nothing." Tim might have said that last bit with an edge to his voice, judging by the slightly apologetic look on Alec's face.

"I'm sorry, Tim. Maybe I shouldn't have asked you to do this." To his credit, Alec did look sorry. "But you were the best option, considering…."

"Considering how I feel about him already?"

Alec sighed. "Yes. You won't need to fake anything, and Newell likes you too." Tim had his doubts about that, but Newell had definitely warmed up to him after Tim had helped some of his pack members following the run-in with the rogue pack. "Anyway, you look knackered, so give me a quick rundown of your plans, and then you can go."

Grateful, Tim proceeded to give Alec a quick recap of what he and Seb had decided. Alec listened without interrupting, and when Tim had told him everything, he sat forward in his seat and clasped his hands together.

"Will it be enough?" Tim asked. The thought had been plaguing Tim since he'd left Nathan's building. "We'll be dating, not moving in together, and I can't keep an eye on him all the time."

Alec hummed, his gaze far away for a moment. When he focused back on Tim, his brow furrowed. "To be honest I have no idea. Newell is adamant there are rogue shifters out there somewhere, and he insists his men have both packs' safety as their main concern. If that's true, then Seb will probably have a P-Pack team watching him most of the time."

"And if it's not?"

"Then short of watching Seb twenty-four hours a day, there's not a lot more we can do. But we hope that knowing you could turn up at any given moment will make them think twice before doing anything drastic. At least until we can get to the bottom of this whole mess, anyway."

An uncomfortable thought slipped into Tim's head. "And if they do harm Seb, as he's a human the police will need to get involved, and then it's out of your hands altogether. Right?"

His lunch threatened to make a reappearance when he saw the answer on Alec's face.

"Out of *our* hands," Alec said softly. "This is your pack too, remember."

"And Seb's now… or so I thought."

"You're right, it is. And we'll protect him to the best of our ability, but things are strained between the two packs at the minute without stirring up more trouble. We need them to hang themselves, so to speak, so there's no margin for error that could mean an opening for Newell to challenge Cam."

*Even if it puts Seb at risk*, he didn't add, but Tim heard it anyway. "All that talk of keeping Seb safe so that Nathan didn't do something stupid—"

Alec reached over and grabbed his arm, making Tim look up and meet his gaze. "Nathan and I have our *issues*, but I don't want anything to happen to him. Or Seb, for that matter. I like him, and more to the point, I know how much *you* like him."

Tim frowned. "But you just said—"

"You're right. Seb would be much safer if someone were around all the time."

"What?" Tim narrowed his eyes. "Are you saying I should…?"

Alec shook his head, but Tim caught the slight twitch of his lips. "I'm not saying anything. We can't order Seb to let you move in with him. We can't order him to do anything. But we can ask."

Yeah, that would go down well. Tim easily imagined Seb's reaction to that little suggestion. "Pretend boyfriends" was pushing his limits as it was. "I don't think so."

Alec let go of his arm and stood—a clear indication that their meeting was over. "It was just a thought."

A thought that Tim now couldn't get out of his head.

*Thanks, Alec.*

At two o'clock the next day, when Tim stood outside Nathan's front door, he was still thinking about Alec's suggestion.

He'd gone to sleep thinking about it, and it had still been there when he woke up. Seb would never agree to it. If Tim pushed, he'd probably back out of the whole thing. Best not to mention it. Besides, it made him feel possessive and slightly out of control, neither of which state was he used to.

He knew people thought of him as soft for a shifter, but he liked that. This urge to protect Seb and keep him close unnerved him. But it was also exciting, and a lick of heat curled around the base of his spine whenever he thought about it. And that was probably scariest of all. Seb wasn't his. Would never be his.

It did nothing to tamp down his smile when he caught Seb's scent drawing closer or to prevent the way his whole body lit up when Seb opened the door and grinned at him.

"Hey." Seb ushered him inside as Tim bit his lip to stop himself saying something ridiculous. "I'm almost ready."

He hobbled off to his bedroom, surprisingly speedy on his crutch, and Tim wandered into the living area where Nathan was.

One look at him had Nathan laughing.

"What?" Tim glanced around to see if Jared was nearby.

"He's in our bedroom, working," Nathan said, seemingly reading his mind. He stood and walked over to where Tim now leaned against the back of the sofa. "And you look far too worked up for just giving Seb a lift home." He made a show of inhaling, and Tim glared at him.

"Don't."

"Want a drink?" Nathan walked past him into the kitchen.

Tim shook his head. "No, thanks." He turned to face him. "Seb won't be that long, I don't think."

Nathan flicked the kettle on and leaned against the worktop, arms crossed. He lowered his voice. "How're you feeling about all this?" He gestured towards Seb's bedroom.

Tim sighed. Out of anyone, Nathan would understand, and after their talk the other day, Tim wanted to confide in him. "Honestly? A little out of control." Nathan paused, a tea bag hanging from his fingers over the waiting mug, and stared at him. "Not like that," Tim hastened to add. "I'm not about to shift or anything."

"Then what?"

How to put it into words that didn't make him sound like a danger to Seb? "I feel overly protective, possessive. Objectively I know it's because I like him and he's in danger, and that all this pretend-boyfriend stuff is messing with my instincts."

"But knowing all that doesn't stop you feeling that way."

"No."

Nathan finished off his tea and glanced at Seb's door from behind which came the faint sound of a zipper. "Listen, I know what it's like to have your instincts take over. I know our situations are different, but if you need to talk or have any questions, call me. Anytime."

"Thank you."

"You're welcome."

Seb chose that moment to come out of his room, looking less than impressed. "Can you help me with my bag, please? Not sure I can manage it and the stairs."

"Of course." Tim eased past him and into his bedroom.

The smell hit him all at once—Seb's scent, thicker and more potent the farther in he went—and he automatically took a big breath in. A low growl escaped him, making him jump.

*Fuck! What the hell am I doing?*

Snatching Seb's bag off the bed, Tim turned and hurried back out.

He waited to one side as Seb said his goodbyes. Jared gave him a fierce hug, but when Nathan stepped up to do the same, Tim's skin prickled with jealousy. Shaking out his shoulders in an effort to calm down, Tim glanced at the ceiling, focusing on the spider web in the far corner.

"Ready?" Seb touched his wrist and Tim barely suppressed a shiver.

"Yeah. Let's go."

"Do you think anyone'll be waiting?" Seb shuffled in his seat, half-facing Tim as he drove. "At the flat, I mean."

They were just about to turn down Seb's street.

"I guess we'll find out soon enough." He indicated to turn right, and they drove down the road in silence; Seb stared out the passenger window, and Tim scanned the parked cars as they passed.

He didn't see any of the P-Pack vehicles, but the shifters could easily be on foot. While Tim was in the car, it made it nigh on impossible to scent them. He would rather know if they had company before they got out of the car, but that wasn't happening. Parking up in front of Seb's building, he turned off the engine. "Wait here," he said, and got out of the car.

The air held the faint scent of P-Pack shifters, but nothing strong enough to imply there were any close by. He opened the door and ducked his head back inside. "Come on, I'll get your bag."

Walking around the car to get Seb's bag from the boot, Tim kept scanning the area. Just because there was no one waiting didn't mean they couldn't appear at any moment.

Barely resisting putting a hand on the small of Seb's back, Tim ushered him up the steps to his front door. Faint scratches marred the red paint, and Seb stopped in front of it. The scent of P-Pack shifters was stronger there, lingering. They'd definitely been back since the night Seb fell down the stairs, but not in the last couple of days. Tim listened for any approaching cars or footsteps, but the road was quiet. "Okay?"

He did touch Seb then, resting his hand lightly on his shoulder.

Seb leaned heavily on his crutch and reached out to run his fingers over the scratches.

Tim gave his shoulder a gentle squeeze. "Seb?"

"Yeah, sorry. I'm fine." He stood up and pulled his keys out of his pocket. "Just wondering why they did it."

"I don't know. They said they were just checking up on you, but…."

But Cam hadn't believed that, and neither had Alec. Tim was inclined to agree with them.

"Yeah… *but*," Seb huffed as he unlocked the door. "They could have fucking knocked instead of scaring me half to death."

The thought of Seb opening the door to a couple of strange shifters made Tim's blood run cold. He slid his hand up to the back of Seb's neck and waited for him to look at him. Then he said, "Promise me you won't open the door to anyone you're not expecting?"

"I promise." Their gazes locked for a long drawn-out moment, and then Seb turned and stepped over the threshold. "It's a shame I've not got one of those cameras like Nathan's," he shot back over his shoulder as he carefully climbed the stairs.

*Why didn't I think of that? Why didn't anyone else?* Tim had his phone out in seconds and sent off a quick text to Alec. When the reply came back that he'd get it sorted as soon as possible, Tim relaxed a little. He glanced up to find Seb waiting for him at the top of the stairs.

"What did you just do?"

*Oh shit. Maybe I should have asked first instead of just taking charge.*

Seb raised both eyebrows. "Now you look guilty. Come on, spill."

Tim sighed and slid his phone into his back pocket as he took the last few steps up to Seb. "I asked Alec to install a security camera. So you can see who's at your front door."

He didn't hold his breath waiting for Seb's response, but his hands curled into fists of their own accord.

"And that makes you feel guilty because….?"

Seb smiled, and it caught Tim totally off guard. "I…um…."

"You thought I'd be pissed off at you for interfering?"

131

Tim nodded. "Basically, yes."

"I'm not stupid, okay?" Seb manoeuvred down the short hallway and pushed the door open with the end of his crutch.

Tim followed closely. "I never thought you were stupid. Just pig-headed," he mumbled. Not quietly enough, though, because Seb laughed.

"Fine, I may be a little stubborn, but not where security is concerned." He stopped, half turned, and waved his crutch at Tim. "I'm doing this, aren't I?"

"True," Tim conceded.

"I actually think it's a great idea. Thank you."

He met Tim's gaze as he said it, and those two small words settled deep in Tim's chest like a warm glow.

Ducking his head to hide the blush no doubt colouring his cheeks, Tim put his hand on Seb's arm and gently steered him into the living room. "Come on. Let's get you sat down and off that leg." When Seb started to protest, he added, "Doctor's orders."

With Seb deposited on the sofa, Tim dropped his bag off in the bedroom and went to investigate the contents of the fridge and kitchen cupboards.

"What are you doing now?" Seb rested one arm on the back of the sofa as he watched Tim opening and closing cupboard doors.

"Seeing what you've got in the way of food."

Seb's brow furrowed as though that thought hadn't occurred to him. "Oh. I usually go grocery shopping on a Monday night on the way home from work, but"—he glanced down at his foot—"I guess that's going to be almost impossible now. Fuck."

After finding very little in either the cupboards or the fridge, Tim leaned against the worktop. "If you give me a list, I can go shopping for you."

"You don't have to do that."

"I know I don't, but I want to." He walked over and sat on the other end of the sofa, careful to avoid Seb's cast. "Going shopping is not something you need to be attempting on your own. It's no trouble for me to pick up what you need before I come to see you." He paused, swallowing down the apprehension of saying the next bit. "And I planned on coming over a lot. If that's okay?"

The silence stretched between them as Seb stared at him, his bottom lip caught between his teeth. "For appearances' sake?"

*No. For mine.* "I suppose." Bollocks to it—it wasn't as though Seb didn't already know how he felt. "And because I want to. I know you don't like to talk about it, and this'll be the last time I bring it up, but thinking about you being in danger brings out my protective instincts in a big way."

"Okaaay?"

Seb eyed him as though expecting him to elaborate. Tim covered his face with his hands and tried to think of the best way to put it. "I'm not out of control or anything, but being this close to you makes me want to—" *Stay with you, keep you safe, because you're mine. Or you could be.*

"Want to what?" Seb licked his lips.

Tim breathed through his mouth, trying to avoid scenting the air because he recognised the look Seb was now giving him—intentionally or not.

"I want to take you into that bedroom and—" *Bite you,* his mind helpfully supplied. *Oh shit.* "—and keep you safe," he added lamely. He stood up and

133

tried to walk calmly into the kitchen while his heart pounded. "I think I'm going to nip out and get you the basics now. Milk, bread, cheese, anything else?"

He needed to get out of there just to get himself together.

"Um…." Seb looked at him as though Tim had lost his mind, and Tim didn't blame him. "Maybe some bacon. Oh, and crisps." He pulled his wallet out, frowning as he peered inside. "I don't have any cash on me, but if you—"

Tim waved him away. "Don't worry about it."

"You don't have to pay for my food. I'm not a charity case, you know."

Seb refused to meet Tim's gaze; obviously money was a sore point.

"I know that." Tim realised he had no idea what Seb did for a living or if he was getting paid while he was off sick. "It's only a few essentials. We can sort it out later."

"Okay."

Seb relaxed a little, and Tim took it as his cue to leave before anything else was said. He paused at the entrance to the hall. The thought of leaving Seb here alone seemed wrong, but he'd have to do it eventually. Might as well use this as a trial run. "You'll be all right while I'm gone?"

Seb huffed out a laugh, albeit a tiny one. "I think I'll manage. And no, I won't answer the door," he added, reading Tim's mind. "In fact, take my keys, then I don't have to get up and let you back in."

"Good idea." Tim scooped them out of Seb's outstretched hand and left before he could change his mind.

Fortunately there was a Tesco Express a couple of hundred metres from Seb's flat. Tim headed in that direction as soon as he'd checked the vicinity was clear of shifters. Pulling out his phone, he then sent Nathan a text as he marched along the pavement.

*Took S home. I want to bite him.*

Nathan's reply was immediate, all in shouty caps.

*WTF? GET THE HELL OUT OF THERE NOW.*

In hindsight, maybe not the best opener. *I'm not going to actually do it, I just wanted to. Never felt that strongly before. Wanted some advice.* Then as an afterthought, because he could easily picture Nathan halfway to his van by now, *And I'm walking to the shop.*

The next reply he got sounded a lot less angry.

*Ok good. He's in danger, it's a natural reaction. Have you scented him?*

*No.*

*Do it. That should help. Having sex would help more, settle down your wolf. Make him smell like he's yours.*

Fuck, just the thought of that gave Tim a semi. He adjusted his jeans as subtly as possible. *I think I'll stick with the scenting for now.*

*Ok. It'll take the edge off, trust me.*

*Thanks.*

Before he knew it, he was back at Seb's front door, fumbling with the keys.

"Sebastian?" he shouted up the stairs, taking them two at a time.

Not that he was worried, but he just wanted to see him—confirm that nothing bad had happened in the forty minutes he'd been gone.

"Just a sec." The reply sounded slightly muffled, and Tim reached the top step just as Seb came out of his bedroom, wrestling a T-shirt over his head while still keeping hold of his crutch. He'd put on a low-slung pair of shorts, and the combination left a wide expanse of skin on show, complete with a dark blond happy trail.

Tim closed his eyes and pinched the bridge of his nose. "Are you doing this on purpose?"

When he looked again, Seb was fully covered and trying to sort out his hair.

Seb's expression turned sheepish. "Sorry. I thought I'd be dressed before you got back."

Part of Tim wished he'd run back from the shop and seen more. He managed to successfully hide that growing part with a well-placed shopping bag. "I'll just put these in the fridge."

"Okay."

Unfortunately, Seb trailed after him, and Tim willed his hard-on to go away. This whole scenario was awkward enough.

"So...." he started.

Seb looked up from where he was buttering a slice of bread. He set down the knife and gave Tim his full attention. "Is this the part where we—?" he gestured to his crotch, and Tim's eyes followed the movement. Although Seb sounded teasing, his eyes didn't match his tone.

"I think scenting you will be enough for now."

"Scenting?"

Tim took a step towards him, raising his hand. "Can I?" He pointed to Seb's neck.

"Yeah. Go for it."

Was he imagining the sudden roughness in Seb's voice? A quick glance confirmed his claws were safely sheathed—which, all things considered, was a relief—so Tim reached out and placed his hand at the base of Seb's throat. Seb swallowed and Tim felt it under his fingers. Taking his time, he slowly and deliberately rubbed his palm around to the side of Seb's neck and up behind his ear until he cupped the back of his head.

Another step closer brought them almost flush. Tim tilted Seb's head to the side, but he froze at Seb's sharp intake of breath. "Relax," he whispered, smiling as Seb shivered in response. "I won't bite you."

"Better fucking not," Seb muttered, but he was already tilting his head more, giving Tim what he wanted.

"Promise."

This close, Seb's scent clung to him, thick and heavy. Tim's eyes fluttered shut as he leaned in and ran his nose along the side of Seb's neck. He always had trouble putting scents into words, but Seb reminded him of the outdoors, something fresh and summery. It filled him with a thrill similar to shifting, something wild and exciting coursing through his veins, and he buried his face in the crook of Seb's neck, greedily breathing it in. "You smell so good."

To his surprise, Seb laughed.

Stung, Tim pulled back and went to take a step away from him, to put some distance between them. Seb's hand on his arm stopped him. "Sorry. It's just such a shiftery thing to say, and… well…."

"What?"

"You're not a typical shifter. It just struck me as funny, that's all."

Tim couldn't decide whether to be offended or flattered. "What do you consider a typical shifter?"

"You know—arrogant, growly, quick-tempered exhibitionists."

*Flattered, then.* He smiled. "I'll let Nathan know what you really think of him. And Alec and Cam."

The look of horror on Seb's face made Tim laugh out loud.

Seb moaned, "Fuck no. They'd eat me."

Tim grinned at him, flashing all his teeth. "And I won't?"

His phone buzzed in his pocket and he pulled it out, still smiling. The smile dimmed a little when he saw it was from Alec.

*Heads up. P-Pack heard S is back home. Coming by later to offer apology.*

"Bollocks." He typed a quick *Ok thanks* and sighed.

"What's the matter?" Instead of answering, Tim angled the screen so that Seb could read. "Oh."

Tim looked up, caught Seb's gaze and held it, hoping he would understand what that meant without Tim having to spell it out. His mouth had gone dry and he didn't trust himself to get the words out.

Realisation apparently dawned; Seb's cheeks flushed and he looked away. "*Oh.*"

# Chapter Nine

Seb focused on his bare feet, curling his toes into the thick pile of the carpet.

Why was this suddenly so awkward? They were both grown men, for fuck's sake, and jacking off next to a hot guy was hardly a chore. Seb was under no illusions that that was what Tim meant with his searching look.

"How long have we got?" he asked, more of a way to break the weird silence.

To his surprise, Tim chuckled. "Long enough." He put a finger under Seb's chin and tipped his head up. "I don't know about you, but I'm thinking it won't take me long at all." He nodded down at the prominent bulge in his jeans.

Seb badly wanted to smooth his palm over the taut denim and feel how hard he was, but he kept his hands to himself, unsure of what the etiquette was in this situation. He'd laid out all the rules for not getting involved beyond what was absolutely necessary, but considering what they were about to do, that seemed absurd now. Seb's shorts were loose fitting, but even so, his hardening cock was easy to see.

*Obviously I want this. Tim must think I'm so full of shit.*

Tim linked their fingers for a second before handing Seb his crutch; then he took a step in the direction of Seb's bedroom. "Bedroom's this way, yeah?"

"Yeah."

"Come on, then."

They walked the short distance in silence, although Seb's heart did a good job of trying to make itself heard. His pulse thudded in his ears as they moved, and his dick bobbed with each clunking step he took.

Tim waited for Seb to go in first, and Seb went straight over to his bed. He lowered himself down, taking extra care, because falling on his arse was not something he wanted to do right then. Tim stood in front of him, just the right height for Seb to lean forward and—

He shook his head to clear it. That wasn't what they were there for. "How should we do this?"

Tim's gaze snapped up from where he'd been watching Seb's mouth, and the flash of disappointment told Seb he wasn't the only one who'd forgotten what this was supposed to be about.

Tim looked down at Seb's cast and frowned a little. "However's comfortable for you." His lips curved up as he spoke. "How do you usually… you know?"

Seb shrugged. "I haven't *you know* since I did this." He held up his wrist and then nodded at his ankle.

"Oh." Tim looked back at Seb's cast and slowly dragged his gaze up over his thighs.

Seb parted his legs instinctively, enjoying the open appreciation. Heat settled deep in his belly as Tim worked his way up.

Tim said, "In my professional opinion, as your doctor, I suggest getting naked and lying down would be easiest."

"Is that so?" Seb sniggered, but Tim just raised an eyebrow at him and carried on.

"Yeah, it is." He dropped to his knees and Seb's breath caught. "Lean back."

Seb obeyed and watched as Tim reached for the waistband of his shorts. He peeled them off slowly, taking great care to lift them over Seb's erection so that his hand barely brushed him over his underwear. Seb bit back a moan, the teasing touches setting his blood on fire.

Dropping the shorts on the floor beside him, Tim returned to do the same with Seb's boxer briefs. "Lift up a little," he whispered, voice rough like sandpaper.

Seb obliged as best he could, leaning on his elbows to avoid his still-healing wrist. Tim managed to not touch him at all that time, and the urge to lift his hips, and chase after Tim's hands was almost unbearable.

*This was your choice, remember?*

With Seb now naked and waiting, Tim stood and looked down at him for a good few seconds before snapping his gaze away. "Scoot up the bed and get comfy." He grasped the hem of his long-sleeved T-shirt and pulled it over his head and off.

Instead of moving into position, Seb lay there staring. He knew shifters were built, their DNA unfairly gifting them with muscles they needed to do little to maintain. But somehow, with Tim being leaner than most, Seb hadn't expected him to be quite as ripped as he was. He licked his lips, tracking the dusting of dark hair covering Tim's firm chest all the way down the middle of his belly to where it disappeared behind his jeans. Tim wasn't heavily muscled like some shifters Seb had seen, but the lean lines, so deceptive under his clothing, were just as defined.

As if it was his own private striptease, Seb watched transfixed as Tim unbuckled his belt and flipped open the button on his jeans. The zipper sounded so loud, and Seb's heart rate increased as each tooth opened. Tight black underwear kept Tim from springing free as he shucked off his jeans and kicked them aside.

He pointed to Seb's pillows. "I thought you were supposed to be getting comfy."

"I am comfy." The last thing Seb wanted to do was move.

Tim eyed him curiously, but didn't reply. He didn't appear bothered by Seb watching him undress, so Seb stayed right where he was as Tim hooked his thumbs under the waistband and drew the underwear down over his hips. Now free, his cock jutted out in front of him, hard and inviting. The tip already wet with precome made Seb's mouth water at the thought of tasting it.

"Move," Tim whispered.

He put a knee on the bed. Seb realised he wasn't going to come any closer until he got into position on the pillows. So he did, shuffling back until he felt one under his head. Then he rolled onto his side and watched Tim climb up after him.

They lay facing each other, both on their sides. Seb itched to reach out and touch him, and once again he cursed his own stupid rules. He settled for wrapping his hand around his cock; it was his bad wrist, and although almost fully healed, it still twinged. Failing to hide the wince, he wasn't surprised when Tim laid a hand on his arm and stopped him.

"Let me?" Tim's eyes, full of want and need, burnt away the last of his resolve.

With his heart pounding, Seb nodded. His eyes slipped shut as Tim shuffled closer and wrapped his long fingers around both of them. "Fuck." His breath caught as his cock rubbed up against Tim's.

Tim's grip, firm and tight, pulled a moan from Seb's lips. Each stroke of Tim's hand sent a shiver through him, pleasure snaking up from the base of his spine and unfurling in a wave of heat. Fuck, Tim had been right. It wasn't going to take him long at all.

A low, rumbling growl broke the silence and Seb's eyes snapped open.

Tim was watching him, his open mouth revealing too-sharp teeth. "'S okay," he mumbled, the words a little distorted. "Still... in control." He ran his thumb over the head of Seb's cock.

"Glad... someone is," Seb groaned, and when Tim growled again, his hand tightening around them, Seb was done for. He came with a shout, head thrown back and eyes closed, riding the wave of pleasure coursing through him.

His release hit his belly, and Seb had the fleeting thought that maybe he should have aimed better. He opened his eyes to watch Tim. Then Tim was coming too, and the sight caught and held his attention. Mouth open on a silent cry, Tim followed him over the edge, managing to hit his own chin, chest, and belly.

"Wow." Seb took in the state of him and grinned. "That's a lot of come."

Hard to tell whether Tim blushed or was still flushed from his orgasm. Tim glanced at Seb's belly, then down at himself, and shrugged. "It's been a while."

They looked up at the same time, and before any awkwardness could creep in, Seb blurted, "So now what?" He ran two fingers through the mess on his belly and held them up. "We do the smearing thing, right?"

Tim's eyes darkened, and for a split second, Seb swore his features started to change, but then he was back to normal as though nothing had happened.

*Maybe I imagined it.*

"Yes," Tim said eventually, not taking his gaze from Seb's fingers. "We do that."

"Here?" Seb licked his lips and then rubbed his wet fingers along the side of Tim's ribs.

Tim flinched as if ticklish. "A little higher."

Seb slid his fingers up, brushing Tim's nipple in the process. "Here?" Tim shook his head. "Show me."

Without saying a word, Tim coated his fingers with his own come and smeared a trail of it down the side of Seb's neck to the base of his throat. "Like that."

Seb breathed deep and felt the brief press of claws against his skin; then Tim's hand was gone.

It felt like they were teetering on the edge of something. None of what they'd just done seemed perfunctory or solely for the good of the pack, and Seb didn't want it to be. He'd been fooling himself into thinking he could do any of this and not get attached. *I'm already attached.*

All he had to do was say the words and all this would be for real. Copying what Tim had just done, he wet his fingers and slid his hand around Tim's neck. "I don't want this to be pretend anymore."

144

Tim froze, his body going rigid under Seb's hands. "But you said—"

"I don't want to be a wolf, and I don't want to be anybody's bonded mate." Seb swallowed, wondering if that was too much for a shifter to handle. "But I'd like to try this. Us. If you do?"

Tim took less than a second to consider his answer. "Yes." With a hand on Seb's waist, he rolled him onto his back and moved on top of him. "Are you sure?"

Seb slid his hand into Tim's hair, tugging him close, whispering the words against his lips. "Promise not to bite me?"

"Never without your consent."

Tim looked so sincere and earnest. *Why did I ever doubt him?* "Then I'm sure." Seb pulled him into a kiss—hard and desperate as he let go of everything that had held him back. Tim's solid weight pinned him to the bed, all that raw power caging him in, yet Seb had never felt safer.

Tim eased his hands under Seb's shoulders, holding him in place while he broke the kiss to nip and lick along the side of his neck. Seb sighed and tilted his head to the side with a soft moan. The faint scrape of teeth made his breath hitch, but Tim's whispered "Trust me" had him melting back into the pillow.

Seb let out a laugh of surprise as Tim's dick began to harden between them. "Already?"

Propping himself up on his elbows, Tim grinned down at him, eyes crinkling at the corners. "What do you expect with you lying there looking like that and smelling of sex?"

Seb peered between them and his grin matched Tim's. "We're a bit of a mess." Tim rolled his hips, sliding alongside Seb's cock, making it stir with interest. "And I've got jizz in your hair."

Tim laughed again. "Shifter, remember. Mess is my thing."

He dipped his head to nose along Seb's collarbone, then up along the strip of skin where he'd rubbed his come earlier. Seb arched into his touch like a cat as Tim licked him clean, shamelessly thrusting his hips to get Tim to move again. He felt Tim's smile against his skin at the same time as he started up a slow, rolling grind that made Seb's toes curl in pleasure.

"That's good to know," Seb mumbled, tightening his hold on Tim's hair and encouraging him to move down his body; after Tim's admission, he didn't care about what was on his fingers or all over their stomachs. Tim wasn't the first shifter he'd messed around with, but he was the first one that hadn't been just a quick fuck or blowjob. Jared had waxed lyrical countless times about how fucking hot sex was with Nathan, but Seb had assumed that was because of their bond. Now he was beginning to think it was more than that.

Christ, if it felt this good now, imagine what it'd be like—*No!* He wasn't going there. Especially not when the wet, warm tease of Tim's mouth had him squirming on the bed. He gave Tim another gentle shove lower; the resulting huff of laughter skittered across his belly and tickled.

"I'll get there soon, enough."

The smile in Tim's voice made Seb's lips curve up at the edges; he was unable to resist a smile of his own. He wiggled his hips; his cock showed definite signs of interest as it nudged up against Tim's chest. The dark hair covering Tim's pecs was

146

surprisingly soft as it brushed along Seb's length, a stark contrast to the rough stubble on Tim's jaw. Seb wanted to feel more of it; his stomach must be pink from all the attention Tim was giving it, and he pushed up, chasing the scrape of it as Tim kissed his way down Seb's happy trail, laving at the salty sweat and come from earlier.

For Seb, it had been a long time since someone had taken such care in getting him off. When he opened his eyes to the sight of Tim glancing back up at him, mouth parted and eyes almost black, and knowing what was on his tongue had Seb fully hard in seconds.

Tim chuckled, obviously feeling it. "You want a taste?" He licked at his bottom lip, and Seb nodded, too turned-on to form words. Far quicker than Seb was expecting—*fucking shifters*—Tim's mouth was on his, his tongue pushing in and sharing the salty bitter taste of what they'd done earlier. Seb kissed him back, greedy for everything, both hands fisting Tim's hair when Tim slipped a hand between them and snaked his fingers around the base of Seb's cock.

Moaning at the feel of having Tim all over him, Seb was certain he could come from this—a few more pulls of Tim's hand while he kissed Seb like that and he'd be done for. No sooner had the thought passed through his mind than Tim was pulling back, sliding down Seb's body. The small whimper Seb let out at the loss of Tim's hand and mouth quickly dissolved into a throaty groan as Tim settled between his legs and whispered, "Pull your knee up for me."

*Oh.* Seb moved quickly, drawing his good leg up until his foot was flat on the bed, thighs wide open for Tim to do whatever he liked to him.

First, Tim wrapped his fingers back around Seb's cock and gave it a couple of long hard strokes that had him pushing his hips up to meet each one. As his hand stilled, resting at the base in a far-too-loose grip, Tim ducked his head and licked a stripe from Seb's hole to his balls, gently sucking one into his mouth as he started up a gentle rhythm with his hand.

"Fuck." Seb pushed his head back into the pillows, eyes screwed shut as a myriad of sensations rushed through his body—his hands still tangled in Tim's hair and he hung on for dear life as Tim slowly worked his mouth down to Seb's hole again. He licked around the rim, the tip of his tongue pressing in again and again until Seb felt himself opening up enough for Tim to slide the tip inside him. His hips bucked as he tried to push for more, needing that tongue so much deeper, but Tim stilled him with a hand on his stomach.

Clinging to the edge of his orgasm, it was almost too much to take and not come, but he needed just a little bit—

Tim thrust his tongue in farther and tightened his hand around Seb's dick, jacking him off hard and fast, and that was it. Seb cried out, pleasure coursing through his veins as he started to come once more. Tim scooted up quickly enough to get his mouth around the head of Seb's cock and catch the last of it, making Seb moan all over again. All he could do was lie there and watch as Tim kneeled up, dick in hand, and got himself off as he licked Seb's jizz from his lips.

"Fucking hell."

It came out breathless and sounding a little in awe, but that was how Seb felt. He glanced down at the fresh mess on his belly, wondering what they were going to do with it just as Tim reached out and ran his fingers through it.

Without a word, he brought his hand up to Seb's mouth, rubbed the sticky wetness across his lips then pushed his fingers inside. Seb sucked on them, drawing the taste onto his tongue. It came as no surprise when Tim withdrew them and leaned down to kiss him, long and deep, until Seb had to push him away to catch his breath.

Tim stretched out on top of him, his weight pressing Seb down into the bed in a way that he desperately needed at that moment. He felt raw, strung out, and he wrapped his arms around Tim's lower back to keep him there.

Leaning up on his forearms, Tim looked down at him, concern etched on his features. "You okay?"

Seb swallowed, taking his time before answering so that his voice wouldn't come out sounding as vulnerable as he felt. Jared hadn't told him it would be like this afterward. Or if he had, Seb hadn't fucking listened. "Yeah," he managed. "I'm good."

"You are." Tim grinned, teeth all normal looking, which got Seb focusing on them—a welcome distraction from everything else.

"How come you didn't... *you know*?" He reached up to gently tap one of Tim's canines.

Tim stared at him for a second before understanding dawned. "Wolf out a little, you mean?"

"Yeah." Seb remembered the way Tim's teeth had lengthened as he touched Seb's cock, and a shiver ran down his spine. "You did the first time."

"I was maybe a little overexcited." He ducked his head, but not before Seb caught the colour blossoming on his cheeks.

Kissing the top of Seb's shoulder, Tim then sighed and rested his forehead in the crook of Seb's neck. His words were muffled but easy enough to make out. "I didn't expect to get to touch you, at least not so soon, anyway." He huffed out a laugh and it tickled. "I wasn't prepared for how good it would feel."

Seb gave him a nudge with his shoulder. "And it wasn't that good second time around?" he teased. Well, half teased. Not that he wanted Tim to lose control while they were having sex, but he had an ego like everyone else and also a few insecurities.

Tim's expression when he lifted his head and met Seb's gaze was far more serious than Seb had been expecting. Tim said, "If anything, it was better. I have a feeling it'll keep getting better, but I just had a handle on my wolf this time." He bit his bottom lip and Seb followed the movement, imagining him doing it with sharp teeth, piercing the—

*Shit.* A wave of arousal swept through him. Since when did he find that hot? Of course, Tim didn't miss the sudden change in him, and he raised an eyebrow, his expression turning curious.

"You like the idea of me losing control?"

Shifter senses were so fucking inconvenient. Seb would have been quite happy to ignore that stray thought and never bring it up. "No." Tim gave him a look that said, "I don't believe you," and Seb sighed, resigned. "Maybe a little."

"I thought that's what had you most worried? That I might lose control and bite you?"

"It was... *is*." Another sigh. His mind was still sex-foggy and finding the right words to explain himself properly was a struggle. "It's just—and I know how this sounds, okay—but... Jared's always going on about how Nathan gets so turned-on, so lost in the moment that sometimes he can't help but lose control. And I suppose...."

God, it sounded even worse when he said it out loud. Was he really *that* insecure?

*It appears so.*

"Sebastian."

Seb couldn't help the automatic smile that caused. Every time. "You're the only one who ever calls me that."

"Oh?" Tim frowned, seeming unsure. "Does it bother you?"

"No. I like it."

Tim's frown smoothed out, replaced by a small soft smile that Seb had a feeling not many people got to see. "You shouldn't compare us to Jared and Nathan all the time."

"I don't," Seb automatically protested. Tim stared at him until he rolled his eyes. "Okay, fine, maybe I do. A bit."

Tim snorted, but that was all Seb was owning up to.

"They're bonded." Tim spoke quietly. "The connection is so much more intense for them."

"Yeah, okay." *Makes sense.* And that wasn't something Seb wanted, so he had no business feeling envious. But by the catch in Tim's voice, Seb

151

wasn't the only one. Would asking make things awkward between them? Probably, but Seb couldn't help himself. "Is that something you want? To have what they have?" His heart rate ratcheted up; Tim's answer was suddenly far more important than it had been a few days ago.

"No." Tim glanced away as he answered. "I used to think so." He shrugged. "But finding a bond like theirs doesn't happen to everyone. It'd be stupid hoping for something that I might never get."

Seb couldn't decide if Tim was trying to convince him or himself. He didn't say that, though, not wanting to open that can of worms; he just slid his hands into Tim's hair and drew him down for a kiss. He hadn't meant to initiate anything, starting out soft and lazy, but then Tim moaned and gripped him a little tighter. Seb moved, spreading his thighs to get Tim settled between them, and then everything moved up a notch.

Could he go for round three? Maybe, maybe not, but Seb was all for giving it a go. He slid his hands down Tim's back, loving the play of muscle under his palms. Just as he grabbed Tim's arse, urging him to move a little, Tim froze. This time, Seb felt the telltale prick of claws against the tops of his shoulders.

"Tim?"

With his head cocked to one side, Tim let out a cross between a growl and a snarl. "They're here."

Seb sat up as Tim climbed off him. "The guys from P-Pack?"

"Yeah." Tim still sounded angry and tense, and Seb watched warily as he searched through their discarded clothes until he found his jeans. Not bothering with any underwear, Tim pulled his jeans on but left the top button undone. He didn't appear to look for a T-shirt either.

Seb went to climb out of bed, but Tim stopped him with a glare. "Where do you think you're going?"

Easing his cast to the floor, Seb gestured to the hallway. "It's my flat. I was going to go and answer the door."

With perfect timing, the doorbell chimed.

"No." Tim took two steps towards him and sank to his knees. "Please stay here until I can make sure it's safe."

"You said they were coming to apologise."

"I know, and I'm sure they are. But just in case, let me go down there first. I can't focus properly if I'm worried about you getting hurt."

Seb wanted to protest. He hated being labelled as someone who needed protecting. But these were shifters, and even if he was fighting fit, he'd never stand a chance against them. Tim fixed him with a pleading expression in his big blue eyes, and the last of Seb's resolve crumbled. "Fine. But shout me when it's okay to come down. I'd like to hear this apology for myself."

Tim smiled, obviously relieved. "Thank you, and I will." He stood and walked towards the door.

"Wait. Are you going down there like that?"

With his jeans left undone and no T-shirt, you couldn't miss the streaks of dried come all over his body, not to mention the mess Seb had made of his hair. There would be no mistaking what they'd spent the last hour or so doing.

"It wouldn't matter if I put more clothes on." Tim grinned at him. "They'll smell me way before I open the door." With that, he turned and walked out of the room. Or swaggered was more like it.

Seb shook his head and smirked. Even mild-mannered shifters could pull off the smug-arsehole look.

# Chapter Ten

Tim heard them muttering on the other side of the front door as he walked slowly down the stairs. They were talking too quietly for him to make out the words, but it sounded like there were only two of them. Not bad odds if it came to a fight.

Tim might not look the part, but he wasn't afraid of getting his hands dirty. Especially with Seb upstairs. His hackles rose as he heard Seb's name, followed by laughter, and he jumped the last six steps and yanked open the door.

The two shifters leaned against either side of the door frame. Neither one looked overly bothered by Tim's warning growl. Their scent was familiar in that it was definitely P-Pack, and Tim thought he might recognise them, but not by name. He stood up straight and crossed his arms.

The one on the right was tall, blond, and kind of cute—not that Tim was interested—and he smiled and let his gaze wander down Tim's chest to his low-slung jeans.

He let out a low whistle. "If we had a pack doctor like you, I'd want to be injured as often as possible."

Ignoring him, Tim turned to the other one, who was slightly shorter, with dark hair and a strong jaw.

The shifter stuck out his hand for Tim to shake. "I'm Mark, and this is Will." He gestured to his pack-mate.

"Tim Walters." Tim took his hand and shook it, then did the same with Will. He'd not washed his

155

hands; the scent of come must be rolling off him in waves, but neither of them flinched.

Mark chuckled and shook his head. "Yeah, we were told you'd be around a lot." He smiled and eyed Tim's belly again. "Have to say I thought it was a way for your pack to keep an eye on Calloway, but now…." Mark breathed in deep and Tim caught the faintest hint of arousal in the air, and it wasn't coming from him. "Well… even if it is, it looks like it comes with some pretty sweet benefits."

Will laughed, and Tim opened his mouth wide enough to let his teeth extend.

Will stopped immediately and held up both hands. "Hey, we were just messing. No offence."

Tim stared at them for a few seconds longer, the urge to half-shift stirring under his skin. He doubted these two posed a threat to him or Seb, but standing there with the evidence of what they'd just done all over him, their combined scents a heady reminder, Tim struggled to back down. There was nothing feigned about his reaction. Whether they were convinced or not, he couldn't tell. "What can I do for you?"

Mark stood up straight, his smile slipping. "We came to apologise for what happened to Calloway."

The hairs stood up on the back of Tim's neck and his fingers itched with the need to let his claws out. "Was it you?" He hadn't paid all that much attention to the scents surrounding Seb's flat that night and couldn't be sure whether they'd been there or not.

"No." Mark glanced at Will, who looked a little uncomfortable.

"Then why are you apologising?"

"You and Calloway are *dating*—" Will's gaze once again dropped to the open button on Tim's jeans. "—so there was a good chance you'd be here when someone from our pack came. We thought it'd be better for everyone if we came instead."

They were probably right. Considering how he'd reacted to these two, if confronted with the idiots who'd scared Seb into falling down the stairs, he might well have done exactly what Alec was trying to prevent. "Fair enough."

But if that was the case, then—"Does Alpha Newell know you're here?"

They shared another look. "No."

Tim eyed them both, trying to detect whether they were telling the truth. The pair seemed on edge, but more from fear than deceit. "I see."

If they were going against their alpha's orders, then they had every reason to be afraid.

Mark glanced behind them, back down the road, and paused as though listening for something. "Look, it's not that we're doing anything wrong. Alpha Newell said that an apology needed to be given to Calloway. He didn't specify who should do it."

"But I imagine it was implied?"

Mark shrugged. "Maybe."

Tim wasn't in the habit of trusting anyone from outside his own pack, but these two had told him more than they strictly needed to. He still had to be careful. The fact that Newell was pissed off over what happened with Nathan was common knowledge. "You realise Newell probably wasn't all that concerned about upsetting me, don't you?"

Mark scratched at the back of his neck. "Yeah, he may have voiced his displeasure with your pack once or twice since the fight with the rogue pack."

Will snorted. "Pack meetings have been… *interesting.*"

"I bet."

"Look,"—Mark lowered his voice to barely above a whisper—"it was my cousin and his friend who were here that night." Tim automatically tensed, but Mark was shaking his head. "No, it wasn't really their fault. They're just young, stupid, and impressionable."

Tim waited. "Go on."

"Wes talked them into it. You know how he had a thing for Nathan?" Tim nodded; he remembered Jared grumbling about it. "Well, he's still pissed off that he chose a human instead of him."

"Nathan didn't just *choose*, Jared. They *bonded*, for fuck's sake."

"Never said he was the brightest member of the pack," Will chipped in. "Since Jared is safely locked away in one of your pack houses, I suppose he thought Calloway was the next best thing."

Tim gestured for Mark to continue.

"Wes said if they did it—scared him a little—it'd put them in good favour with Alpha Newell, and like a pair of idiots, they believed every word of it."

Tim wanted to believe them, they seemed sincere enough, but—"Why are you telling me all this, exactly? If Newell or his betas find out, I can't imagine they'd be impressed."

In fact, he would put money on Newell being royally pissed off that Will and Mark were speaking this candidly with a member of Cam's pack.

Mark sent a quick glance to Will, who nodded. "I know our two packs don't have the best relationship right now, but not everyone…." He trailed off and ran a hand through his hair. Tim sympathised—saying anything against one's alpha wasn't an easy thing to do. "We don't want to start a pack war, and there's a few of us in P-Pack that think it's headed that way. If we can stop that from happening, we will."

What did he say to that? Tim was the pack doctor; he didn't have the authority or experience to handle something like this. *Fuck. I wish Alec was here. He'd know exactly what to do, what to say.*

Mark and Will were watching him expectantly, waiting for his response.

He finally answered. "That's good to know. What about the rogue shifters? Are they an actual threat?"

He didn't really expect them to tell him the truth if Newell had made it up, but it was worth a shot. Body language told him a lot about a person.

Mark frowned and Will seemed just as confused. "Yeah, why wouldn't they be?"

"Because I was under the impression that they all died at the raid on the warehouse."

Now they both looked a little shifty.

Mark sighed as he ran a hand through his hair again. "We can't talk about that. But Alpha Newell had a full pack meeting about it. The threat's real."

Tim didn't know how to feel about that. On the one hand, it was a good thing Newell wasn't lying to Cam, but the thought of rogue shifters running

159

around, intent on some payback for Nathan and the rest of the pack, filled him with dread. If the rogue shifters were alone, isolated from what used to be their pack, then what did they have to lose? A wolf like that was as dangerous as they came. Tim couldn't help but move closer to the open door to scent the air.

"Relax." Will glanced behind him as he spoke. "Why do you think we've been watching this place? There's no sign of them around here."

"Have they been here at all?"

Another look passed between Mark and Will, and Tim's stomach sank.

"Maybe." When Tim's lip curled up in a snarl, Mark added, "Hey, it was hard to be sure as there'd been a shitload of rain that night."

A familiar scent wafted down from the top of the stairs and all three shifters glanced up.

"Hey." Seb stood there in his pyjama pants and a T-shirt, one hand holding his crutch, the other loosely gripping the stair rail. "You were taking ages, so…."

The smell of sex and Tim was all over him, heavy enough to make Tim growl a warning. His teeth itched and his fingers tingled with the need to shift and protect what was his.

"We're no threat," Mark murmured.

With a slight nod and a roll of his shoulders, Tim shook off the possessiveness trying to take over and smiled up at Seb. "Hey, sorry. I should have called you." What he wanted to say was "What the fuck are you doing? You promised to wait until I said it was okay. Anything could have been going on." But the truth was he'd forgotten about shouting for Seb at all, much preferring him tucked away in the bedroom, as safe as possible under the circumstances.

"Am I okay to come down?" Seb raised an eyebrow, as though he knew just what Tim was thinking.

Tim sent a quick warning glance at Will and Mark, then said, "Yeah, come here. Let me introduce you."

Holding on to the rail, Seb carefully descended the stairs, his gaze flicking up to the two P-Pack shifters every few seconds. When he got to the bottom, Tim reached out for his hand and drew Seb in behind him, thankful Seb just went with it and didn't make any smart-arse comment. What he did do was slip his hands around Tim's waist, hook his thumbs in the waistband of his jeans, and place a soft kiss on the top of Tim's shoulder.

Tim shivered, both from the feel of Seb's lips against his bare skin and the way his thumbs rubbed just above his pelvis. He caught the expression on Seb's face out of the corner of his eye— mischievous. *Fucker.* This wasn't a game, but Tim wasn't about to say that in front of Will and Mark, who were staring as if Tim and Seb were the most amusing thing ever. It stirred Tim's wolf again, and he let out a low snarl in warning.

Mark held up his hands. "Sorry." He smiled. "It's just we didn't expect you two to be so...."

"So what?" Seb asked, his thumbs still rubbing back and forth in the most teasing rhythm ever.

"Full-on. If it's all an act, then it's a bloody good one."

Mark laughed, and Tim just pulled Seb closer behind him until he was virtually plastered to his back.

161

He didn't realise he was growling until Seb leaned up to whisper in his ear. "Hey. Shh. It's okay."

"Fine, I get it." Mark said, more serious this time. "Not an act."

They'd both been surprisingly honest with him, and Tim felt compelled to share a little more than he normally would. "It might have been suggested that a relationship between us would be beneficial to the pack." He slid his hands over Seb's. "But I can assure you, for me, this is all real."

Mark's eyes widened; he appeared to grasp that Tim had told him more than he needed to. He nodded and smiled. "I understand."

Seb rested his forehead against the back of Tim's neck and exhaled. Tim waited for him to speak, but Seb remained silent. Tim was aware this thing between them wasn't the same for Seb, but his silence still stung. As did the look of pity that flashed in Mark's eyes before he masked it.

"Now Seb's here you can offer him that apology in person," Tim said, wanting the whole conversation over and done with. He didn't need pitying looks from anyone, let alone a pair of shifters from another pack, no matter how friendly they were being. His raised eyebrows prompted Mark into speaking.

Mark turned to face Seb, wisely keeping his hands to himself. "On behalf of the Primrose Hill pack, I'd like to offer our sincerest apologies for causing your injuries by our careless actions. Those directly responsible have been spoken with, and nothing like that will happen again. You have our word."

Mark waited, focus entirely on Seb, even though he could probably feel Tim's gaze on him.

Seb sighed, his body relaxing into Tim's as if Tim was a solid weight he trusted to keep him upright. Tim tightened his fingers around Seb's where they still rested on his waistband, reassuring him that he had him. It felt good to have Seb lean on him like that.

*Too good.*

Seb lifted a hand and gestured at the two shifters in front of him. "Thanks, I suppose. Is that all you came here to say?"

Mark nodded. "Basically, yes." He glanced at Tim, and that wry smile was back. "And to check if you two were an actual couple, or if Alpha Harley was full of shit." When Tim snarled, he added, "Newell's words, not mine."

Seb slipped a hand back to Tim's waist, and something inside Tim settled. "Well, as you can see, we are."

Mark's smile was genuine and wide. "See, smell, practically *taste*."

Smug satisfaction curled in Tim's chest, but he buried the reaction, not wanting Seb to notice. "I think we're done here."

"I think so too." Mark nodded and gestured for Will to leave. "We'll be around as long as the rogue shifters continue to be a threat." He turned and ran a finger over the scratches in Seb's door. "But that won't happen again." With another nod at Seb this time, they were gone.

Tim walked forward and shut the door, locking it behind them. He listened to them walk down the road and get inside their car; then he turned to face Seb.

Seb asked, "They gone?"

"Yes."

Seb sighed, running a hand through his hair. "Anyone else lurking out there?"

Tim stepped towards him and set his hands on Seb's shoulders. "Not that I can sense."

"Okay." He seemed to relax at that. "What happens now?"

*Good question.* "First things first. I need to let Alec know." In fact, he should probably do that now. "Come on." After turning Seb around, he steered him towards the stairs. "I'll give him a call, and hopefully that'll do until I go and see him tomorrow."

As Seb climbed the first few steps, he looked back over his shoulder. "You can go and see him now if you need to. I'll be okay here by myself, you know."

Just the thought of it made Tim's wolf unsettled. "*No.*"

It came out far sharper than Tim intended, and this time, Seb stopped and half turned to glare down at him.

"No?" Seb's incredulous expression told Tim he was on shaky ground.

He took a deep breath, and making sure to sound much less like he was giving an order, he said, "I'd rather not leave you alone tonight, if that's all right with you?" Seb narrowed his eyes but didn't answer, so Tim forged ahead. "I'm not trying to tell you what to do, I promise. This is all about me. I can't—" He scrubbed his hands over his face, trying to calm the way his wolf longed to be the big, bad protector. His instincts in this case would only send Seb running for the hills, and Tim refused to

164

scare him off after only just getting to have a little taste of him. "It's hard for me to even think of leaving when the scent of another pack still clings to your front door." He looked up and met Seb's eyes. "Please."

Seb swallowed. Tim waited for him to say something, anything. The silence was killing him.

And then Seb whispered, "You can stay."

Tim's breath left him in a whoosh of relief. "Thank you."

"But if you're calling Alec, I'm calling Jared and Nathan."

"Maybe that's not such a good idea" was on the tip of his tongue, but Seb's glare had him swallowing them back down. "Okay."

Judging by Seb's smirk, he knew what Tim had been thinking. "You're not giving them enough credit. Nathan listens to Jared, and Jared would never let him do anything stupid."

"I know that. But Alec…." Alec would probably be pissed off that Nathan was involved. Although, considering Jared and Seb's friendship, it was unavoidable. "He and Nathan don't exactly—"

"I know all about Nathan and Alec." Seb leaned against the wall, taking the weight off his ankle.

"You do?" Not that it was a secret; all the pack had been there that day, but it wasn't something anyone discussed, let alone with a human. Even one adopted into the pack like Seb was. "Did Jared tell you?"

"No. Nathan did."

"Oh." Tim guessed that made sense. Although… "It happened a long time ago. I can't imagine how that came up in conversation." Seb

165

slumped against the wall a little more, and Tim glanced down at the cast on his foot. "Is it giving you trouble?"

"It aches a bit, that's all."

Tim made a shooing gesture with his hands. "Go and sit down, then. There's absolutely no reason to be chatting on the stairs when we could be on the sofa."

Seb turned around and started back up the stairs, but not quickly enough for Tim to miss the wince as he moved. Tim frowned and vowed to keep a closer eye on Seb for the next couple of days. He'd studied both human and shifter anatomy at college, and since the majority of his everyday cases were human, he knew first-hand the fragility of their bodies. "You need to take it easy."

"I have been taking it easy." Seb lowered himself onto the sofa with a sigh. "I've done nothing but lie around for the past week."

Which reminded Tim of something he'd been meaning to bring up. Two things, really. "When are you thinking about going back to work?"

Seb's mouth curled up into a lazy smile. "Well, thanks to my doctor, I've been signed off for another week."

"I never actually asked what it is you do for a living." Tim had happily scribbled out a doctor's note for Seb to send to his boss, too concerned about everything else at the time to be bothered asking questions. Which wasn't all that professional of him, but whatever.

Seb leaned his head back on the sofa and closed his eyes. "I work in an office." He waved his hand about. "Doing some data crap that I won't bore you with." He looked as though he had no intention of elaborating, so Tim let it drop. "My boss said I can probably do a couple of weeks working from home after that, maybe more. He just needs to check it with his boss and HR."

"That would be better, surely?"

Cracking one eye open, Seb turned to face him. "I knew you'd think that."

Tim looked pointedly at Seb's leg. "Are you saying that getting to and from work every day with that on would be fun?"

"No."

"Well, then." He pulled his phone out of his pocket and held it up for Seb to see. "I'm going to call Alec. Okay if I use your bedroom?"

Seb nodded. "Be my guest."

With a smile of thanks, Tim left the living room and headed for Seb's bedroom, closing the door behind him once he was inside.

Alec answered after the first ring. "Just a second." He sounded like he was walking, and Tim heard a couple of doors shutting before "Everything okay?"

Tim sighed and walked over to look out of Seb's bedroom window. "We had a couple of visitors from P-Pack."

"They give you any trouble?"

"No. The opposite, in fact. They came to apologise."

Alec's laugh was humourless. "Did they now."

"I know you don't trust any one of them right now, but the ones who came seemed genuine, as far as I could tell."

"Did you recognise them?"

Tim automatically shook his head. "Not by name." He gave Alec a quick rundown of what was said, the silence on the other end giving away nothing. "What do you think?"

"I need to talk to Cam."

"Yes, of course. Sorry." Tim was closer to Alec than most members of the pack, and sometimes he forgot that there were things Alec couldn't tell him. Tim might be the pack doctor, but he wasn't high enough in the chain of command to be privy to everything.

"It's nothing personal, Tim."

"It's fine. I understand." He heard Seb talking in the living room. "Nathan and Jared know about it."

Telling Alec felt almost like a betrayal. It shouldn't. Alec wasn't just his friend; he was also his beta and one of Cam's right-hand men. But a small part of him was conflicted, and he shifted uncomfortably. Thankfully, Alec didn't say anything other than to acknowledge what Tim had told him. He probably expected as much. If he and Nathan didn't dislike each other so much, maybe this wouldn't be such an issue. Tim debated whether to voice it. "Maybe it's been long enough. If you and Nathan could just—"

"No." Alec sounded more resigned than angry, but his tone still made Tim drop it. "I understand how you might feel caught in the middle of this, but Nathan and I can work perfectly well together without needing to dredge up the past."

Tim managed to hold back his huff of laughter. "Work well together" was a bit of a stretch. "Okay."

"Thank you for telling me. I'll suggest to Cam that we include Nathan in any discussions that involve him, Jared, or Seb."

"Oh." That was a big concession and Tim faltered, not sure how to reply. Alec was usually the last person to want the rest of the pack involved until absolutely necessary, and given his feelings about Nathan….

A couple of seconds passed before Alec spoke again. "So," he began, and Tim immediately sensed the change in tone, "they believed that you and Seb were together?"

"Yes." Tim's cheeks heated. "The… um… evidence spoke for itself."

Alec's burst of laughter was unexpected and made Tim smile. "I see." Another pause. Tim waited. "Be careful." Alec's voice was softer now, no trace of amusement or authority. This was Tim's friend talking. "I know I actively encouraged you to do this."

Tim huffed. "That's one way of looking at it."

"All I'm saying is it's easy for us to get attached. We don't do prolonged casual sex well. It's not in our nature to continually mix our scents like that and not form some kind of connection. He won't necessarily feel the same."

"I know that." He did know, all too well. And he'd given this same lecture to countless young shifters before and seen the consequences when they didn't listen.

"Sorry. I know I don't need to tell you any of it." Alec sighed, and Tim pictured him rubbing a hand over his face. "I suppose I feel guilty for using your attraction to Calloway to get you to agree."

Another thing that didn't happen often. Alec very rarely apologised for anything, because he was very rarely in the wrong.

Tim leaned his head against the window and watched the street below, empty of people this late. "I knew what I was getting into, so let's just drop it."

"Done."

"What I need to know is what happens now? Sebastian's off work for the next week and then hopefully working from home for the two after that. I doubt he'll stray too far from home in that time. But I can't keep an eye on him all the time, even if he'd let me."

Alec hummed, and the faint sound of fingers drumming on a tabletop sounded on the other end. "Cam has another meeting with Newell tomorrow. I have a few suggestions for him that might work. Can you stay there tonight?"

"Yes."

"Good. The meeting's at eight in the morning. I'll call you after."

"Okay. Thank you."

Tim held the phone against his chest for a minute, mulling over the day's events. It felt a lot longer than a few hours since he'd picked Seb up and brought him here. If this was how he felt after just one day... *Fuck*. He might have told Alec he knew what he was doing, but standing in that bedroom, surrounded by the scent of sex and *them*, Tim had never felt so out of control.

# Chapter Eleven

"Yep, two of them."

Seb sat hunched over the coffee table where his phone lay, Nathan and Jared on speaker.

"And they apologised?" Jared asked.

"Yes."

"Did you believe them? Did Tim?"

Jared again. Nathan had been oddly quiet for most of the call. Seb was starting to wonder if he was still there. "I've not really had chance to discuss it with Tim. He disappeared into my bedroom to call Alec,"—Nathan grunted at that. *Still there, then*—"but they seemed pretty genuine."

"Was it the ones from that night?"

Nathan's voice was lower, rougher than Seb was used to hearing it. "Um... not sure."

"How did Tim react?"

Seb frowned at his phone. "What do you mean?"

"Did he shift?"

"What? No, he didn't shift." A week ago, Seb would have laughed at the idea of Tim shifting in anger. Not now, though, but he still found the idea hard to imagine.

Nathan let out a sigh that sounded like relief. "Not the same ones, then." He didn't give Seb time to comment as he barrelled on, the whole thing beginning to sound like an interrogation. "Did they mention anything else? Like why someone from their pack thought it'd be a good idea to scare you like that? Did they mention the supposed rogue shifters roaming around?"

Seb ran the conversation back through his mind. "No, nothing else that I can think of. Tim spoke to them for a while before I got down there, though. I can ask him when he gets off the phone. Oh—they did say they'd be around as long as the rogue shifters continued to be a threat."

"Hmm, okay."

Nathan said nothing else, and Seb struggled to decide whether that was a good *hmm* or not.

"Is Tim staying the night?" Jared asked.

"Yeah." Seb felt the blush creep over his cheeks. Thank God neither of them could see him. "Something about not wanting to leave while another pack's scent was all over my front door."

"I bet." Nathan then muttered something that Seb didn't quite catch. *I'm probably better off not knowing.* "He'll have to leave at some point tomorrow. You going to be okay?"

Seb's usual flare of annoyance didn't surface at Nathan's question—a clear sign he was knackered. "Yeah. I don't have work. Might try and do a trip to the shop down the road, see how I get on. And before you say anything, the guys from P-Pack said they'd be keeping an eye on me."

Hushed whispers were followed by the slamming of a door. Then Jared came back on. "I don't think Nathan finds that reassuring."

Seb sighed and settled back into the sofa cushions. "Yeah, I know no one seems to trust them, but the two who came round seemed all right to me. And it's not like they'd do anything to me in broad daylight, right? There are laws against that sort of thing."

172

He tried to remember what Tim had told him yesterday—*Was it only yesterday?*—but a huge yawn interrupted his thought process.

"You should get to bed. You sound knackered. Tim worn you out already?"

Jared laughed as he said it, and Seb knew he meant it as a joke, but it wasn't anymore. Jared was his best friend; they'd been through a lot together. If anyone would understand the confused mess of feeling this whole situation stirred up, it would be him.

"Something like that. Listen, are you busy tomorrow?"

"Yeah, I've got a project to finish by Thursday. Why?"

*Oh.* "No reason. Just bored with not being at work."

"You're always welcome to come and hang out here, Seb. I'll be working most of the time, but I can take breaks, and Nate'll be here for a few hours."

Seb mulled the idea over for a second. Nathan would know what he and Tim had been up to as soon as Seb stepped within twenty feet of him. *Do I care?* "I'll let you know. Thanks."

"No problem."

The bedroom door opened and Seb glanced up to see Tim paused in the doorway. "I'm going to go. Talk to you tomorrow. Bye."

"Bye. And if you do go out tomorrow, be careful, yeah?"

"Course." He ended the call and shuffled around to half face Tim, who hadn't moved from his spot. "Everything okay?"

173

"Yeah." Tim smiled and walked over to stand next to the sofa. He narrowed his eyes. "You look tired."

"Thanks." Seb tried to sound offended, but he yawned again and gave up. "Yeah, I feel it. It's been a long day." He glanced up, caught Tim's gaze as it dropped to the soft bulge in his lap, and everything they'd done earlier came flooding back in a rush of heat. He knew the second Tim noticed.

"We should—" Tim breathed deeply and curled his hands into fists at his sides. "—should go to bed. You need rest. And food, probably. We seem to have missed dinner."

"Who's fault was that?" Tim's jeans still gaped open, the undone button now at Seb's eye-level, and he found it increasingly difficult to tear his gaze away. Now he'd made the decision to embrace their new friends-with-benefits status, his body was totally on board with it. "Bed sounds like a great idea."

He reached out a hand, and Tim grabbed it, gently guiding him to his feet; then Seb stepped forward until they were chest to chest. Seb was taller, but he knew what strength lay hidden in Tim body, and the thought of it sent a shiver through him.

"I meant we should sleep," Tim whispered, already leaning forward. His lips met Seb's, and Seb closed his eyes, losing himself in the kiss that followed. "But we need to eat first. Come on."

Seb watched, propped up against the worktop, as Tim insisted on making them both a sandwich. Despite his protests that he wasn't hungry, his stomach rumbled as soon as he took his first bite.

Tim laughed at him. "See. Doctor knows best."

174

As soon as they finished, Tim tidied up their mess while Seb went to use the bathroom.

After Tim had cleaned his teeth, he walked into the bedroom and then paused just inside the door. He glanced at where Seb lay, already in bed, looking uncertain for the first time that evening.

Pushing himself up onto his elbows, Seb peered up at him. "What's the matter? I thought you said we should go to bed?"

Tim ran a hand over his stomach; dried come flaked off under his fingers. What they really needed was a shower. The words were on the tip of Seb's tongue when Tim cut him off with "I wasn't sure…."

"Really?" Seb pulled the quilt back, then pointed at the empty spot. "Don't be ridiculous. I'm not going to make you sleep on the sofa."

Tim shrugged but got in next to him. "I didn't want to assume."

That made Seb laugh and shake his head. "After all we've done tonight, I think it's safe for you to assume we'd sleep in the same bed. Besides, won't it help with all the"—he waved a hand between them—"scent stuff."

"Yeah." Tim smiled at him, but this time it didn't quite reach his eyes. "Good point."

Seb got the impression there would be no more sex on offer tonight, and he was knackered anyway, so he scooted around until he lay with his cast in the best position, and closed his eyes.

The faint sound of an alarm going off slowly worked its way into Seb's consciousness, tugging him awake. He reached out, searching for his phone, but his hand came up empty. "Fuck's sake."

Soft laughter sounded beside him. "Sorry, it's mine. I forgot to turn it off."

Seb opened one eye to find Tim propped up on an elbow, watching him. "What time is it?"

"Seven."

"Fuck." Usually he was up and out of the house by then. This past week had done a number on his body clock. Thankfully, Tim had shut off his alarm but didn't seem in any great hurry to get up. "When do you have to leave?"

"I usually have surgery at eight fifteen, but I swapped with one of the other GPs."

"I thought you were the only pack doctor?" Seb was almost certain that was what Jared and Nathan had said.

Tim pushed a lock of hair back from Seb's face and smiled at him. "I am, for shifters. They don't need a doctor all that often. But there are plenty of humans, both in the pack and associated with it. We treat local residents too."

"Oh. How many of you are there, then?"

"Three in our practice."

That made sense, Seb supposed. "You don't have to stay here with me all day. You know that, right?"

Tim smiled, looking a lot more relaxed than he was last night when Seb had said almost the exact same thing. "Yes. You've made that quite clear. I'm actually meeting with Alec at eleven, so you can have your peace and quiet back then."

Oh, well, that was… great.

Tim continued. "Unless you wanted me to drop you off somewhere? Jared's maybe?"

Seb narrowed his eyes. "Were you listening to my phone call last night?"

"Unintentionally, I promise." Tim put his hand on Seb's cheek and drew him in for a quick kiss. Which was unexpected, but nice, and probably had the effect Tim had been aiming for. "I heard Jared mention it, that's all."

As tempting as that offer was, Seb had only just left Jared's. After all the fuss he'd made about coming back to his own place, he needed to stay in it for more than one day. "No, thanks, anyway. I want to venture out a little with that thing." Seb pointed over to where his crutch leaned against the wall. "See how easy it is to get to the shops."

To his credit, Tim only tensed for a second or so but didn't comment.

Seb smirked. "Nothing to say?

"I know you wouldn't listen."

"No warning to stay inside and not go anywhere?"

Tim shook his head, but then tensed again, as though listening for something.

"What?"

"You remember when we spoke about security cameras, yesterday?"

Seb cocked his head to the side. "Vaguely."

Tim nodded in the direction of the front door, just as a knock sounded. "They're here."

"Who?"

"Get some clothes on, and come and see." Tim hopped out of bed as he said it, grabbing his jeans from yesterday and slipping them on, again foregoing a T-shirt.

Seb got out of bed more gingerly, still wearing his T-shirt and pyjama bottoms from the night before. After settling his crutch, he gestured to himself. "This do?"

Tim grinned. "Yeah."

"What's so funny?"

"Nothing."

Seb glanced down. The front of his pyjama bottoms was slightly tented from his morning wood. "And you weren't going to tell me?"

Tim shrugged.

Another knock on the door, and Seb's brain put two and two together. "Is that another shifter down there?"

"Two of them."

"You don't look especially bothered, so I'm guessing they're from your pack?"

"*Our* pack, and yes."

Tim fastened the button on his jeans, the movement drawing Seb's attention to his fingers and the outline of his cock, definitely a little more visible than usual through the denim.

Seb pointed at Tim's bare chest and then at the semis they were sporting. "You want them to see?" Tim's blush said it all, though he didn't appear at all sorry. "Why? If they're your own pack-mates?" He didn't get shifters at all. Jared deserved either a medal for dealing with all this shit, or his head seeing to.

Tim walked towards him slowly, stopping when their bodies were only an inch or two apart. He placed a hand on the side of Seb's neck, rubbing his thumb gently back and forth. Seb shivered.

In a deep, husky voice, Tim said, "I know we'll only be together for a short time, and it's not—"

*Not what?*

"—I'm supposed to be acting like you're mine. Now I've started this, I don't seem to be able to turn it off." He swallowed, and Seb glanced down at the bob of his Adam's apple. Dark stubble covered Tim's throat; Seb had the sudden urge to bend down and get his mouth on it. "I want…." Tim slid his hand up to cup Seb's jaw.

"What?"

"For as long as we're doing this, I want people to know." With his other hand on Seb's waist, Tim backed him up against the wall, pinning him there with his hips and thighs. "Can I?"

"Yeah." Seb barely got the word out before Tim closed the distance between them, the kiss hot and dirty, all tongue and desperation as Tim ground against him, his cock hard and pressing insistently against Seb's belly.

The thud of Seb's heart beat loudly in his ears and his pulse raced. He'd never been this turned-on from kissing someone. Maybe Jared was onto something, after all. With Tim's hand still rubbing back and forth on his jaw, occasionally dipping to his neck again, Seb had the vague thought he was being scented. Normally that would have pissed him off, but with Tim pressed against him, his soft moans escaping as they kissed, it barely registered.

The knocking on his front door turned to banging. Tim seemed more than happy to ignore them, but Seb got his hands on Tim's chest and eased him back so he could speak. "Shouldn't we go and answer the door?"

"They know we're in here."

*Of course they do.* "My neighbours'll complain if they get any louder."

With a deep sigh, Tim smiled and took a step back, his hands staying on Seb until the very last second, as though he couldn't bear to let go. "Come on, then."

Seb trailed after him out into the hallway and down the stairs to the front door. When Tim finally opened it, with Seb standing just behind him leaning against the wall, two youngish guys stood on the other side. One looked familiar, and it took a moment or two to place him. "Luke, right?"

The guy smiled. "Yeah." He glanced at Tim, eyebrow raised. "Morning, Tim. Saw Nathan earlier."

Tim snorted. "And?"

"He said he hoped you took his advice."

Seb caught the quick look Tim shot him. "What advice?"

"Nothing." Tim waved a hand in front of him. "You know what Nathan's like."

Yeah, Seb was well aware of what Nathan was like. He very much doubted the advice was nothing.

Luke cleared his throat and indicated the guy stood next to him, silently watching them with an amused smile. "You ready for me and Jack to get started?"

"With what?" Seb peered around Tim to get a look outside and spotted a couple of boxes along with a new, very sturdy front door. "Oh!"

Two hours later, after showering separately—covering his cast was too much of a hassle to shower together—Seb was in clean pyjamas, but Tim was dressed and looking far too good for a Monday morning. The security camera was well on the way to being installed next to his new, scratch-free front door. Luke and Jack had worked on it while Tim and Seb finished eating breakfast upstairs, trying not to feel uncomfortable that the installers could hear everything they talked about. Seb tried to keep their conversation bland and boring.

Jared constantly complained about shifters and their unfair advantages, and Seb heartily agreed with him. He'd often wondered if Jared only moaned so much because he was jealous.

Seb had to admit—if only ever to himself—that recently, he'd started to envy their extra speed, strength, and everything else that came with it. Must be nice to know you would come out on top in most fights, and if you didn't, you'd heal quickly anyway.

"So Luke'll be around today."

Seb looked up sharply. He'd been too lost in his own head to follow the conversation. "Sorry, what?"

Tim cocked his head to one side, studying him. "Are you okay? You've been a bit… off this morning."

"No, I'm fine."

"Is it the door and the cameras? I know I should have asked if today was okay, but Alec suggested it and I agreed without thinking. It wasn't my business to do that on your behalf. I'm sorry."

Surprisingly Seb hadn't thought about it from that angle; he was more than happy to see that old door go as soon as possible. But even so… "Yeah, you're right. It's not your place to make those kinds of decisions for me." Tim's face fell immediately and guilt prickled at Seb's insides. "Not that I don't

181

appreciate it being done so quickly, because I do. I'll feel a lot safer knowing who's outside my front door before I go down to open it."

"But?" Tim prompted.

They both knew a but was coming.

"But it's my home. You should have asked me first."

"Yes, I should have."

Tim was one of the gentlest shifters Seb had ever met: easy-going, not arrogant in the least, and always careful not to overstep. Well, that had all been true a week or so ago, anyway. "Why didn't you?"

"I—" Muted laughter from downstairs halted him midsentence, and Tim sent a glare in the direction of the front door—not that Luke or Jack could see him. He sighed, looking sheepish. "I suppose I forgot."

"Forgot what?"

"That you aren't actually mine to protect," he said. Tim's voice was so quiet that Seb doubted the others would hear him. "If we were together properly, then I'd do everything I could to keep you safe, and as my ma—*boyfriend*, you'd let me."

Ignoring Tim's slip of the tongue, Seb sat forward. "And that'd work the other way around too, then? If you could make decisions without consulting me, then I could do the same for you, right?" Tim smirked. "Hypothetically speaking, of course." Seb added, just so Tim didn't get any ideas.

"Of course. And yes." His smile turned soft, and by the way his gaze slipped down to Seb's hand, Seb got the feeling he wanted to hold it. "If you wanted to do something like that for me, I'd be more than happy."

182

"Okay." Seb didn't know why it mattered to him so much that Tim acknowledge they'd be equals in a relationship because they were never going to end up in that situation. Ever.

"Okay."

Silence settled between them, so Seb took the opportunity to finish the rest of his tea. Their closeness yesterday evening suddenly seemed like a lifetime ago. He was seconds away from broaching the topic when Tim cleared his throat.

"I meant to ask you earlier, about family. You never mention anybody, and I was curious."

Seb set his mug down on the table and met Tim's gaze. Family wasn't a subject he enjoyed talking about in general. Apart from one other person, Jared was all the family he had or needed. "I have a sister, Kelly."

"Parents?"

"Both dead."

It had happened a few years ago now, but his voice still held that edge when he talked about it. Which always surprised him, as they hadn't been all that close as a family.

Tim did reach out then, taking Seb's hands in his. "Sorry, I didn't mean to drag up bad memories."

Seb shook his head. "No, it's fine. I don't mind." He squeezed Tim's fingers to let him know he meant it and then sat back. "It happened about four years ago. Car accident. We weren't... I mean, it was awful, don't get me wrong, but we weren't what you'd call a particularly loving family. Not like Jared and his parents." He shrugged as though it was no big deal.

"Oh."

Tim looked… well, horror-struck was the phrase that came to Seb's mind, and for some reason that struck him as funny. "With everything that's happened over the past week or so, *this* is the thing that shocks you the most?"

"It's just… the pack is my family. There's arguments, yes." He laughed. "Fights too. But we're all close, the individual units even more so. Everyone has each other's backs."

"I didn't say that they wouldn't have been there for me if I'd needed them." Seb stopped, not sure if that was strictly true but not really wanting to examine it further. It didn't make any difference now. "What about Nathan and Alec? They don't seem all that *close*."

Tim hesitated. "They have their differences, true."

Seb laughed. "Mm-hm. Differences, okay. Are you telling me Alec would have Nathan's back in a fight?"

"Absolutely."

No hesitation that time. Another few seconds passed, with neither of them speaking. The tension in the room was weird, unsurprisingly. Not bad, exactly, but not entirely comfortable either. Talking about family never ended well in Seb's experience. Unless you were Jared.

"So," Tim asked finally, "you have a sister?"

"I do."

"Older or younger?"

Seb smiled, thinking about her surly attitude at times—exactly the same as him. "Older. By six minutes. She's my twin."

"Do you keep in touch?" Tim glanced down at Seb's cast, then back up.

"Yes, we keep in touch. And no, I haven't told her about this." Seb could see the questions forming on Tim's face, and he sighed. "She's on holiday with her friends, so there's really nothing she can do and I didn't want her to worry. After everything that happened with Jared that time...." He didn't want to explain further.

Thankfully, Tim nodded in understanding. "You want to keep her out of this?"

"As much as I can, yes. She still lives in London. I try and visit her more than she comes here, and I don't want her anywhere near me until this fucking mess is resolved." *Christ, that'd better be soon.*

Kelly was as headstrong and stubborn as he was. If she had an idea of what was going on, she'd probably offer to move in with him or something stupid like that. No way was he putting her in danger.

"I understand. And I agree. Her scent is nowhere around here, and you should keep it that way."

Seb wrinkled his nose. "Please don't talk about my sister and her scent. It's just wrong."

"Sorry."

Eager to change the subject, Seb stood and hobbled to the sink with his empty bowl. "Any idea how long they'll be with that?" He pointed in the direction of the stairs.

Tim paused, listening. "Luke says about another hour or so."

"Good, because I want to go out later."

He waited for Tim to protest, tell him it wasn't safe, but he said nothing.

Seb turned and leaned against the worktop. "Still nothing to say about that?"

His mood was so different from last night. Seb almost missed Possessive Tim, although he'd never tell him that.

"I got a text from Alec earlier."

Seb waved a hand for him to continue.

"Apparently Cam insisted that Newell let one of our pack tag along today to see if they can pick up the rogue shifters' scent and give us an idea of what to look out for."

"And…?"

"And Newell agreed. Luke will be joining a couple of the P-Pack guys."

*Ahh.* "And you asked him to keep an eye on me?"

"Cam asked Luke to ensure you were safe and that the immediate area around your flat was shifter-free." Tim didn't quite meet Seb's eye as he said it.

"Is that all?"

"Fine. I might've have asked Luke to keep an eye on you if he could—but only because I was worried about you."

Seb wanted to tell him it was okay, that he appreciated it this time, but Tim was on a roll.

"If the threat is real, then you could be in serious danger, Sebastian."

Seb shivered at the use of his full name, and Tim noticed. His expression changed from concerned to interested in a heartbeat. Warmth settled in Seb's chest; having someone so focused on him was fast becoming addictive, and words tumbled out without his brain having any input. "I probably should have someone stay with me all the time. Just to be on the safe side."

# Chapter Twelve

Tim stared at him.

*Did I hear that right?*

Seb shuffled in his seat and looked down at the table. Maybe he hadn't meant to make the offer, but neither was he retracting it. Tim swallowed, taking his time to answer and not come across as eager as he really was. "I think that would be a very wise decision on your part."

Seb glanced up, looking at him for a few moments. His lips twitched as though he was fighting back a smile. "Do you reckon Luke would do it?"

The low growl took Tim totally by surprise, and it filled the space between them, making Seb jump. "Shit sorry, I—"

More laughter from downstairs.

"It's okay. I probably deserved that." Seb sucked his bottom lip into his mouth; Tim watched it, helpless to look away. "And I know I'm taking advantage here, considering everything…." He gestured between them, and Tim assumed he meant their non-relationship. "But would you want to stay in the flat with me until this is all sorted out?"

There were a lot of reasons why that was a bad idea. He'd get even more attached than he was now. His scent would be all over Seb's home, mixing with Seb's and forming 'their' scent. He'd get too used to it; he knew he would. It would be too close to what he wanted for it to be healthy. And it would kill him when he had to leave.

But staying would make Seb that much safer. Sure, he had the camera now, but that wouldn't help much if they got through the door or grabbed him when he was out on the street. "Yeah, I'll stay."

*As if there was any other option.*

Nathan's words rang like a reminder in his head: *"Get to know him better. If his opinions of shifters are anything like Jared's were, then you need to show him that you're not like that."*

Tim tried to tamp down the hope that flared in his chest. Glancing at the clock on Seb's kitchen wall, he cursed. "Shit, I need to get going. I have a meeting with Alec in an hour."

"And I'm sure he hates people being late," Seb said, scoffing.

Tim stopped, halfway out of his chair. "He's not that bad, you know. His relationship with Nathan isn't indicative of his personality."

"Nathan says he's like that with everyone."

Tim paused and tried to think of the best way to explain Alec. Alec had done a lot for Tim these past few years, and Tim always felt the need to defend him when people bad-mouthed him. "Alec holds a position of authority within the pack. He takes it seriously, and sometimes that comes across as cold or stand-offish. I've known him for a long time, and I can tell you now, he's one of the bravest, most loyal shifters I've met. Trust me, if there's anyone you want on your side, it's Alec."

Seb only appeared half-convinced, so Tim let it drop. Not many got to see the side of Alec that he did. Alec was always too busy acting the part of responsible beta to let his guard down. Tim had frequently tried to get him to loosen up, but to no avail. Alec was as stubborn as… Nathan. No wonder the two of them couldn't sort out their differences. "Anyway, it's not that Alec'll be mad. I don't like to be late, and I have to go into work for the afternoon surgery."

Standing up too, Seb lowered his voice a little—not that it'd prevent Luke from hearing them, but Tim wasn't about to remind him of that. Seb asked, "You coming back here tonight?"

"Yes." As though anything would stop him.

He took a step closer and hesitated. Despite Seb agreeing to a friends-with-benefits kind of deal, the boundaries of their new relationship still felt undefined. Tim wanted to lean in and kiss him, rub his scent all over him and mark him up for any shifter to know he was taken. But could he? Strictly speaking, it wasn't necessary—what they did last night would linger for a day or so. Despite his shower, Seb smelled like sleep, and warmth, and sex, a heady combination at the best of times, without adding in the subtle undercurrent of Tim's scent there too. It set his instincts on edge and his body alight with the need to touch and be close.

Seb met his gaze, eyes darkening as he seemed to grasp the situation. "Do you need to touch me before you go?"

He licked his lips, seemingly unaware of the effect it had on Tim, but he had to know, right? Tim swallowed down the wave of longing that swept through him. "I don't *need* to…."

Seb took another step towards him, close enough for Tim to feel the warmth of his breath as he spoke. "But you want to?"

"God, yes."

With a tilt of his head and a soft smirk, Seb offered up his neck.

*Fuck!*

190

Tim slid one hand around Seb's waist and cupped his jaw with the other, burying his face in the juncture of Seb's neck and shoulder. "You smell so good," he moaned. Seb laughed, the vibrations running through his body, and Tim grinned against his skin. "I could stay right here all day." He could too. Seb's scent was addictive and Tim held him tight while trying to get his fill.

"I don't think anyone's been this excited about the way I smell before."

Tim had his eyes closed, skimming Seb's soft skin with his nose, breathing him in. An image flashed through his mind of Seb with other men, other *shifters*, and the spike of jealousy took him by surprise. He fought to push it back down because he had nothing to be jealous about. For now, Seb was his, but—"We have to be exclusive while we're doing this."

"Hmm… what?"

Tim drew back enough to see that Seb had closed his eyes, a soft smile on his face. "While we're together here, it needs to be just the two of us."

Seb's lashes fluttered as he slowly opened his eyes, his expression morphing into a frown. "I thought that was a given?" As he curled his fingers in the front of Tim's shirt, Seb reeled him back in. "I know how possessive shifters get." He grinned. "Even you."

"Even me?"

"Well, you're the mild-mannered doctor. No one expects you to be all—" He scrunched up his nose and bared his teeth.

Tim laughed at him. "Growly?" he supplied, only a little offended now.

"Yes, that."

Ever so slowly, Tim let his teeth extend, a small thrill running through him as Seb's gaze locked onto them. It hurt a little to do it this slowly, but was worth it for the way Seb's pupils dilated and his pulse raced under Tim's palm. Careful not to move too quickly, Tim leaned in and set his teeth to base of Seb's throat, using enough pressure for Tim to feel it, but not breaking the skin.

His heart thudded in his ears, and the seconds seemed to last forever as he catalogued Seb's reaction. It was a risky move, considering how Seb had no desire to be bitten and changed, but Tim wanted to know how he *felt* about this. If last night was anything to go by, then Tim's control wasn't as complete as he might like, and the last thing he wanted was for Seb to freak out if he shifted like this.

Tim also liked it—liked letting his wolf out a little and feeling the soft slide of Seb's skin against his teeth.

If he fantasised about biting in deep, claiming Seb as he fucked him, sealing their bond, then no one had to know. Tim would never do it, no matter how attractive the idea was. Forcing Seb into a bond he didn't want wasn't the way Tim wanted to get a mate. The thought made him shudder and he stood up straight, retracting his teeth. "Okay?" he whispered, relieved to smell a hint of arousal coming off Seb, but no fear.

"Yeah." Seb's voice came out rougher than normal and he cleared his throat, his gaze dipping to Tim's mouth and back up. "You sure you can't stay for a bit?"

Tim grinned at the groans and mumbled protests from downstairs as they started hammering extra loudly.

Seb flinched at the sudden noise. "Shit! I forgot all about them."

Tim hadn't, but he didn't really care. He'd learned to live with lack of privacy years ago. "I have to go, but I'd like a kiss goodbye." He slowly backed Seb up against the wall and pressed a thigh between his slightly spread legs. "If that's okay?"

In answer, Seb slid his arms around Tim's neck and tugged him the rest of the way in.

Flush as they were, Tim felt Seb's shiver as if it was his own, and he rolled his hips in response. He held on tightly to Seb's waist, kissing him deeply and insistently, loving the soft moans that escaped Seb as he worked his tongue into Seb's mouth.

*Fuck, I really don't want to leave.*

Throwing Seb over his shoulder and taking him back to bed seemed like a much better plan, and Tim was half considering it when his phone vibrated in his pocket, startling them.

Seb gently pushed him back. "I guess you should be going, huh?"

"Probably." Tim sighed and reluctantly stepped out of Seb's embrace, putting some much-needed distance between them. His phone buzzed again, and after giving Seb an apologetic look, he pulled it out of his pocket.

That it was from Alec was no great surprise.

*Cam joining us this morning. Gareth, Mike, and Daryl too.*

Fuck, he really did need to get going. Alec might not be bothered if he was a little late, but he didn't fancy keeping his alpha and the other betas waiting. Especially when they would all smell the reason why.

He typed back a quick *On my way* and slipped it back into his pocket. "Okay, I definitely need to leave now."

"Everything all right?"

Seb was still leaning against the wall where they'd kissed. Tim smiled, smug satisfaction hard to contain as he took in Seb's puffy lips and the redness of his skin from Tim's stubble.

"Just Alec, informing me Cam and the other betas will also be there this morning."

"War meeting? Planning how to take out Newell and get away with it?"

Tim laughed. "I very much doubt it."

Seb shrugged. "From what I've heard so far, sounds like it'd be no great loss."

Now was not the time to get into pack politics. "I'll tell you all about it later. If I can," he added.

Seb rolled his eyes. "Go on, then. I'll see you later."

"Be careful today."

Seb waved him off, then put two hands on his shoulders and steered him towards the door. "I've got my own security camera and shifter bodyguards. What could possibly go wrong?"

"Don't tempt fate like that, please."

"Oh for fuck's sake, go!" Seb laughed as he all but shoved Tim towards the door.

Tim attempted to shake off the feeling of dread Seb's words had brought on. Nothing would happen. It was ridiculous superstition, and he was just overly touchy because—well, for reasons he'd rather not think about.

After stealing one last kiss, Tim grabbed his keys and headed for the stairs. Luke looked up at him as he started down them. He had his eyebrows raised, looking far too judgemental for Tim's liking. "What?"

Luke glanced back up the stairs behind Tim. "You seem awfully attached for a friends-with-benefits kind of setup. I'm not going to find a nice fresh bite mark on Seb's neck when I get up there, am I?"

"I would never—"

"That's what Nathan used to say, too."

"Not the same situation at all, and you know it."

Luke sighed, the deep, long-suffering sigh of someone who'd been through this whole thing before. "You know as well as I do how this goes, Doc. Nathan was lucky with how it all worked out."

*And I won't be.*

Tim stopped when he reached the bottom; he faced Luke, his helper out of sight for now. "I appreciate your concern, and I'm aware of how this will probably end." The thought already made his chest constrict, and from the look on Luke's face, he suspected. "I know what I'm doing."

"Okay. I won't mention it again."

"Thanks." Tim manoeuvred past the new door leaning upright in the hallway and paused before stepping outside. "Keep him safe."

To his credit, Luke didn't groan or roll his eyes. He just nodded, but then a small smile appeared. "I had the same talk from Jared and Nathan. Not sure I dare let Seb out of my sight."

That brought a smile back to Tim's face. "Sounds like a great plan."

Feeling a little better about going, he walked through the doorway and headed to his car.

Alec met Tim at the doors to his building and escorted him inside. "They're waiting for us in Cam's flat," he said, holding the stairwell door open and gesturing for Tim to go through.

"Not in the meeting rooms?"

The floor below Cam's flat held two large meeting rooms that opened to make a room big enough to house the whole pack, plus visitors if necessary. For some reason, Tim had expected to use one of those spaces. He glanced over his shoulder in time to see Alec shake his head.

"No. This isn't exactly a formal gathering."

*Okay, then.*

They walked the rest of the way in silence until they got to Cam's floor. There Alec paused before leaving the stairwell. Tim turned to face him. "What's wrong?"

"I wanted to apologise."

Tim frowned. "For what?"

Alec gave him a pointed look and took a deep breath in. Tim felt some of the colour leave his face. "If I'd known you'd get this involved so soon, I would have insisted someone else do it."

Anger flared inside Tim at the thought of anyone being that close to Seb, and he closed his eyes, willing himself to calm down. "It's not like that."

When he opened his eyes again, Alec was watching him, nonplussed.

"It's *exactly* like that. Maybe not for him," Alec conceded when Tim went to protest, "but for you, definitely."

Tim sighed, no point denying it. It wasn't just their one night together. All the buildup beforehand, then Seb being injured and letting Tim take care of him. Getting to kiss, touch, and taste him had just brought it all together. Alec was far from stupid, though. "You had a fair idea how I felt when you suggested it. That's *why* you suggested I do it." He trusted Alec completely, but he wasn't naive enough to think that Alec wouldn't push those boundaries for the good of the pack.

"It is."

"Then why are you apologising?"

Alec glanced at the floor before meeting Tim's gaze again. "I thought… *hoped* you'd get it out of your system once you'd fucked him a few times."

Tim scoffed. "That's not—we've not—"

"From what I recall, he doesn't want the bite or to bond." Alec waved his hand in a semicircle. "Or any other part of this."

"I know that."

"Do you?" Alec asked, voice hard. Tim had never been on the receiving end of this side of Alec and really didn't like it. "He's not Jared, and you're not Nathan. You can't just go ahead and bite him and hope he forgives you afterwards."

"I would never!" Tim ground out, his anger back in full force. He grabbed Alec by the front of his shirt and slammed him back against the wall, teeth bared and claws slicing through the material like butter. "Yes, I want him. Yes, I wish he'd let me bite him and let a bond form. But I would *never* do it without his permission. *Never.*"

197

"Even when you're deep inside him and he tilts his head just so…. All that skin begging for your teeth?"

Tim stared back at him, letting his words sink in, and imagined Seb spread out like that underneath him, neck bared. Would he want to bite him? *Yes.*

But then he pictured Seb's horrified face, betrayal marring his features, and Tim shook his head. He didn't want that. Having Seb look at him like that would break him. Even with the bond, he'd always know that he'd stolen something from him, that it hadn't been given freely. "Not even then."

"Good." Alec met his gaze steadily, keeping eye contact until Tim caught on.

"You were testing me?"

"As your beta and head of Cam's security unit, I had to be sure. One illegal bite in the pack is enough for this year, don't you think? We don't need to give Newell any leverage against us." He looked pointedly at Tim's hand, still fisted in the material of his shirt, until Tim retracted his claws and let go.

Five slits remained in the cloth, but Tim was unrepentant. "I understand the need for you to be sure about my intentions, but as my *friend*, that was a shit thing to do."

"It was necessary." Tim shook his head and reached for the stairwell door, but Alec stopped him with a hand on his arm. "But as your friend, I'm sorry." He squeezed Tim's shoulder; a rare look of contrition on his face was gone as quickly as it appeared. "Come on. They're waiting."

After recounting his run-in with the two shifters from P-Pack, Tim sat back in his chair. He wasn't used to being the centre of attention like this or being involved this closely with pack affairs. It unnerved him to some extent, and the relative peace and quiet of afternoon surgery suddenly sounded very appealing.

But his curiosity was also piqued, and he never could resist asking questions. "Were they telling the truth about the rogue shifters?" He directed the question to Alec and the other betas, but it was Cam who answered.

"I believe so. Alpha Newell is of the opinion that his units did their jobs at the warehouse." The implied "but ours didn't" was there, but Cam didn't voice it. "Regardless of who was at fault then, it seems likely that some of the rogue pack escaped the warehouse."

Tim immediately thought of Seb. "You think they'll go to the flat, hoping to find Nathan?"

"I've spoken to Luke," Cam said, as if reading Tim's mind. "Mr Calloway hasn't left his flat. He's safe for now."

The "for now" didn't sound good, and Tim leaned forward again to rest his elbows on his knees. "How many got away? Do they know?"

"Not for certain. Best guess is at least two, possibly four. There were a lot of bodies that day."

"But some."

"So it would seem."

"And you think they'll go after Sebastian?"

Alec sighed, and when Tim glanced at him, he was sharing a look with Cam.

Cam nodded, and Alec focused on Tim. "It's possible. But I'm more concerned with how Newell will use this situation to his advantage. He said some borderline threatening things after the attack on the warehouse. He wanted Nathan punished—read *dead*—because of the risk he caused not only to our pack, but Newell's own pack by association, and he made noises about going to the alpha council anyway."

Tim's gaze shot immediately to Cam. "Could he do that? Our packs had an agreement. He'd be going against—"

Alec stopped him. "Our agreement would hold and his claims would likely be thrown out. They were empty threats, and he knew it. The council won't concern themselves with a matter that's already been resolved, especially now that we have the proper paperwork in place."

Tim relaxed slightly, but his mind worked feverishly to connect the dots. "But he's still angry about the whole thing."

"Yes," Cam answered. "I believe he feels I let Nathan get away with a crime he would have punished by death or at least banishment. He suggested—in a roundabout way, of course—that I make a poor alpha in his eyes."

Tim wanted to laugh at that statement. There was a reason the P-Pack was a lot smaller than theirs: no one with any sense would follow Newell. "You think Newell let the rogue shifters go on purpose?"

Silence.

Then Alec spoke. "It's a possibility, but we have no evidence to support it, and getting any proof without giving Newell grounds for complaint is tricky, to say the least."

Tim turned to face Alec, struggling to wrap his head around it all. "What does Newell have to gain by Seb getting hurt, though? I know you said he's trying to goad Nathan into doing something rash, but how does that help him get back at Cam?"

The other three betas had stayed mainly quiet throughout the discussion, but now Gareth sat forward and cleared his throat.

"Nathan already has one black mark against him. If they can get him to react and attack without provocation, or maybe somehow blame him for an attack on Seb, then they would have grounds to call Cam's leadership into question. Newell will suggest that if Cam had dealt with Nathan properly the first time round, then none of this would have happened. Anything that involves human authorities gives shifters as a whole a bad name, and that's something the council *will* act upon."

*Fuck.* There was logic in there somewhere. Tim rubbed at his temples. The alpha council weren't something he thought about often, if he could help it. Not that they weren't necessary—the pack wars were testament to that—but having that many alphas in a room together made his wolf incredibly unsettled, and he was pretty sure everyone else would feel the same way. The idea of his alpha being subjected to the others' scrutiny didn't sit well either. "So now what?"

"Well," Alec paused, again looking to Cam for confirmation. "With you now in the picture and your relationship with Seb being what it is, I'm not sure Newell will see Nathan as an option for them anymore. If Nathan doesn't go near Jared's old flat and stays with other members of our pack, it's harder for them to get at him. And besides,

201

Nathan's no longer the one who feels most protective over Mr Calloway."

Tim refused to feel embarrassed about that. Everyone in the room had sensed it as soon as he walked through the door. "That's a good thing, though. Right?"

"Possibly. But Alpha Newell isn't the sort of alpha to just let things go."

*Fuck.* "What do you think he'll do now?" He looked from face to face, not liking their expressions.

"We have no idea."

# Chapter Thirteen

Seb sat there tapping his fingers on the table top, debating whether he could be arsed to go to the shop or not. Luke and Jack had left about an hour ago, leaving the new door and security camera all installed. After a quick demo of how to use the security system, they'd gone with Luke's assurance that should Seb want to go out later, him—plus a couple of P-Pack shifters—would be keeping an eye on him.

That knowledge was both reassuring and invasive. Seb wasn't in the habit of being watched, and even though the observers were out of his sight, it still made him uncomfortable.

*Can they hear me right this second?* He stilled his fingers, suddenly conscious of every sound.

A walk down the street, with six pairs of eyes tracking his movements, suddenly didn't seem all that appealing. He grabbed for his crutch and headed to the kitchen to set about making some lunch. It was almost one thirty, and breakfast had been ages ago.

Sandwich in hand, Seb carefully made his way over to the sofa. His book lay on the coffee table, waiting for him, and he set his plate down beside it before lowering himself to the seat and getting comfy.

Five hours later he was still lying there when he felt a hand running through his hair.

"Hey."

Seb smiled, leaning into the touch, and a soft chuckle sounded close to his ear. Opening his eyes, he found Tim looking down at him. "Oh, hey." His voice was scratchy and thick from sleep. He cleared his throat a little and tried again. "You're back. What time is it?"

Tim smiled. "Just gone half past six. Surgery finished on time for once."

Seb raised his arms above his head and stretched. The pull on his muscles felt good after being stationary for so long, and he let out a low moan of satisfaction. When he looked up, Tim's gaze had dipped to the waistband of Seb's pyjamas and his lips had slightly parted… and if Seb wasn't mistaken, his teeth looked sharper than normal.

Seb glanced down at where his T-shirt lay rucked up against his stomach, a wide strip of skin on show. *Oh.*

Heat curled in his belly; he slowly reached down to palm his cock through the material.

A low, rumbling growl filled the quiet of the room.

Seb grinned. An afternoon on the sofa had left him well rested, and Tim looked good—all windswept and fresh-faced. Seb wanted to tug him close and breathe him in.

So he did.

Tim came willingly, stretching out above Seb along the sofa, taking care not to touch his cast. "This okay?"

Seb parted his legs and lifted his injured ankle so it rested on the back of Tim's calf. "Yeah." He ran a hand through Tim's hair, the black curls sliding through his fingers, and tugged a little. Tim's breath caught. "How was the meeting?" Seb whispered, lips brushing Tim's in the barest of touches.

"Don't want to talk about it." A slight shake of his head accompanied the words, and then Tim kissed him.

Stubble scraped against Seb's mouth and chin, the roughness sending a tingle down his spine. He arched up as best he could, grabbed Tim's arse with his free hand, and pulled him closer, needing the full-body contact. The day had been a strange one and Seb felt off, but couldn't put his finger on why, exactly. He clung to Tim as they kissed and moved against each other in a slow dirty grind. The constant press of Tim's groin had Seb hard, but with both of them still fully clothed, each roll of his hips was like a tease of what could happen if only they were naked.

He caught sight of the camera monitor out of the corner of his eye and a thought struck him, working its way into his mind until he had to stop kissing and pull back a little. "Is anyone close enough to hear us?"

Tim took a second or two to answer, his mouth busy as he trailed kisses along the cut of Seb's jaw. "Hmm?"

"Is anyone listening?" Seb tried again, his voice going a little breathy at the end when Tim reached that spot below his ear.

"Don't think so. Hard to concentrate." Tim ground his erection against Seb's belly to emphasise his point. "Does it matter?"

Seb opened his mouth to say yes just as Tim bit down, teeth sharp but safe. "*No*" came out instead, and he closed his eyes, turning his head to the side to give Tim all the access he wanted. Offering his neck to a shifter like this, especially when they weren't in full control, should scare him or at least make him wary, but the only thought running through Seb's mind was *more*.

Which was probably why he had no handle on what words came out of his mouth. "I want your scent all over me. So everyone knows." Tim immediately stilled, and Seb whined at the sudden loss of friction. "Don't stop."

Tim's sigh tickled the side of Seb's neck as he rested his forehead on the sofa cushion. That didn't bode well. "We don't have to."

He took the opportunity to get his hands on Tim's arse and trail his fingers along the curve of his arse cheeks.

Tim's groan was gratifying, but he remained still. "We still smell *together*, if that's what you're worried about. We don't have to do anything for another day, probably. As long as we share the same bed." Tim sounded disappointed, and Seb took that as a good thing.

Seb let his fingers slide along the seam of Tim's trousers, tracing the line all the way down between his legs. "That's not why I want to do this."

"No?"

"No."

"Then why?"

"Because—"

Seb stopped; no immediate answer was forthcoming. *Because I'm horny? Because Tim feels so good sprawled out on top of me like this? Or because we've started this thing, so I might as well make the most of it?* None of those seemed like the right answer.

He shrugged as best he could, pressed down by Tim's heavy weight. "Because I want to."

And then another thought hit him, and it unsettled him. Tim wasn't hiding away in his flat all day, he was out there with all the other humans and shifters, and the idea of anyone thinking they could hit on him set Seb's teeth on edge. "I want you to smell like you're mine. That you're taken." Tim buried his face in the crook of Seb's neck, hands gripping tight to his shoulders. Seb added, "For however long this lasts."

He tried not to think about the last part, because as much as he liked what they were doing now that he'd embraced the idea, he couldn't be what Tim ultimately wanted.

*And that will never change.*

"Want that too," Tim murmured. Seb groaned in relief as he rolled his hips, starting up that slow, dirty grind again. "I want...."

"What?" Seb muttered, thighs spread wide now, urging Tim on with his hands on Tim's strong arse.

"Want to fuck you." Teeth scraped across Seb's collarbone, almost too sharp, and he cried out and pressed his head back into the cushions. "Can I?"

*Oh God....*

Tim's muscles bunched and contracted under Seb's hands, and the thought of all that raw power focused solely on him made his dick throb in the confines of his boxer briefs. "Yeah," he whispered, not caring if he sounded hoarse. The one thing he'd vowed not to do now seemed like the best idea. Seb hadn't been this turned-on in ages. *If ever.*

Tim was up and gone, leaving a rush of cool air in his wake, and Seb blinked up at him, taking a second to realise Tim was now standing. *Wow, I forgot how quickly shifters move.*

"Bed."

Tim held out his hand and Seb took it, allowing himself to be helped up. He grinned as Tim steadied him with a hand on his elbow. "You going to carry me to the bedroom too? I was kinda hoping you'd pin me against the wall."

He said it as a joke, but Tim got a gleam in his eye. He pushed Seb's crutch out of reach as Seb went to grab it. "Like this, you mean?"

With that, he picked Seb up, forcing him to wrap his legs around Tim's waist—a little awkward with his damn cast, but they managed. Then Tim took the three steps over to the wall and pressed Seb up against it.

"Yeah." *Exactly like that, only*— "But with less clothes."

Tim laughed, eyes shining with heat and excitement.

Something tightened in Seb's chest, but he ignored it in favour of drawing Tim into another kiss. They stayed like that for a few minutes longer, Seb supported—easily, he thought—by Tim's hands underneath his thighs. He could feel the hard line of Tim's erection, hear the way his breathing had roughened, and it set his pulse racing. "Bedroom," he gasped out, wanting to get naked but also not wanting to move. "Or I'm going to come in my pyjama bottoms, and that would just be a waste."

Tim growled at that, and it must have been the right thing to say, because the next second Tim carried Seb through the bedroom door as though he weighed nothing. He landed on the bed on his back, lowered down in a surprisingly gentle fashion, and raised an eyebrow in question. "I'm not a Disney princess."

The laugh that elicited rang loud in the bedroom and Tim crowded him back against the pillows, smiling wide. "I know that." He ran a hand along Seb's thigh, up towards the clear outline of his dick, thumb brushing upwards along the length of it. "Believe me."

This time Tim leaned down and mouthed over it, his breath hot through the cotton covering Seb. "Didn't want to hurt your ankle."

*Fucking ankle.* For a second there, Seb had forgotten all about it. Frustration made him blurt out without thinking, "I'm tempted to let you bite me just so I could fucking heal already."

Tim's head snapped up and his teeth slid out so quickly Seb gasped. They both went stock-still; the air in the room crackled with the sudden tension.

"*I didn't mean that,*" Seb whispered urgently—a knee-jerk reaction to the hungry look in Tim's eyes.

"I know." The words came out slightly slurred through teeth too big to form them properly. In that moment, with his teeth bared, eyes dark, and wearing a wild expression, Tim seemed more otherworldly than human.

*Because that's exactly what he is.*

Even with everything he'd witnessed so far, Seb had separated the two facts and not equated Tim with the primal version of a shifter. Up until that moment, he'd never pictured him as half-shifted and dangerous, or as a full wolf. It just hadn't seemed possible. But now... now he could see it.

He glanced to the side, not surprised to see long, sharp claws buried deep into the mattress. *Probably have to replace that.*

Such an unhelpful thought, but his mind was all over the place. Still, his cock was as hard as ever, and when Tim licked at the edges of his canines, Seb had to reach down and rub himself to ease the ache.

Tim didn't miss it, either. "Give me a minute."

He closed his eyes, breathing deeply until he shuddered and his shoulders sagged.

Seb watched, fascinated, as Tim's teeth returned to normal and his claws disappeared.

But when Tim met his gaze again, the wildness was still there, and Seb liked it. It made him want to be reckless, to push Tim as close to the edge as he could without tipping him over.

That thought should probably scare him more than it did.

Seb had his hands flat to the bed. Tim looked at them, then back to Seb's face. "Unless you want to stop? I'd understand—"

"No." Seb shook his head. He took hold of Tim's hand and placed it on the prominent bulge in his pyjama bottoms. "I definitely do not want to stop."

Tim's smile started slowly, but grew wide as he stroked Seb's length, drawing a low moan out of him. "So I see."

Seb had a feeling they'd be talking about this some more later, but right then Tim curled his finger in the waistband of Seb's bottoms and underwear, then pulled them off him. Seb took care of his T-shirt, tossing it onto the floor somewhere; he lay back and watched as Tim undressed. It was a sight he wouldn't tire of any time soon—broad shoulders, slim hips, toned muscle on display wherever his gaze landed. The dark happy trail drew his focus to where Tim's cock jutted out, thick and hard.

Tim stroked himself once, twice, and Seb licked his lips imagining it sliding into his mouth.

Tim's soft chuckle snapped his gaze up. "Keep looking at me like that and it'll be all over before I get anywhere near you."

Seb grinned back at him. "We can't have that, can we?"

"No." Tim crawled up the bed, taking care to help move Seb's cast to the side, out of the way as Seb spread his legs wide. He really couldn't wait to get that thing off.

Lying back on the pillows, fully expecting Tim to come up for a kiss, Seb cried out, at the first swipe of Tim's tongue on the head of his cock. "Oh fuck."

The bottom sheet bunched under Seb's fingers, the tears from Tim's claws widening as he pulled.

Wet warmth enveloped him as Tim sucked him deep, the stroke of his tongue driving him wild. Blindly groping under the spare pillow next to him, Seb searched around until he found the lube he'd shoved under there that afternoon, when wanking had briefly crossed his mind. Now it seemed like excellent forward planning.

"Here." He shoved it towards Tim. "You don't need condoms, right?" Of course, Seb always played safe with humans, but one of the pluses with shifters was that you could go without.

Tim hummed what sounded like a no.

The vibrations around Seb's cock made his toes curl. "Good." He pushed up a little, not wanting to thrust hard but helpless to stop his hips chasing the heat of Tim's mouth. "Fuck me," he whispered, voice strained. "*Come on.*"

With his eyes shut tight, he listened to Tim grab the lube and snap it open, felt the slick slide of fingers over his hole, teasing around the rim, back and forth so many times he ached with the need to have them inside. Finally, Tim put him out of his misery; two fingers stretched him open and made him cry out.

By the time Tim pressed his cock inside, Seb was back to gripping the sheet again, clinging on for dear life. Pushing Seb's good leg up towards him, Tim slowly bottomed out, resting for a second before reaching up and cupping Seb's jaw.

"Hey." He waited for Seb to open his eyes and meet his gaze. "You okay?"

"Mm-hmm"

"Your leg's not—"

"'S fine!" Seb reached for him, grabbing hold of Tim's shoulders and urging him to move. "I'm good. I swear."

The first few thrusts were slow, steady, but as nice as it felt, it wasn't... *them.* "Come on, Tim," he whispered against his ear. "Fuck me like you want to. Like we both want to."

As though it was the permission he'd been waiting for, Tim sat back a little, hooked Seb's leg over his arm, and pushed into him hard.

"Yeah," Seb breathed out, closing his eyes and losing himself in the steady rhythm. Already so turned-on from the buildup to this point, he fought not to come. But with each slide of Tim's cock in just the right spot, his control slipped a bit more, and he couldn't resist getting a hand on his dick. "*Fuck.*"

The growl he got in response made him look up. Tim stared back at him, lips parted and a hint of

212

fang peeking out. Seb went hot all over. For a split second, he wondered how it would feel to have those teeth sink into his skin, claiming him…

Then he was coming, coating his hand and his belly as his orgasm rushed through him.

Tim gripped Seb's thigh, fingers digging in just shy of too hard as he fucked into him twice more, threw his head back, and shuddered. He stilled and closed his eyes for a moment, and Seb watched a soft smile spread across his face. When he finally looked down, expression lazy and content, Seb reached out to pull him close.

The breath Tim took filled his chest, and he held it in a moment before exhaling on a sigh.

Even to Seb's unrefined nose, the air around them smelled like sex and sweat. For a shifter, it had to be ten times as strong.

Running his hands up and down Tim's back, he laughed softly. "How do we smell now?"

Tim smiled against his shoulder as he took another long, deep breath. "Perfect."


Tim stayed that night and the one after that. He went to work in the day and came back to Seb in the early evening. They hadn't fucked again, but Seb was pretty sure all the sex they'd had was enough to make them smell like each other for weeks. He also hadn't seen hide nor hair of anyone from P-Pack, or Tim's pack, for that matter. The subject seemed to be off limits between the two of them for now— either that or they were both ignoring it.

The only thing Tim said on the matter was that Seb was still being watched for his own protection. By whom, exactly, Seb wasn't certain.

Sunlight streamed through the living room windows and Seb smiled, basking in its warmth for a second or two. He'd not been out of the house since coming back to live there. He needed to change that.

Putting off his walk to the shop had been easy with the weather being shit the last two days, but since today was glorious…

Seb headed to his bedroom, mind made up.

Halfway through getting dressed, his phone buzzed with a text. Jared's name lit up his screen, and Seb smiled as he reached for it.

*What you up to? Fancy some company?*

As appealing as that sounded, he replied with *Tim's already left, and you can't come here, remember?*

*Get a taxi.*

He could do that. Taxi fare from his place to Jared's wouldn't be extortionate, and at a push he could always catch the bus. A quick glance down at his foot reminded him that no, he really didn't fancy braving public transport yet. Besides, it was a beautiful day; did he really want to spend it cooped up in Jared's flat?

No, he didn't. *What about tomorrow? I'll get Tim to drop me off.*

*Yeah ok. It'll be good to catch up*

Seb sat with his phone in hand, staring at the screen long after it had gone black. A lot had happened since he'd left Jared and Nathan's apartment. News travelled fast around the pack, he had no doubt Luke would have reported back to Nathan. If nothing else, Jared would be aware Seb's relationship with Tim wasn't entirely for show, and he'd want to talk about it, discuss how Seb felt about it all.

214

That thought alone was enough to make Seb's head ache. They were having fun, that was all. Seb was taking advantage of the shitty situation he found himself in. When his phone buzzed again, he almost dropped it in surprise. The sender's name brought a big smile to his face.

*Hey bro. Still ok for a lift tomorrow? We land at 10:30, North Terminal Flight EZY8682 xx*

Shit. Was that tomorrow? In all the excitement of the past few days, he'd forgotten all about picking up his sister from the airport. *Bollocks.* He'd planned on borrowing Jared's car again, and he hated letting her down, but he couldn't go with his foot like this, and no way was he asking Tim or Nathan to get her.

Shifters were everywhere in London, more so than the rest of the UK, but that didn't mean he wanted his sister involved in his crap. Ever since Jared's hospital stay, Seb had urged Kelly to stay away from them. He'd tried to tell her what to do, and that had gone down about as well as he should have expected. But his current predicament? Yeah, he could keep her well out of that.

*Sorry sis. Somethings come up and I can't get you. I'll arrange a car to pick you up. Don't worry. X*

A taxi back from Gatwick to his sister's flat would eat into his budget for the month, but it wasn't as though he needed it for going out or anything. He made a mental note to google airport taxis when he got back.

*Everything ok?* she sent back, and he pictured her typing it, brow furrowed. It wasn't like him to let her down.

He had every intention of telling her everything, but he'd do that when she was home, not on the last day of her holiday while she was still hundreds of miles away.

*Yeah, nothing to worry about. Tell you when you get back. Enjoy your last day x*


With his newly installed security monitor situated on the kitchen worktop, Seb got into the habit of checking it whenever he was in there. Even though all it ever showed was the empty front step and the path beyond—and the postman every morning—it had become habit to stop and watch for a few seconds. A small part of him still expected a couple of shifters to pop into sight, teeth and claws out, marking up his new door.

His foot throbbed as though stirred by the memory of that night, and Seb rubbed a hand over his eyes. He was a big guy, six foot three, and though not overly muscular, his size tended to make people think twice before giving him grief. Despite knowing shifters were amongst them all the time, and even after seeing Jared all banged up, he'd never been scared for himself. Until now.

The fear wasn't as bad as it had been when he'd fallen down the stairs, but suddenly, knowing that only the front door stood between him and one or more potentially violent shifters unsettled him.

And just like that, the sun-filled warmth of the outdoors lost all its appeal.

Seb closed his eyes and leaned back, resting against the edge of the worktop. It wasn't something he wanted to admit even to himself, but if he let himself dwell on it, going outside knowing what could be waiting for him was enough to make his hands shake.

Which was ridiculous. Tim had as good as said the threat was minimal, just speculation and caution on their part. Seb had nothing to worry about. And unless he wanted to spend the rest of his life cooped up in his house or continually looking over his shoulder, he needed to suck it up and go outside. People were looking out for him; he knew that. Just because he couldn't see them didn't mean they weren't there.

He made his way downstairs and then stopped to send a quick text to Tim, just to be on the safe side. *Finally going to test my limits.*

The *Dare I ask?* he got back made him smile.

*Taking a walk to the shop.*

*Be careful. Call me when you get back.*

Tim's concern warmed him instead of irritating him as he'd expected, and Seb sent a quick *Will do* before slipping his phone into his back pocket and unlocking the front door.

As expected, no one was on the other side, but his heart raced and still he breathed a sigh of relief.

*For fuck's sake, get a grip!*

Shaking off the wariness clinging to him, Seb locked up, pocketed his keys, and set off along the path to the road. Over the past week and a half, he'd become relatively proficient at getting around on his crutch. His hand still got sore sometimes if he used it a lot, but the shop was only about a ten-minute walk away. Fingers crossed, he should be okay. He'd also remembered to take his rucksack, so there'd be no awkward carrier bags to manage on the way back. Not that he planned to buy much on this first trip.

The road wasn't a main one by any stretch of the imagination, but cars still travelled up and down

217

it, the intermittent flow of traffic a reassuring sight. He glanced behind him and then up ahead, trying to spot any suspicious cars or people, but nothing stood out. In all honesty, he had no idea what to look for anyway.

He reached the small Tesco Express without mishap and felt a little foolish as he walked inside. Nothing was going to happen in broad daylight. In fact, nothing would probably happen at all, ever. In the cold light of day, back in the outside world, it all seemed foolish. What would anyone have to gain by messing with him?

Tim, Alec, and whoever else might think he was in some sort of danger, but they were wrong. Seb wasn't a shifter, wasn't anyone's bonded mate, wasn't even part of their pack, regardless of what Tim said. No one in their right mind would waste their time on him.

Feeling slightly better, Seb paid for his pint of milk, chocolate bar, and newspaper, shoved them in his backpack, and left the shop with a smile on his face, finally able to fully enjoy the sunshine.

That lasted for all of two minutes.

Not quite sure what had suddenly changed, Seb slowed his pace, glancing around him to try and see what had made the hairs on the back of his neck stand up. Nothing looked any different than it had twenty seconds ago, but Seb *felt* it: that niggling awareness of someone watching him.

He shrugged it off and carried on walking. Tim had said P-Pack were still keeping an eye on him. They were obviously keeping their distance; that was all it probably was.

He resumed his earlier pace, trying not to speed up as he headed for home, but his gaze darted back and forth, continually scanning for anything out of the ordinary. Every car or van that drove past set Seb's nerves on edge, and he couldn't stop himself from peering inside, trying to get a look at the occupants.

*Like I'd be able to tell a shifter from a regular human.*

The feeling persisted, though, and the closer Seb got to home, the worse it got. Rationally he knew it must be his mind playing tricks, but that didn't make it go away.

A white van sat parked on the kerb outside his flat, and Seb stumbled as he came to an abrupt stop. It hadn't been there when he left, and it had no identifying marks or logos that he could see. Just as he reached for his phone to call Tim or Jared, *someone*, the passenger-side door of the van slid open and one of the P-Pack shifters who'd come to apologise to him—*Mark?*—got out.

He turned, saw Seb, and grinned at him, pointing at Seb's crutch. "Pretty quick with that thing, aren't you?"

Seb shrugged, his heart still pounding. Seeing a familiar face should have reassured him, but it hadn't. "How long have you been here?"

Made sense they'd been following him, so of course it was their presence he'd felt. But no matter how many times he repeated that thought in his head, it still sounded hollow.

"About twenty-five minutes. We saw you leave the house, so Will followed you on foot and I brought the van around."

Mark pointed back up the road, and when Seb glanced behind, he recognised the guy jogging towards them. Even though it was unlikely, he had to ask. "And you haven't seen anyone else?"

Mark cocked his head to one side. Seb wondered if he was scenting the air, or whatever it was they did at times like that. "You mean like the rogue shifters?"

Seb nodded and Mark shook his head. "No. Nothing. There's a few from our pack around here somewhere. I caught a faint trace of them earlier…." He trailed off with a shrug. "No one's around here who shouldn't be."

*And yet….* Seb shook himself, trying to get rid of that not-right feeling once and for all. "Okay." He smiled, unsure what they expected of him now. "Thanks for looking out for me. I'm just going to"—he pointed his crutch at his building—"go inside."

"No problem. See you later."

Seb gave them one final glance over his shoulder, then hurried inside, only relaxing with a huge sigh of relief when he had the door locked behind him.

He was on edge the rest of the afternoon, unable to sit still for longer than twenty minutes. Watching TV or reading a book was out of the question, and he found himself logging into his work laptop to catch up on what he'd missed at the office—something he never usually did.

By the time Tim arrived, he was ready to climb the walls with frustration. He pulled himself to his feet and met him at the living room door. Not giving Tim chance to say anything, Seb put a hand on his hip and walked him backwards, using his height advantage to crowd him against the wall.

Tim beamed back at him, eyes dancing with a mixture of amusement and heat. "Hello to you, too." He slowly seemed to register Seb's agitated state of mind and quickly reached up to cup his jaw, concern replacing everything else. "Are you okay? Has something happened?"

Seb shook his head, not wanting to talk, but Tim was having none of it.

"Tell me."

With a sigh, Seb led him to the sofa and replayed his trip to the shop, including the feeling of being watched and then seeing Mark and Will. "So, just my overactive imagination, right?"

He met Tim's gaze, looking for conformation that he'd overreacted, that everything was fine, as it should be.

Tim frowned. "Maybe."

He didn't seem 100 per cent convinced, and that was not what Seb needed to hear. "Hey, you're supposed to reassure me." He slapped Tim lightly on the arm.

"Sorry. If Mark and Will said no other shifters were nearby, then it was probably your imagination." He quirked an eyebrow. "How's that?"

"It'd be more convincing if you sounded like you meant it."

Twining their fingers, as if absentmindedly, Tim focused on some far point over the other side of the room. "Sorry. It's just… this whole situation has me on edge."

Seb bristled; he thought they'd been having fun. Had Tim had changed his mind?

Maybe sensing Seb's sudden tension, Tim snapped his gaze back to him. "I don't mean us."

"Oh." Seb tried to tamp down his smile, but his lips had a mind of their own. "So what's bothering you, then?" He gave Tim's fingers a squeeze. "I told you mine. Fair's fair."

A few seconds passed in silence. Tim's thumb rubbed over the back of Seb's hand, and Seb watched the slow, repetitive motion until Tim sighed again.

"Okay."

# Chapter Fourteen

Where to begin?

Tim had so many thoughts and theories running through his head at present, he had trouble sorting through them sometimes. He almost longed for the days when all he had to do was get up, go to work, then come home.

Human ailments took up the majority of his time at work, and usually he found their various illnesses and complaints fascinating. Being the pack doctor either involved maternity cases, the odd queries about the full moon, or patching up wounds that were too serious to heal on their own. Sometimes he got to oversee the transition from bite to full change or no change, as with Jared, but that didn't happen as often as it used to.

Seb nudged him, and Tim realised he'd been staring into space again. He cleared his throat.

"All this stuff with the escaped rogue shifters, it's got me on edge all the time, and I'm not used to feeling this way."

Tim didn't get stressed; it was one of the things that made him a good doctor. He didn't panic, tried not to overreact to situations, and generally remained calm. But the last few days he'd been antsy, emotions all over the place, and as he stared at Seb, he was pretty sure he knew why. "That meeting I had with Cam, Alec, and the rest of the betas…."

"What about it? You never did tell me everything you discussed." Then Seb hastily added, "Not that you have to, of course, and I understand if they asked you not to."

Glancing down at their joined hands, Tim started to speak. All his concerns spilled out as he let the frustrations of the last two days get the better of him. "After they raided that warehouse, I thought that was the end of it. For the most part, we've had peace amongst the packs for the last ten years. There's been the odd incident, but nothing bad. I've not had to deal with injuries that severe for ages—Nathan's in particular." He looked up, expression serious as he met Seb's gaze. "I know what shifters are capable of, and if any did escape from that warehouse, they're going to be angry, out for revenge with nothing to lose."

Seb frowned, biting at his lip for a second. "What about Newell being behind all this? I thought—"

"I know what I said before. But Alec seems to think the threat from the rogues is real. Whether Newell is involved or has an agenda of his own, we can't be certain."

"They'll be waiting for Nathan, though, right? All of them seem to have a grudge against him, not me. And if he's not coming here, then I'm not in as much danger as you thought, am I?"

Seb's hopeful expression made something twist inside Tim. Was he so eager for all this to be over?

"I'm not sure. I mean, Alec and Cam suspect that with me here and not Nathan, Newell's plans might have changed—if he had any in the first place. But they have no idea what he might do now."

Seb rolled his eyes. "Wonderful. And what about the other ones?"

"Nathan's scent is all over this building—faint, but still there. They might not stop to ask questions."

"Great." Seb stared at his hands in Tim's for a second; the slight tremor in his fingers was the only sign that the conversation unnerved him. "But all this could still be for nothing. I might not be on anyone's radar."

Every one of Tim's instincts said Seb was in danger from something, but he forced himself to think rationally. "It's a possibility, I suppose. But after today, I think it's safer to assume that it's not for nothing." He held his hand up when Seb started to protest, knowing full well what he was going to say. "It probably was the P-Pack guys you sensed following you back from the shop. But what if it wasn't?"

"Mark and Will didn't scent anyone nearby." Seb eyed him curiously as though he wasn't making sense. And maybe he wasn't, but Tim couldn't shake the feeling that Seb wasn't safe.

He took Seb's hand in both of his own again. "I can't explain this in a way you'll understand, but please trust me. I can *feel* that something's wrong—" He brought their joined hands to his chest. "—in here. Whether it's Newell and his pack or the escaped rogue shifters, I don't know. But there's something or *someone* out there. And they aren't friendly."

Seb's gaze flicked from his face, then to where their hands were still pressed to his chest, and then back up. "So you're asking me to trust your instincts? Right?"

"Yes."

Seb shuffled closer and Tim breathed in the scent of him, letting it fill his lungs. "You want me to ignore all the facts and put my life on hold because of a feeling."

"Yes." Daring to risk a rebuff, Tim tugged him closer and leaned in to nuzzle the base of his throat. Seb's sharp intake of breath gave him the green light, and he trailed barely there kisses up the side of his neck until his mouth rested on that spot behind Seb's ear that made him shiver. Seb didn't disappoint this time, either. In a deep, growly voice, Tim asked, "Can you do that?"

The moan he got in answer wasn't exactly a yes or no, and Tim pulled away to meet Seb's eyes. He added, "We don't know what Newell has in mind, if anything, but neither Alec nor Cam trust him."

"What are you suggesting?" Seb lay back on the sofa, spreading his thighs and tugging Tim down to settle between them.

Tim went willingly, keeping a careful eye on Seb's cast so as not to knock it. "Keep doing what we're doing."

Seb's fingers were in his hair now; the loose grip was enough to keep Tim where he was. With his eyes closed and Seb wrapped around him like this, Tim let himself imagine what it would be like to have this for real, not some convenient, friends-with-benefits scenario that had an expiration date.

Another deep breath in filled his lungs with Seb's scent once more, its nuances so familiar to him now, he could pick it out anywhere. Opening his mouth, Tim set his teeth—still human—against the thrumming pulse point in Seb's neck. If he bit down hard, Seb would be his, maybe even a wolf to run at his side during full moons.

226

A surge of want rushed through him, the force taking him by surprise, and he immediately pulled back with a gasp, away from temptation.

Seb tensed underneath him. "What's wrong?"

Tim hesitated until his teeth were safely back to normal. It took longer than he was comfortable with.

"Tim?"

As his control returned, Tim placed a soft kiss on Seb's skin, relieved. "I'm fine, just got a little carried away. You always smell so good, but this spot right here?" He smiled as he trailed his lips up behind Seb's ear again. "This is my favourite."

Seb tilted his head to the side, sighing as Tim took the invitation and carried on kissing him there. "That spot's good, but are you sure it's your favourite?" As he spoke, Seb thrust his hips up, the hard length of his cock pressing into Tim's stomach.

Tim laughed. "Okay… maybe *one* of my favourite spots."

"That's what I thought." Seb continued rubbing up against him, small movements, but enough to get Tim straining against the fabric of his work trousers. "We should make sure I still smell like you. Don't want it to wear off."

The smell of *them* had hit Tim as soon as he walked in the door. A strong hint of sex lingered in the flat, and anyone coming into contact with either of them would know what they'd been up to. "No," he whispered, leaning up on his elbows, and meeting Seb's gaze. "We don't want that."

They kissed, and it was just as desperate and all-consuming as every other time. He'd never get enough of this, never get tired of having Seb in his arms, and the thought that he might soon have to give this up made him slip his hands under Seb's shoulders and hold on tight.

With each scrape of Seb's stubble over his skin, Tim pictured the red mark it would leave behind. The redness wouldn't last long, fading after a few seconds, but for the moments before that, Tim would be marked as Seb's. A jolt of excitement raced through him and he bucked his hips hard, making Seb cling to him and moan loudly.

"Need to get off this sofa and naked." Contrary to his words, Seb hooked his foot around Tim's calf, slid his hands down to rest on his arse, and pulled him closer.

Tim chuckled against his lips. "You need to let go of me for that to happen."

"I know," Seb muttered, not showing any signs of moving. "But you feel so good."

With the way Seb writhed against him, coupled with the heady scents filling the room, Tim wasn't going to last much longer if they kept this up. And he wanted to take his time, make the most of whatever time they had together. Failing that, he at least wanted to get Seb naked as often as possible.

Decision made, he forced himself to sit up, ignoring Seb's protests and grabbing hands. "Come on."

Seb looked up at him, wearing a betrayed expression as though Tim was the worst. Tim grinned down at him, taking a moment to consider how to do what he wanted, then reached down and scooped Seb up as if he weighed nothing. Always wary of his ankle, Tim gently slung him over his shoulder and smacked his arse.

"Put me down," Seb protested, but laughter followed his words as Tim carried him towards the bedroom.

"I'm going to." After depositing him on the bed, Tim climbed on too, crawling up to lie alongside him. He reached for the waistband on Seb's trackie bottoms. "Now get these off."

Seb shimmied out of both them and his boxers, laughing when it all got caught up around his cast.

Tim stood to take off his work trousers and shirt, offering no help at all.

With one eyebrow raised, Seb stopped his struggling and glared up at him. "If you want this to go any further, you might want to give me a hand."

Tim let his gaze wander up Seb's legs, from where the material caught round his ankle to the pale hairs covering his thighs. His hard cock jutted out, brushing against his belly as he leaned forward to try and free his foot. He grinned. "I'd love to give you a hand."

Seb rolled his eyes, but he couldn't hide the accompanying smile. "Get down there and help." He sat back on his elbows, then wrapped a hand around his dick, stroking it slowly. "Or I'll just get myself off like this."

Not that Tim was opposed to watching Seb wank, but right then he wanted to touch him all over and get his hands and mouth on him, not sit back and enjoy a show. He unzipped the lower part of Seb's bottoms and gently eased them over his cast until they were free. Tossing them to one side, he glanced up to find Seb watching him, still lazily stroking his cock. Tim took a moment to appreciate the sight, desire burning low in his belly, each breath in fanning the flames. Slowly he crawled up the bed, his gaze fixed on Seb's hand, tracking the movement until he got close enough to peel Seb's fingers away and replace them with his mouth.

"Fuck."

Seb moaned above him, the sound rough and needy, and Tim revelled in the knowledge he'd caused that. He sank down lower and lower, gripping the base of Seb's cock to keep him steady, and ran his tongue along the shaft as he went. With Seb's fingers tangled tightly in his hair, Tim eased off and then sucked him deep again, repeating the pattern as Seb shook and writhed beneath him.

The scent of sex filled the air, making Tim a little light-headed with the need to make Seb come. He drew back and sucked two fingers into his mouth, getting them good and wet. Glancing up, he caught Seb watching him, lip drawn between his teeth and eyes dark as he drew his legs up and spread his thighs. Tim kept eye contact as best he could as he took Seb back into his mouth and slid his spit-slick fingers towards Seb's hole.

Seb's grip tightened, his hold on Tim's hair just this side of painful, and that felt so good, keeping him grounded. Tim focused on the sharp tug as he slowly pushed his fingers inside. Seb arched up immediately, thrusting into Tim's mouth with a strangled cry.

The room filled with the sound of harsh breaths and soft moans as Tim sucked Seb's cock and worked his prostate.

He closed his eyes for a second and let the sounds wash over him. His own dick throbbed where it lay trapped against the bed and he pressed down, searching for a little friction to ease the ache.

"Close," Seb whispered. He let go of Tim's hair and clutched at the bottom sheet, fingers curled into tight fists. Tim hummed around him, keeping a steady rhythm and not letting up until Seb's whole body tensed and he came in a rush down Tim's throat. "Fucking hell."

Seb collapsed back onto the pillows with his arms over his face.

Tim pulled off and kneeled over him. Seb looked thoroughly used with his sweat-covered skin, messy hair, and sated expression.

Tim's wolf stirred under the surface; he had put that expression on Seb's face, made him come so hard he was out of breath.

The instinct to crawl up over him and take what was so clearly his warred with the knowledge that it wasn't real. Seb didn't feel that way about him, didn't want to be tied to him forever. Tim rolled his shoulders, only shuffling forward when he had his wolf back under control. He leaned over Seb, balancing on one hand as he stroked his cock with the other. Already on edge, it didn't take long before he was striping Seb's stomach, head thrown back as his orgasm rushed through him.

Seb's soft laughter brought him back down to earth and he glanced at him with a frown. "Something funny?"

Gesturing to his messy stomach, Seb grinned up at him. "Such a typical shifter move. I thought you were more original than that."

The playful lilt to his voice just about kept Tim from bristling. "Sorry to disappoint."

Seb shrugged one shoulder, then ran a finger through the cooling come and sucked it into his mouth. "Who said I was disappointed?"

He scooped up another fingerful, but Tim grabbed his hand, drew it towards him, and licked it clean.

"Fuck," Seb whispered.

It was Seb's expression more than anything, all hungry-eyed and vulnerable, that had Tim surging forward to pin him to the bed. Seb's behaviour curled around his heart, tugging at the emotions already held there, and he needed to be as close to him as possible.

Sticky come clung to their stomachs and Tim growled low in his throat at the feel of it. He twined his fingers with Seb's and kissed him, chasing the flavours on his tongue.

When they finally came up for air, Seb smiled up at him, just as his phone chimed with a reminder from the pocket of his bottoms somewhere on the floor. Seb glanced over in the direction and frowned for a second. Then, "Oh, shit."

"What?" Tim propped himself up on his elbows.

"I need to sort out a cab from the airport for my sister tomorrow." He slithered out from under Tim and leaned over the bed to find his phone. "Aha!" He sat back up triumphant, phone in hand.

"What time does she land? I could go and fetch her if you want?"

Seb stilled and looked up at him. "Er…."

"It's no problem. I can get someone to cover for me at the surgery."

"Yeah, it's not that." Seb scrubbed a hand over his eyes and sighed. "I'd rather keep her away from this mess if I can."

"Ahh. That's fine, I understand."

And he did. It just hurt that he couldn't do anything to help, that Seb didn't feel he could ask him without putting his sister in some kind of danger. Tim rolled onto his back, listening as Seb called the taxi company and rattled off his sister's name and flight details.

Seb placed a hand on Tim's chest after he hung up. "Sorry. I'm grateful for the offer, but I'd really rather keep her away from shifters if I can help it."

"You know they're everywhere, right? She's bound to run into one at some point. In fact, it wouldn't surprise me much if that car you just ordered was driven by one. Packs are involved with all sorts of businesses these days."

"I know, but with everything going on around here, around *me*... I just don't want her near anyone involved with it."

"Fair enough."

Silence settled between them as they lay on their backs, looking up at the ceiling.

For Tim, Seb's flat felt more like home with each day he spent there. He shouldn't think of it that way, but his scent overlaid Seb's everywhere, especially in the bedroom, and not one part of him wanted to ignore it.

Seb nudged him in the side. "So, do I smell enough like you again?" He ran his fingers over the traces of dried come on his belly, drawing Tim's gaze.

Tim smirked, transfixed. "I'm not sure. Maybe?"

Catching on, Seb turned onto his side, facing him. "Well, we can't have uncertainty, can we?" When he reached out to place his hand on Tim's chest. Tim grabbed it and tugged him closer, and

Seb laughed and let Tim arrange him how he wanted, then said, "Got any ideas how to fix it?"

If Seb wanted to forget everything going on around them, then Tim would go with it. He wanted to grab every opportunity with both hands. Who knew how much longer he'd get to have this. With a soft smile, he tilted Seb's chin towards him and kissed him. "I've got one or two."

# Chapter Fifteen

Tim dropped Seb off at Jared and Nathan's flat the next morning, insisting on walking him to the front door and waiting until Nathan came down to meet them.

"I'm fine, really." Seb didn't like the slight edge to his tone, but Tim was overreacting. "We're in the building, for fuck's sake! You can stop fussing."

"Shit." Tim sighed and immediately stepped back to give him some space. "Sorry. I'm just a little tense."

Seb snorted. "You don't say." He heard the stairwell door creak open on the floor above them, and he gave Tim a gentle shove. "Relax. Nothing's going to happen here."

"I know that, I just…." He sighed again and glanced towards the door, just as Nathan wandered through. "Never mind."

"Hey," Nathan grinned broadly as he greeted Tim with a hug and a slap on the shoulder. His gaze flicked between Seb and Tim, and if possible, his smile widened.

Seb groaned inwardly. In his excitement to see Jared, he'd forgotten all about Nathan and his shifter senses.

Nathan said, "Well, I see you two have been busy. And thorough," he added, gesturing for them to follow him inside and holding the door open for Tim. "Good to see you're taking this whole pretend-boyfriends thing so seriously."

Seb stopped halfway through the door, leaned on the frame, and pointed his crutch at Nathan.

"Like you did with Jared?" As Nathan laughed at him, he realised how that sounded.

"Yes, *exactly* like that from where I'm standing."

Seb tried to backtrack quickly, because he and Tim were *nothing* like Nathan and Jared. "No, that's not what I meant, and you know it." He hadn't wanted to go into it, but as usual, Nathan had riled him up. "We're just making the most of the situation. Having a little fun." Shooting Nathan a glare, he eased past him into the hallway. "Not everyone has to rush in feet first and bond for life."

He expected Nathan to laugh or give him a shove, but when he looked back, Nathan's gaze was fixed on Tim, their expressions unreadable.

Tim cleared his throat and gestured with his thumb towards the front door. "I don't want to be late for morning surgery, so I'll see you later."

Seb frowned; he'd clearly missed something. "Okay."

Tim was almost at the door. "About half past five?"

"Yeah, sounds good."

With a short nod, Tim left and didn't look back.

"What's up with him?" Seb stood rooted to the spot, watching the space where Tim had been moments before and feeling like he'd messed up somehow.  Nathan stared at him, eyebrows raised, as if Seb was the one behaving strangely. "What? I didn't do anything."

"Fucking humans," Nathan muttered, but his voice didn't have any bite to it. "Jared's waiting upstairs for you."

Seb turned to see that Nathan wasn't following him. "Not coming up?"

236

"No." Nathan shook his head and gestured at the door Tim had just gone through. "Luke's waiting for me in the van. We've got a shift at the warehouse."

"Oh." Even better, a day with just Jared. It had been a while since he'd had his best friend to himself, and Seb had a lot of questions for him.

Nathan took two steps towards the door, then stopped.

Seb knew it had been too good to be true. For a second there he thought he'd escaped without Nathan's usual teasing.

Nathan's pained expression made Seb think that whatever was about to come out his mouth would be uncomfortable for the pair of them.

"Tim's a good guy."

"I know that."

"Just—" Nathan sighed and muttered something Seb didn't quite catch. "I know you don't want to be involved with a shifter for any length of time. And that's fine. I'm not saying you should be." Good, because Seb had some words for him if he was. "But for us it's not so simple. We get… *attached*. Easily."

"Whatever point you're trying to make, just spit it out."

"He likes you. You know that, right?"

"Yeah." Seb nodded. "I like him too."

Nathan pinched the bridge of his nose. "But for him it's…."

Seb waited for him to elaborate, but he didn't. "It's *what?*"

"Fuck." Nathan met Seb's gaze, expression torn. "Not for me to say." With that, he pointed to the stairs. "Go on up."

And then he was gone, leaving Seb staring after him open-mouthed.

Seb cursed him out all the way up the stairs, grumbling to himself and wondering why there wasn't a bloody lift in the building. It might only be one flight, but it was awkward and slow getting up them with his crutch.

Jared opened the door when Seb knocked, took one look at him, and laughed. "What did he say now?"

He stepped aside and ushered Seb in.

"How can you tell?" Seb shrugged off his coat and gave it to Jared to hang up.

"You have that pinched look that only Nathan can give you."

Seb huffed. "He has a gift." He followed Jared through to the kitchen and leaned against the worktop as Jared set about making them each a drink.

"Seriously, though, what did he say?"

"Something about Tim." Seb sighed and rubbed at the bridge of his nose as he tried to recall Nathan's exact words. "That he likes me, and how it's different for shifters, that they get *attached* easily." He made air quotes with his fingers. "Then he refused to say anything more and left. He's so annoying. I don't know how you put up with him." The way Jared ducked his head and smiled made Seb roll his eyes and groan. "God, stop it already. I might be ill."

"Here." Jared carefully slid a coffee towards him. "And stop being an arse." He eyed Seb closely, narrowing his eyes as if he'd be able to see into Seb's mind if he looked hard enough. "You don't usually let him get to you like this. What's the matter?"

Seb looked away, focusing on his cast instead. *Has it only been on for ten days? It seems so much longer.*

He finally answered when Jared nudged his foot. "I don't know."

But that wasn't strictly true. Seb took a sip of his drink, blowing on it first as he debated what to say.

"Seb?"

"I don't..." *know.* He stopped himself repeating it and set his mug down. "Do you reckon you and Nathan would be together if you hadn't bonded?"

The question obviously took Jared by surprise. He stopped with his mug halfway to his mouth and stared at him. "How do you mean?"

"If you'd not fucked and activated whatever creepy shifter magic you did, do you think you'd be together now?"

He watched a little guiltily as Jared seemed to struggle with an answer. It was a shitty question to ask, but even after all these months, the idea that Jared had never had a choice still bothered him to some extent.

Jared glanced up at the ceiling, sighing heavily. "We've been over this."

"I know, but humour me."

"I can't answer that the way you want me to. Yes, I thought he was hot when I first saw him, but I also thought he was an arrogant dick. We didn't fuck right away, remember, and I was starting to like him, I think."

"Even though he essentially kidnapped you? There's a name for that, you know."

239

Jared laughed. "Yeah, I know. But it wasn't like that. Even before our bond kicked in, there was something there, something that drew us together."

"But how do you know that wasn't the shifter magic already at work? He *bit* you. All his whatever-it-is was swimming around in your blood." Seb waved his hands around to emphasise his point.

"I guess I don't know for sure." Jared set his mug down and crossed his arms. "But does it matter? So what if Nathan and I have some freaky chemistry that makes it work even when I'm human. I love him. He loves me. I'm happier than I've ever been, Seb, and that's not going to change, because we're bonded." He met Seb's gaze, expression earnest. "How many people get to say that? To have that?"

Seb had nothing. He drank his coffee in silence, mulling Jared's words over in his head, while Nathan's opinion tried to sneak back in too. But even for all Jared's assurances that he wouldn't want it any other way... *how does he know for sure?*

Ugh, his head hurt just thinking about it.

"Why are you so interested again? Thinking about asking Tim to bite you?"

Seb choked on his coffee, coughing violently before turning to glare at his grinning friend. "What? No! Definitely not."

"You're fucking, though, right?"

"What makes you say that?"

Jared rolled his eyes. "Luke was here this morning."

*Oh. So no point even trying to deny anything.* "You've seen how hot he is. Might as well make the best of the situation."

"Mm-hmm."

240

"What the hell does that mean?"

"Well, the last time we spoke about this, you were adamant you weren't going to get involved with a shifter, just in case. Remember?"

*Did I say that?*

Jared was carrying on, clearly on a roll. "And now Luke says the two of you smell like you 'rolled around in each other's jizz.' His exact words," he added when Seb wrinkled his nose.

"We didn't roll around in it."

They drank their coffee in silence for a few moments.

Seb contemplated letting the subject drop, but he still had questions. "Hypothetically speaking…."

Jared turned his head to face him. "Yes?"

"If Tim were to bite me now, would I turn into a wolf and would we bond, or would I have to wait until after the full moon to find out, like you did?"

"Er…." Jared stared at him open-mouthed. "*Hypothetically?*"

"Yes."

"Well, I'm no expert. You'd be better off asking Nathan." He paused. "Or, you know, Tim."

*So not happening.* Seb glared at him and motioned for him to carry on.

"Well, as I understand it, if you're already fucking and a shifter bites you, then *bam!*" He slapped his hand on the worktop, startling Seb. "Instant bond. I don't know about the wolf bit, though. I think that's maybe still a case of wait and see."

"But the bond would stay whatever the outcome?"

"I think so? But I'm really not the one to ask, Seb." Jared flicked a quick glance at the clock on the wall.

Seb suddenly realised that he might be keeping him from working. "Do you need to be somewhere?"

"What? Oh, no. I left my laptop upstairs with Gareth last night. I just need to go get it before eleven, that's all."

"Oh."

"Are you sure you're not thinking about Tim biting you?"

"Not a chance. Even if it would fix my leg."

Jared didn't look all that convinced, so Seb busied himself with the last of his coffee. Did he want Tim to bite him? *No.* Well, maybe the thought had crept into his head when they were having sex, but that was different. He wasn't thinking with his brain then. But something about what Nathan had said… "Can bonds be one-sided?"

"What?"

"Like, without the biting bit, can shifters form bonds to humans but not have it reciprocated?"

Jared studied him again and Seb fidgeted under his constant scrutiny.

Jared said, "Is that what you think's happening with Tim?"

"I don't know. Nathan said they get easily attached, so… maybe?"

"Um…." Jared blew out a breath and shrugged. "I have absolutely no idea."

"Great help you are."

"Fuck off." Jared punched him on the arm, laughing. "If I'd known there was going to be a quiz, I'd have prepared."

Seb grinned back at him and they lapsed into silence again, until Jared kicked Seb's shoe.

"I do know that shifters can bond with other shifters, and obviously they don't need the bite."

"Can they?" For some reason, Seb had never thought about that.

"Yeah. I'm sure I remember Nathan saying it doesn't happen all that often, but it can."

The idea that Tim could suddenly be bonded to another shifter left a nasty taste in his mouth. "They'd still have to have sex, though, right?"

Jared shrugged again. "No idea. I assume so."

Seb hummed to himself. "Well, at least Tim's in no danger of that happening." He didn't realise what he'd said until he caught Jared smirking at him. "What?"

"Just making the most of things, eh?"

He gave Seb a knowing look, and Seb scowled back at him.

"Oh, fuck off."

His phone chimed, distracting him from saying anything else. The text was from his sister.

*Just been picked up. Thanks for sorting. X*

He replied with *No problem. Call me when you get home. X*

*Will do*

Jared was grinning at him when he looked up.

"That was from Kelly, before you say anything."

Jared perked up at that. "Oh, how is she? Back from her hols?"

"Yeah, just got picked up from the airport. I booked her a taxi." He knew what was coming even before Jared glanced down at his cast and frowned.

"Me or Nathan would have picked her up, you know."

"Yeah, I know, but—"

"You wanted to keep her out of it?"

Seb nodded. Out of everyone, Jared understood how he felt. "Yeah."

"Fair enough. But let me know if you want a ride over to see her. That goes for anything else too. I know we don't see each other as much these days, but I'm always here if you need me."

"Thanks."

Seb smiled, and a rush of warmth filled his chest as Jared put his arm around him and hugged him close.

About half an hour later, they had firmly pushed aside their earlier conversation, mainly due to Seb's refusal to discuss it further. Jared's phone chimed, and he glanced at it as Seb paused their game.

"Shit. Forgot all about my laptop." Jared glanced at Seb sprawled out in the corner of the sofa. "I wouldn't go, but I need to do a bit of work this afternoon."

Seb waved him off. "Go get it. I'll just leave this paused while you're gone."

"Want to come up?"

"No, thanks." Despite Jared's assurances that Gareth was great, Seb had no desire to walk up more flights of stairs, only to have to turn round and come all the way back down.

"Okay. Be back in ten minutes, tops." Jared slipped on his shoes, grabbed the flat keys from the table, and headed for the door.

Seb stretched and yawned, and when his phone vibrated in his pocket, he jumped a mile. His smile faded when it wasn't his sister's name that appeared. "Hello?"

"Mr Calloway?"

"Speaking." Seb pulled the phone away from his ear a second to check the number. It looked vaguely familiar, but he couldn't place it.

"This is Caroline from Airport Xpress Taxis. Our driver has been waiting at the airport for over almost an hour now, and there's no sign of Miss Calloway. Can you confirm the flight details were correct?"

Seb sat there, stunned, not sure what was going on. "Um, I'm sorry, there must be some mistake. I got a text from my sister a while ago saying she'd been picked up and was on her way home."

"I'm afraid that's not possible, sir. Well, it wasn't our firm, anyway. And since she's obviously no longer at the airport…"

She carried on talking, something about him still being charged the full amount, but Seb wasn't really paying attention any longer. He gripped the phone tightly; his hand shook as the implications began to sink in.

"Mr Calloway? Are you still there?"

"Yeah, do whatever's necessary. Bye."

He hung up, not caring what he'd just agreed to. Jesus Christ! Some fucking stranger had picked up his sister from the airport and could be taking her to God knew where. He ran a trembling hand through his hair, gripping hard at the long strands while dialling his sister's number. His phone buzzed with a text as the call went to voice mail.

Seb left her a terse message to call him back immediately, then checked the text.

It was from Kelly. *Heading to your flat first. Hope that's ok. X*

Fuck no, it wasn't okay. Who the hell was she with? And what if they left her waiting outside on her own? Christ, what if those fucking rogue shifters chose that moment to pay him a visit!

*Shit. Shit. Shit.*

He called her again as he stood and grabbed his crutch. No reply. *Again.*

*Come on, Kelly!*

Jared came through the door, carrying his laptop, just as Seb was frantically pulling his trainer on. "Going somewhere?"

"Grab your car keys. We need to go back to mine."

"What? Why?" Jared grabbed Seb's arm as he reached for the door. "Seb? What the hell's going on?"

"Kelly didn't get in the taxi I arranged."

Jared looked confused, but fuck, there was no time for that. Seb reached past him for the door handle.

"Someone else picked her up, J. She's in a car with some fucker, and on the way to my flat. I need to get there right the fuck now." He glared when Jared took too long to respond. "Jared!"

"Okay, okay, but we can't go on our own. Nathan would kill me, and I suspect Tim wouldn't be too pleased either."

"I'm not fucking bonded to Tim," Seb snarled, pushing his way out of the door. "I don't care whether he'll be pissed off or not."

That wasn't true—he did care—but at that moment the only thing that mattered was getting to Kelly.

"Everyone'll be pissed off if we do this, Seb. Let me just call Nath—"

"Nathan's at work and so is Tim. I'm not waiting. Tell them to meet us there, whatever, I don't care."

Jared had his phone out dialling someone, but he was finally hurrying towards the stairs, so Seb didn't give a shit who he called.

"We're going back to Seb's flat," Jared said to whoever was on the other end. "Family emergency." He gave a quick rundown of the situation, then hung up. "Gareth'll meet us at my car."

"Fine. But he better hurry, because we're not waiting."

Contrary to his words, Seb relaxed a little at the news. As everything started to sink in, the realisation that this was maybe a bad idea dawned on him. He and Jared were human; they'd be absolutely no help to Kelly if shifters were involved.

But she was his sister; he couldn't just sit around and do nothing. Gareth was a beta, stronger than either Nathan or Tim, and having him there swung the odds considerably in their favour.

"I'm sure it's all fine," Jared said as they hurried down the stairs. "She probably just got in another cab."

Seb clung onto the rail tightly as he went faster than was probably safe for him. *Fucking cast.* "You honestly believe that?" Jared's silence spoke volumes. "Thought not."

"How would they know about Kelly? Or when her flight got in? Who did you tell?"

"Only Tim, last night." For a second he considered it, but no, Tim would never—

*Could someone have overheard?*

Gareth caught up to them before they reached the front door. "Wait here." He rushed past them and out the door, returning after a few moments. "Come on."

Jared was parked close, thank God, and they piled into the car. Gareth insisted on driving, and Seb managed to refrain from rolling his eyes. Of course the beta wanted to be in charge.

"Don't call Nathan," Gareth said when Jared got out his phone.

"Why?"

"He can't be there. Neither can Tim." Jared went to protest, as did Seb, but Gareth spoke again, cutting them off. "If anyone is waiting at your flat, then the last thing we need is Nathan and Tim going into protective mode. I don't need them killing anyone if we can help it."

Seb understood why it might be a bad idea for Nathan to be there, but why Tim? "Tim and I aren't—"

"Whatever you think you are or are not, if you're in the slightest danger, Tim would protect you."

Gareth's voice had a warning edge to it that Seb didn't exactly care for, but he let it go without comment. There were bigger things to focus on.

Gareth went on issuing his orders and information, fully in control now. "I've called Alec. He'll bring one of his unit and meet us there."

Oh. Well, that made Seb feel better. With three shifters on their side, surely the odds were in their favour?

He tried calling Kelly repeatedly as they headed through the Thursday traffic towards his flat. Each time it went straight to voice mail. Either she'd run out of charge—possible—or there was no signal. Considering where Seb lived, the latter was extremely doubtful. With his phone gripped in one hand and the edge of his seat in the other, Seb counted down the minutes until Gareth indicated and turned into his road.

Everything appeared as innocuous as ever. Seb wasn't sure what he'd been expecting, but seeing the street looking completely normal threw him off.

Gareth lowered the window and leaned out.

*Is he sniffing the air?* Seb poked Jared in the shoulder to get his attention, then gestured at Gareth. "What?" he mouthed.

"He's scenting the air." Jared spoke out loud for Gareth to hear, and Seb slunk lower into the seat, glaring at him. Jared shrugged. "What?"

"Nothing."

Gareth glanced back at him before resuming whatever it was he was doing. "Just trying to get a feel for who's about."

Seb strained to look out the windows as much as possible, up and down the road. *As if I'd be able to spot anyone even if they were there.*

The closer they got to his flat, the thicker the tension inside the car became. He was practically vibrating in his seat, cast forgotten as he twisted this way and that to try and see any sign of foul play near his building.

The tree-lined pavement looked eerie in a way Seb had never noticed before, and scenes from countless horror films flooded into his head.

Gareth pulled to a stop in the middle of the road outside Seb's building. There were no spaces for him to park, so they sat with the engine idling, staring up at it.

Seb bit his lip, waiting for Gareth to say something, until the silence got too much and he couldn't stand it any longer. "Well?"

"It smells like you, but different."

Seb relaxed a tiny amount. "So that's probably Kelly, right? She has a key to my place. She's more than likely already inside." He reached for the door handle.

"Wait." Gareth's lip curled up in a snarl, teeth lengthening as his gaze focused on the path up to Seb's front door. "That's not all I can smell. We need to wait for Alec."

Seb's heart pounded. He glanced up at his home, almost afraid to ask, but he had to know. Tightening his fingers on the door handle, he followed Gareth's line of sight and whispered. "What else?"

"P-Pack shifters and maybe someone from another pack. I can't be sure."

It sounded like there was more, and Seb was so tired of shifters treating him like he couldn't handle it. "And?" he spat, gripping Gareth's shoulder and giving it a shake without really meaning to.

Gareth's head turned sharply; his angry glare fixed on Seb for a terrifying second until his features softened. "And blood."

Seb didn't have to ask if it was human, he just knew from the expression on Gareth's face. His

250

heart clenched as though invisible fingers had wrapped around it and were steadily squeezing the life out of him. That was his sister, the only family he had left apart from Jared.

Visions of her lying broken and bloody flooded his mind, chasing all rational thought away. In possibly the stupidest move he'd ever made, Seb opened his door and tumbled onto the pavement, miraculously not tripping over as he started to run towards his flat.

"Seb!"

"Fuck!"

He ignored the angry shouts behind him and ran-slash-hobbled as fast as he could, the pain in his ankle a dull throb that barely registered through the haze of terror clouding his mind. "Kelly?"

No answer.

It shouldn't have been much of a surprise when he only reached less than halfway up the path before Gareth caught him.

"What the fuck—"

One minute Gareth was yanking him around by his shoulder, the next Seb was flying through the air, arms pinwheeling as he fought to get his bearings. He hit the ground hard and the breath exploded out of his lungs on impact, but he'd landed on his side and managed to cradle his head in his hands. That did nothing to protect his arm or his wrist, though, and the sickening *crack* made bile rise in the back of his throat.

*For fuck's sake! That's only just healed!*

Pain radiated throughout his body, but Seb pushed himself into a sitting position in time to see Gareth rip a huge chunk of flesh out of—*Oh God, that's someone's ribs on display, or what's left of them.*

Unable to look away, Seb was sure a couple of bones were missing. The injured shifter slumped to the floor, howling and clutching his side, but he still made a swipe at Gareth, catching him in the thigh. Three of them were fighting Gareth, though, and while Gareth was distracted, one of the others zeroed in on Seb and grinned, blood dripping from its teeth. All four had half shifted, their extended jaws giving them a grotesque half-wolf, half-human appearance, with rows of sharp teeth on display as they snarled and snapped at each other.

Every part of Seb urged him to get up and run for the car, his flat, anywhere to get away from the advancing shifter, but now his ankle throbbed in earnest—God only knew what damage he'd done to it—and his arm felt as though it was on fire. He forced himself to stand, ignoring his body's protests in the face of all those teeth and claws, and hobbled as fast as he could manage to the closest point of safety—Jared's car. Which, in hindsight, probably wouldn't afford him much safety, and if Jared was still in there… *Fuck!*

Seb tried to change direction, but in the end it made no difference. He made it two paces before his back erupted in trails of white-hot fire. Pain exploded in his shoulder blade, radiating out and down, and Seb crumpled in a screaming heap on the ground.

*Is this it? Is this how I'm going to die?*

He had so much more he wanted to do with his life, and he'd promised his sister he'd never leave her. They'd only been young at the time, but the thought of her all on her own made his chest ache. *No.* After all his worries that getting involved with a shifter would ruin his life, take away his free will, he hadn't thought it would kill him.

An image of Tim smiling and laughing filled his mind, and Seb clung to it like a lifeline as blood pooled underneath his shoulder, trickling from his back, down the side of his neck to the ground.

That he was still breathing was a miracle at this point. Seb had braced for more, been expecting it ever since he'd hit the floor, but so far another attack hadn't come. More snarling from the direction of the road, and Seb lifted his head enough to see two blurry shapes flying up the path. *Alec.*

He couldn't see the shifter who had attacked him, but from the sounds of it, Alec and whomever he'd brought with him had already found him. Everything hurt, and Seb struggled to see Gareth, but his head swam and his vision began to blur at the edges.

It might have been his imagination, but as he felt his body succumbing to unconsciousness, Gareth's soft voice sounded in his ear and strong arms lifted him from the ground as though he weighed nothing.

"Kelly?" Seb muttered, desperately clinging on as he waited for the answer.

"We'll find her."

Everything after that was a mixture of noise and light fading in and out, nothing discernible, just sounds and images. Seb tried to make sense of what was going on around him, desperate to know more about Kelly, but it was a losing battle. Easier to just close his eyes and sleep.

# Chapter Sixteen

Tim paced the length of the hospital room, willing Seb to wake up so that he could kill him already.

What the hell had Seb been thinking? For what seemed the fiftieth time that day, he dropped heavily onto the hard plastic chair next to the bed and ran his hands through his hair. He'd done it so often now, he was probably a horrendous mess, but fuck it, he felt so helpless just sitting around.

"Hey."

Tim looked up as his brother came in brandishing Seb's chart. "Tell me."

David hesitated, then said softly, "You're not down as family, Tim. I should really check with the patient before I—"

"Please. I'm his doctor. Won't that do?"

David frowned and stared at him for a couple more seconds, then walked into the room with a sigh and closed the door behind him. "Technically you're not listed as his doctor, but since he's classed as pack and you're the pack doctor, I guess I can bend the rules this time."

Tim smiled, grateful it was his brother on shift tonight. "Thank you." He pointed to the chart. "How bad is it?"

"Well, it's not good, but it could have been a lot worse, as I'm sure you're aware."

Yes, Tim was all too aware how bad a shifter attack on a human could be. He'd treated a few and had identified two fatal cases in the past year. On the surface, Seb looked virtually untouched. He had a graze across his cheek and forehead from where he'd hit the ground, but that was all. The real damage would be on his back and inside his body. "Just tell me."

"Fine."

Tim closed his eyes and slumped back in his seat willing himself to remain calm—something that had been increasingly difficult since he'd received Gareth's call three hours ago.

"Mild concussion, broken right ulna and radius, two-inch cut on right palm that required stitches. Bruised ribs on the right and five lacerations on his back, crossing from right shoulder to left hip. Three of them were deep enough to require stitches. He lost a lot of blood."

"Fuck."

Tim felt sick; something he'd not experienced much of until Seb came along. Unfortunately that kind of pain wasn't anything his shifter DNA could fix, and Tim rested his head in his hands in an attempt to will the feeling away. Falling apart wouldn't help anyone, and he didn't want Seb to see him like that when he woke up. "Is that everything?"

"They had to recast his ankle too."

"Bollocks."

"But at least it didn't need surgery."

Tim stood, needing to move or do something, anything to relieve the stress of waiting around at a hospital. He walked over to the side of the bed, his gaze sweeping over the sharp lines of Seb's face. "Can I stay?"

He trailed a finger along the edge of Seb's jaw; soft stubble prickled his fingers.

"For a little while. I'm due to check his vitals in a sec. You can stay for that, and then I'm going to have to kick you out."

Tim nodded. "Okay."

He didn't want to leave Seb's side, but Seb would probably be in and out of sleep for the rest of the evening. Plus, Tim wanted to speak to a few people about what had happened.

His hands curled into fists as he remembered getting the call; he closed his eyes again, breathing through it. Getting angry wouldn't help.

A few moments later, David touched his arm. "I'm about to wake him. You ready?"

Tim rolled his shoulders and reached for Seb's hand, the one not currently wrapped in bandages. Again. "Yeah."

David carefully roused Seb from deep sleep and began checking his vitals and asking him a few questions. Seb answered, his voice thick with sleep. When David moved to one side, Seb's gaze landed on Tim and he smiled.

Tim's heart stuttered. He hadn't realised just how close he'd come to losing him until that moment. Squeezing Seb's fingers, he smiled back. "Hey."

"Hey." Seb swallowed and licked his lips, his eyes already dropping closed. He blinked them open and took a second to focus again.

"You should go back to sleep," Tim said. "You've had a rough afternoon." He rubbed his thumb across the back of Seb's hand, carefully avoiding the cannula taped there.

"Time's it?" Seb glanced lazily down his body, frowning at his arm and the way his ankle was raised off the bed. The morphine must be doing its job, because his back wasn't giving him any pain.

"Just after 10.00 p.m."

When Seb focused back on Tim, his eyes seemed far more alert. "Where's Kelly?"

*Shit.* Tim sighed and ran his free hand through his hair. "They haven't found her yet?"

Seb tried to sit up, but Tim darted forward, placing a hand on his chest. "Don't—your back."

"Oh." Seb frowned and let his head fall back onto the pillow. "I can't really feel much, although it's tight across my shoulders."

"It's bad. So be careful, please." Tim hadn't seen the damage for himself, but he was well acquainted with what a shifter's claws could do to skin and flesh. "I spoke to Alec, briefly. They're doing everything they can to find your sister."

Seb yawned, his eyes fluttering shut, then snapping open again. He looked exhausted. "Anyone call the police?"

Tim hesitated, and Seb was alert enough to notice.

"Jesus Christ, why the hell not? She's human. They should be—"

"Sebastian." Tim squeezed his fingers, shushing him. "Her scent was all over the shifters who were at your house. We'll have a much better chance of finding her without getting the police involved."

Seb grunted, not looking at all convinced, but then his eyes closed; they stayed closed this time. "Tired," he mumbled, barely audible.

Tim smiled and reached out to push a stray lock of blond hair away from Seb's forehead. His gaze travelled down Seb's body, slowly cataloguing his injuries, matching them to what David had told

257

him earlier. The low-level anger he'd been carrying around all day flared hot and insistent, and for just a second, Tim let it consume him.

Releasing Seb's hand, he stumbled backwards, claws and teeth sliding into place at an alarming rate, and before he realised what was happening, he'd already half shifted. A low growl reverberated around the room, and oh God, it felt so good to let his wolf out. He wanted to get his hands on those who'd hurt Seb, wanted to rip them apart and burn whatever was left.

"For fuck's sake."

Tim whirled around, teeth bared, to see David pressed up against the door, hands up in front of him. Tim let out another growl before he could stop himself. The instinct to protect Seb overrode everything else.

"Calm yourself down. I'm not going to hurt him."

Tim closed his eyes, willing his wolf to fade back to lie just under the surface, but he couldn't do it. *Shit.*

He sighed and focused on David's scent instead, the warm feeling of *family* slowly allowing him to relax. "Sorry."

He opened his eyes to see David nodding over at the bed. Tim turned to find a sleepy but surprisingly alert Seb watching him, mouth open.

Seb stared at him, gaze flicking from his eyes, to his mouth, down to his hands. "Tim?"

*Fuck.* Tim couldn't tell whether Seb sounded frightened or disappointed, but he'd never wanted him to see him like this. Shame flooded through him, and his half-shift fell away easily.

"I want you to bite me," Seb whispered, not taking his eyes off Tim.

"What?" Tim took a step closer to the bed. *Did I hear that correctly?*

Desire flared in his chest, hot and encompassing, and his gaze automatically slid to Seb's neck.

David, still glued to the door, cleared his throat. "I'll just give you two a minute."

Tim didn't bother to acknowledge him other than to nod his thanks. As the door shut softly behind David, Tim pulled the chair close to Seb's bedside and sat down, taking his hand again.

"I said"—Seb's voice was a lot clearer this time—"I want you to bite me."

"No." Tim shook his head. "How much fucking morphine did they give you?" He moved to get up, intent on checking Seb's chart, but Seb's hand on his wrist stopped him.

"I'm serious." Seb sounded steady enough, but it was obvious that keeping his eyes open was a struggle. "I want to help find my sister." He pulled his hand free from Tim's grasp and waved it down the length of his body. "I can't fucking do it like this."

"You don't have to. Seb, we have people looking for her. They'll find her."

Seb tried to sit up again, and again Tim stopped him, but not before Seb winced in pain.

"*Fuck.*" He screwed his eyes shut, placing his palm against his ribs.

Tim could smell the pain rolling off him, and he couldn't stop the small sound escaping.

Seb slid his hand back into Tim's. "I felt so useless when Jared got hurt. There was nothing I could do to help him, and there was nothing I could do to help Kelly today."

"None of that was your fault."

"I know that. But it doesn't change the fact that when it comes to protecting the people I love, I'm going to fail, every single time."

"Sebast—"

"No!" Seb gripped Tim's fingers, urging him to listen to him.

And God, part of Tim wanted to agree, say it was an excellent idea and he'd do it right now if Seb wanted. But… "You don't want this." He gestured to himself. "You saw what I turn into, didn't you?"

"Yes."

"You told me you never wanted to be a shifter, never wanted to be tied to one for life because of a bond you had no control over." He looked Seb in the eyes, his heart beating so fast he'd be light-headed if he were human. "Has any of that changed?"

The sudden silence in the room was almost too much for him to bear.

But thankfully, Seb broke it. "*Yes.*"

Tim tried not to hold on too tightly, his fingers now curled around Seb's. "Which bits?"

"I'm tired of not being enough, of never being enough. I'm three inches taller than you, for fuck's sake, yet you make me feel small. You could probably pick me up with one hand."

"Seb—"

"I want to be able to protect myself. I want to feel safe when I go home, or when I walk down the street to the fucking shop." He took a shuddering breath and closed his eyes. "And at this minute, that's the last thing I feel."

"I can protect you—"

"I don't want you to protect me!"

Tim felt the words like a physical blow. He sat back in his chair as though struck, and words flew out of his mouth, unfiltered. "Well, if *I* bit you that's exactly what would happen, whether you want it to or not. We'd be bonded, *for life*, or have you forgotten that part?"

Seb's quiet, resigned "No" did nothing to appease Tim's hurt.

"You would be my mate—to love and protect. And I'd be yours. And you'd want it. You'd be happy."

He almost added "you'd love me," but he couldn't force the words past the lump in his throat. This was a conversation he never thought he'd get to have with Seb, and though he'd imagined it once or twice, it hadn't gone like this.

"I haven't forgotten." Seb let go of his hand. He tried to shrug one shoulder, gasping at the obvious pain.

Tim was about to ask him if he was okay— Seb's welfare took priority over everything else— but Seb's next words floored him.

"I just figured it's not that big a deal anymore. And I'd be able to protect myself and the ones I loved."

Seb might as well have put a knife through Tim's heart; the pain felt like a real, tangible thing as it tore through his chest. "Not that big a deal?" he whispered.

Seb's brow furrowed as though he didn't understand Tim's problem. "Yeah. I like you. I know you like me. So we'd be bonded. Everyone's happy."

"I don't just *like* you, Sebastian." Tim stood up quickly, making his chair screech across the floor. "I *love* you. I would give anything for you to ask me to bite you, to have you as my bonded mate. There's nothing I want more. But only if you love me back, not because you feel you have no other option."

He covered his face with his hands, trying not to fall apart. A deep breath in filled his lungs with Sebastian and *pain*, and it was too much. "If you're serious about wanting the bite—and it's not just the painkillers talking—speak to Cam. I'm sure he'd agree and would organise the necessary paperwork." He turned and headed for the door. "I need to go. I think Nathan and Jared are coming in the morning. Night, Sebastian."

"Tim, wait—"

Tim stopped with his hand on the door. "What?"

"I—"

Tim waited. Waited for Seb to tell him that he loved him too.

The room remained silent. Tim pressed his forehead against the door, collected himself as much as he could, then left.

David stood just outside. The hospital rooms were soundproofed to some extent, but that close, David had probably heard most of it. Grasping Tim's shoulder, he pulled him in for a quick hug. "You going home?"

Tim sighed. "Yeah. Need to talk to Alec, see if they've had any luck finding Kelly, but I'll call him from the car."

"Okay. Will I see you tomorrow?"

Although he'd had every intention of coming back first thing in the morning, Tim wasn't sure now. "Maybe."

"He's on pain medication, Tim. Don't take everything he said to heart." David patted him on the arm.

Tim nodded. "Yeah, I know."

"Go home, get some sleep. I'll call you if anything happens."

"Thanks."


Tim arrived at the hospital ten minutes before visiting hours the next morning. There was never any doubt he'd be there, and David probably knew it, because he smiled when he saw Tim walking towards him.

"Thought I'd see you bright and early."

"What are you doing here, anyway? Thought you worked till twelve last night?"

David yawned on cue. "I did, but a couple of nurses called in sick this morning, so I offered to cover a shift." He accompanied Tim down the long corridor that led to Seb's room.

The door stood ajar about an inch. Several voices sounded inside, and Tim recognised them all. Turning to David, he gestured inside with his thumb and mouthed, "When did they get here?"

"About twenty minutes ago."

*Fuck.* Tim had been hoping to get some alone time with Seb before everyone showed up. The conversation paused inside, a sure sign that the shifters in the room knew he'd arrived.

Seconds later the door opened wide and Alec stood there, his expression a little strained. "Are you coming in?"

Tim nodded, then turned to David. "I'll catch you later, yeah?"

"Nope." David put his hands on the small of Tim's back and gave him a little shove into the room. "I need to check a few things before—"

"David," Alec interrupted. His warning tone sent a ripple of unease down Tim's spine. "Is there anywhere private where I can talk to Tim for a second?"

"Yeah." David pointed behind him. "Third door on the left. It's the toilet, but it's probably the most heavily soundproofed room around."

"Thank you." Alec put his arm on Tim's shoulder and ushered him forward.

The feeling of unease blossomed, and Tim wondered what the hell Alec needed privacy for—*Is it Kelly? Is she dead? Oh God, Seb will be—*

"It's not what you're thinking." They reached the bathroom and Alec opened the door, inclining his head for Tim to go in first. "Still no news on Kelly, although we have some promising leads."

"How did you know I was thinking about that?" Tim leaned against the wall and crossed his arms. Thank God it was a fair-sized bathroom, or things would be a lot more awkward.

Alec rolled his eyes. "It's written all over your face, Tim. You're in deep with this one." Alec wasn't asking a question, so there was no point in even trying to deny it. "Why did you refuse to bite him, then?"

"What?" Tim's gaze snapped to Alec's. "How do you know about that? He only asked me last night."

The sigh Alec let out wasn't a sound you'd normally hear from him. "What time did you leave here last night?"

"Just after ten, why?"

"Because Mr Calloway has been a busy boy since then."

Tim shook his head. "He was half-asleep when I left. What could he possibly have done overnight?"

Even as he said the words, Tim got that sinking feeling in his belly, and he just knew. The full moon was tonight. "He asked for the bite, didn't he?"

"Yes."

"Fuck." Tim covered his face with his hands and let his head fall back against the wall. He thought it had been the drugs talking, that Seb would have forgotten about it all. But no. And why the fuck hadn't David told him? "How?"

He looked around uselessly for a clock. Visiting hours in this section of the hospital started at ten thirty, but alphas, and betas to some extent, could come and go as necessary.

*Has Cam been in to see him already?* "It's been less than twelve hours since I saw him. How the fuck has it all happened so fast?" There were applications to be filled out, permission to be granted, unless—"Is it an illegal bite? Surely there's been no time to—"

Alec shook his head, stopping Tim's outpouring. "Cam called in a couple of favours. And anyway, there's special dispensation for cases like this."

265

"That's if the injuries are *life-threatening*. Last time I checked, that wasn't the case." Tim spoke through gritted teeth, trying not to lose his temper. It'd only piss Alec off, and that would help no one. With his hands curled into fists, he forced himself not to snap or shout. "Why has Cam agreed to this so quickly? Seb is under the influence of painkillers. Who knows what state of mind he's in right now?"

Alec had an answer for everything. "They took him off the good stuff late last night. His mind is clear, and Cam spent the last three hours in there talking with him. He wants this, Tim."

Aware that his mouth was hanging open, but unable to do anything about it, Tim stood there, shocked. How had everything snowballed so quickly? He hadn't expected Seb to take him at his word when he suggested asking Cam to do it.

*Fucking hell.*

"So let me ask you again." Alec looked him in the eye, searching for an answer. "Considering the state of your relationship, why aren't you the one biting him?"

Tim groaned. Alec's words set off the flare of want and possessiveness he'd tried so hard to tamp down. "*Because I love him.* And I want to be bonded to someone who loves me back, not someone who likes me well enough, but really just wants to heal quickly. Call me old-fashioned, but…."

Alec snorted, and the sound pulled a reluctant half-smile from Tim. "What a fucking mess."

Tim couldn't agree more.

The walk back to Seb's room felt like a funeral march. Even if Tim wasn't biting him, he should still be thrilled that Seb might become a fully fledged shifter by this time tomorrow. But all he

266

could picture was someone else sinking their teeth into the base of Seb's throat, and it made him want to hit something.

Jared's voice drifted out of the room as they got nearer. "It's not too late to change your mind, you know."

"I know," Seb replied. "I want this."

"But you were so anti-shifter, and now you want to be one?"

A heavy sigh, as if they'd already discussed that several times. "Look at me, J. I'm useless like this."

"You'll heal. It's not irreparable."

"You heard what the doctor said. He's hopeful I'll get full mobility back in my ankle, but there's no guarantee, and I'd be worse off than ever then! I thought you out of everyone would understand."

Silence. Then, "Yeah, I do. Of course I do. Sorry." Jared sighed, the sound audible in the quiet. "What about Tim?"

Tim froze midstep, and Alec almost bumped into him.

"What about him?"

*Yes, what about me?* Tim held his breath, not moving a muscle.

"Why didn't you ask—?"

"*Jared.*" Nathan's voice cut through the air, low and urgent. Tim wanted to strangle him.
The door swung wide open and Nathan stood in the doorway, his expression cool. *Yeah, he knows we've been listening. Fucker.* "Tim."

"Nathan."

Nathan stepped to one side in invitation, and Tim couldn't do anything other than go in.

"Hey," he said, managing a small smile for Seb, who almost mustered one in reply.

"Hey." Seb's cheeks had more colour in them this morning and he was sitting up in bed, not lying down.

The greeting was all they could manage.

Thankfully, Alec stepped in before the silence got awkward. "I just got a text from Daryl."

Tim glanced at him and Alec smirked. Had he? Tim hadn't heard his phone go off, too busy listening in on another conversation.

Alec sobered. "He's awake."

Seb glanced between them all. "Who's awake?"

"One of the shifters who attacked you," Alec answered.

Seb immediately looked at Tim, his accusation as clear as day. "Why didn't you say anything last night?"

"You never asked about them." Tim didn't mean to sound so defensive, but Seb was making him feel guilty.

"I—" Seb turned his attention to Jared and Nathan, frowning.

"We just got here." Jared offered, hands out in front of him.

"I assumed they were dead," Seb muttered, then closed his eyes and rested his head back on the pillow.

It was only then that Tim noticed the dark shadows under Seb's eyes. If he'd been talking to Cam since early this morning, he must be shattered. Tim wanted to talk to him alone, tell him that he didn't need to do this. Asking for a shifter's bite wasn't something to be decided when you were in hospital, for fuck's sake.

Alec cleared his throat, garnering everyone's attention. "Two are dead, one was touch-and-go for a while, but he pulled through."

Seb met Tim's gaze. "Did you treat him?"

Tim couldn't tell what answer Seb was hoping for. Whatever it was, he couldn't stop the harsh laugh that burst out. "Are you kidding? If I got within ten feet of him, he'd never wake up again."

His teeth slid out as he thought of them attacking Seb, hurting him so badly they put him in hospital. His low growl filled the room, surprising no one by the looks of it, except maybe Seb, who stared at Tim wide-eyed, bottom lip pulled in between his teeth.

"Where are you keeping him?" Nathan spoke, either oblivious to the tension building between Seb and Tim, or trying to take everyone's focus away from it.

"Somewhere safe." Alec glanced up at the clock, then at Seb. "If we're going to do this, it needs to be now. The room's ready. It won't be the full pack—just Cam and the betas." He looked around at the rest of them. "And anyone else who wants to be there."

Tim curled his hands into fists to stop himself reaching for Seb and shaking him. Instead, he tried to catch Jared's eye. Surely, as Seb's best friend, he couldn't have been on board with it?

Jared met his gaze, held it, and sighed, and Tim knew that he was the only one in the room who thought this was wrong.

"I've been where Seb is, Tim." Jared glanced at the bandages on Seb's arm and the grazes along his face, and Nathan slipped his arm around him, pulling him close. "I know what it's like to be that scared, but powerless to do anything about it."

"But you didn't ask to be bitten."

Tim only realised what he'd said when Jared laughed softly.

"No, I didn't. But I was. It didn't take, but it did leave me stronger than before, and I heal a little quicker too. I'm not sorry it happened, and I wouldn't give either of those things up. I understand how Seb feels, and if it's what he wants, then I'm 100 per cent behind him."

*Fuck.* Tim ran his hands through his hair, lost.

Alec moved towards the door. "I'm heading down to join the others. David will bring Seb as soon as he's checked him over."

Before Alec reached the door, Jared elbowed Nathan in the ribs. Nathan grumbled, but called after Alec. "Wait a sec."

"Yes?" Alec turned to face them.

Nathan swallowed as though the words hurt to get out. "Thank you."

Alec's eyes widened, clearly not expecting that.

Nathan continued. "For saving Seb's life and protecting Jared when I couldn't."

Alec stared at Nathan. Tim willed him to take the olive branch Nathan had just extended. Finally Alec nodded, his lips curling up at the edges—not a smile, but so very close to one. "You're welcome."

He left the room, and to Tim it felt like everyone else breathed a collective sigh of relief.

Jared opened his mouth to speak, but Nathan shook his head. With the door ajar, Alec would hear them.

Jared settled for kissing him instead, then grabbed his hand as David came in. "We'll see you down there," he said to Seb, then walked out tugging Nathan after him.

David eyed Tim, looking a little sheepish—as well he might. David said quietly, "I didn't know until I came in this morning. And by then you were already on your way in." He took Seb's temperature and then his blood pressure. "I would have told you."

"Yeah, I know." Tim waited until he'd finished, then stepped closer to the bed.

Seb glared at him. "Whatever you're about to say, just don't. Okay?"

*I changed my mind. I want to be the one to bite you. Choose me, not Cam.*

The words sat there on the tip of his tongue. Tim couldn't ask, though, couldn't do it knowing that Seb didn't feel the same about him. He swallowed down the lump in his throat. "Good luck. I hope the change takes and you get what you want." He leaned down and placed a soft kiss on Seb's forehead.

Seb grabbed his hand as he went to move away. "Will you be there?"

Watching his alpha bite the man he was in love with was quite possibly the last thing Tim wanted to see at that moment. But the sudden vulnerable look in Seb's eyes tugged at his heart.

"Please?" Seb whispered.

A faint hint of fear and anxiety surrounded him. For all Seb's apparent bravado, underneath it all, he was scared. Against everything he felt inside, Tim took Seb's hand and gave it a gentle squeeze. "Yeah. I'll be there."

271

# Chapter Seventeen

As David wheeled him down the corridor, with Tim walking alongside them in silence, Seb fiddled with the edges of the blanket draped over his legs. His mind swirled with what seemed like a hundred different emotions; his damaged body hurt, yet felt strangely alive at the same time. That probably had everything to do with what awaited him at the end of the corridor.

He'd never imagined finding himself in this position, never dreamt of becoming a shifter, something both he and Jared used to despise with a fiery passion.

*How times change.* But Kelly had been missing for almost twenty-four hours, while Seb sat helpless and broken in a fucking hospital bed.

Despite his constant comments to the contrary, Seb had enjoyed being accepted as part of Tim's pack. The sense of belonging it afforded wasn't something he was used to, and it stirred something inside him that he couldn't name but wanted to feel more of. He could only imagine how much more intense it would be when he changed.

*If.*

*If* he changed. He needed to remember that there was no guarantee—look at Jared.

They came to a set of innocuous double doors. Seb frowned as he waited for David to swipe his card and open them.

Tim put a hand on his shoulder and leaned down to whisper. "Under normal circumstances, this would be done in Alec's building, in front of the whole pack. Just because the room itself looks nothing special, don't think for one second that those inside will treat it as anything other than the honour and privilege it is. For the pack, and for you."

Seb swallowed past the lump in his throat as Tim's words sank in. *An honour and a privilege?* Not just a way to make himself strong enough to protect those he loved.

For the first time since he'd made the decision, a frisson of doubt crept in. But then the door opened. Gareth and Alec held them wide as David wheeled Seb through.

The room was a little larger than it looked from the outside, obviously a meeting room, judging by the chairs and tables pushed back against the walls. Cam stood in the centre of the room, with his two other betas off to one side, and Jared and Nathan just inside the door. David wheeled Seb towards Cam, then turned him to face the rest of the room.

Alec and Gareth took their place on the other side of Cam; Tim hung back to stand beside Nathan. Seb wanted him closer than that, wanted to hold his hand and feel the reassurance that Tim's touch always brought, not have him so far away. It felt wrong.

Seb tried to catch his eye, but Tim had his head down, gaze focused on his hands. Seb caught Jared's attention instead. Jared's encouraging smile faded a little as he glanced from Seb to Tim and back again. Seb gave a tiny shake of his head, hoping to convey that he was fine.

Cam stepped forward and addressed the room. Although Seb had spent the early hours of the morning talking to him about what it meant to be a shifter, Cam hadn't looked anywhere as serious as

273

he did now. Tim was telling the truth; this was a huge deal for the pack. Inviting a new member to join them wasn't an everyday occurrence, and Seb started to wonder if he'd been as grateful and appreciative as the gesture called for.

The others in the room, Jared included, gave Cam their full attention as he recited what must be pack lore or something. Seb's gaze flicked over each of them in turn, finally coming to rest on Tim.

Tim had his hands fisted at his side, and from where Seb was sitting, they looked white. His face betrayed nothing, but when he glanced at Seb, their eyes met. For a split second, Seb saw nothing but hurt and longing.

Tim focused on Cam again.

*Fuck. I did that. I've hurt him… am* still *hurting him.*

Cam turned to him and Seb's mouth went dry. *This is it.* He'd thought there'd be more talking before they got to the actual biting part. His hands felt clammy as Cam took the few steps forward that brought him to stand in front of Seb.

"The full moon is tonight. Hopefully, with its arrival, we will welcome a new member into our pack." He slid a hand into Seb's hair, gently tilting his head to one side, and as he started to bend down Seb's gaze shot to Tim.

He was gone.

Only Jared and Nathan were there now.

Cam's hot breath washed over the base of Seb's throat… the barest press of teeth on his skin.

*Oh fuck!* Every part of Seb screamed out that this was wrong—wrong scent, wrong shifter—*but it's too late.*

Seb's whole body tensed, waiting for the press of teeth and the pain of Cam's bite, but Cam shifted a little, bringing his mouth to Seb's ear.

"It's not too late to change your mind."

Seb sucked in a breath. Had he changed his mind about the bite? *No, but—* "I still want it," he whispered, "but I—"

*Fucking hell, can I really tell the pack alpha that I'd rather not have him bite me? After practically begging him to do it?*

To his surprise, Cam hummed in what sounded to Seb like satisfaction before he spoke.

"Good. I hate to see one of my pack in such pain. Tim's bite will work just as well as mine, if not better."

Cam stood straight, and Seb stared up at him, open-mouthed. Had he said any of his thoughts out loud? How did Cam know? Cam smiled and ran his hand down the side of Seb's neck to rest on his shoulder. "What sort of alpha would I be if I couldn't recognise when two of my pack are in pain?"

With Seb still reeling at being called pack, Cam addressed the rest of the room. "Find Tim and take him to Seb's room. Tell him Seb's waiting for him."

Closest to the door, Nathan immediately slipped out to go and find Tim. Jared looked about as stunned as Seb had felt moments before, but Seb's shock was quickly being replaced by a growing sense of excitement and anticipation.

Cam beckoned Jared over. "Will you take Seb back down to his room?"

"Of course." Jared quickly moved to stand behind Seb's wheelchair.

Seb's gaze flickered over the betas in the room, as he wondered how to word his next question.

Cam followed his gaze, then smiled down at him. "Alec and Gareth will stand guard outside your door, but should you choose to go through with this, it will just be the two of you. A bonding bite is a private affair."

Seb vaguely remembered Tim mentioning something like that, but it was good to have Cam confirm it. The idea of Tim biting him in front of witnesses wasn't something he liked the sound of.

*Assuming I can persuade Tim to do it.*

As soon as Jared wheeled him out of the room and into the corridor again, Seb opened his mouth, not caring that the others could probably hear him. Hell, half the hospital could listen in if they wanted. "What if he refuses?"

"Why would he refuse?"

"Because he already did it once," Seb hissed, and maybe he did care about people hearing, after all.

Jared leaned down close to Seb's ear. "You didn't see his face when Cam was about to bite you…. He looked… *broken*."

Seb's heart constricted; his chest was too tight to breathe, and he rubbed at it with the heel of his hand. "He could still say no."

"Well, now's your chance to ask him."

They reached the door to Seb's hospital room, and Seb glanced up to see Nathan and Tim walking towards them. God, his palms were sweaty all over again; he'd never felt so nervous before. Unable to meet Tim's eyes, Seb focused on the blanket again as Jared wheeled him into his room and parked him next to the bed.

Jared asked, "Do you want to stay in the chair or get back in bed?"

"Um…." It had been okay being in the chair when Cam was going to bite him, but if Tim agreed to do it, then he wanted them to be close. Closer than you could get with him sitting upright in a wheelchair. "Bed, I think."

Jared pulled the sheets back, then looked from Seb to the bed and back again. "If we—"

"I've got it." Tim walked into the room; Nathan lingered just outside the door. Gareth and Alec had also arrived, flanking Nathan, but all Seb saw was Tim. His hair stuck up all over the place, as though he'd constantly had his hands in it from the moment he'd walked out.

Seb barely noticed Jared pat him gently on the shoulder, whisper "Good luck," and then leave, closing the door behind him.

"If you could give me a hand, maybe?" Seb put his good hand on the armrest to lever himself out of the chair, but before he could even try to push up, Tim scooped him up as if he weighed nothing.

"I said I'd got it." Tim's voice was rough, a little slurred. "Is your back okay?"

It hurt where his stitches were, but when Seb carefully looped his arms around Tim's neck and looked up, Seb's gaze caught on the fangs slowly extending downwards, and he forgot all about the pain.

A hot, desperate feeling unfurled inside him, starting at the base of his spine and echoing outwards in a warm rush. Seb imagined those fangs pressed into the base of his throat, breaking the skin, and his stomach clenched, a nervous excitement coursing through his veins. "Why did you leave?"

Tim sighed. "I couldn't stay and watch him bite you. Not without losing control and doing something incredibly stupid."

He turned and gently deposited Seb on the bed, but he made no move to step back, looming over Seb with a hand on either side of him.

When Tim closed his eyes, Seb reached up to palm his jaw. "Hey." He ran his thumb along Tim's bottom lip, brushing the tips of his teeth, making his breath hitch. "I'm sorry."

"What for?"

"For not realising sooner."

Tim's eyes snapped open, their beautiful blue almost eclipsed by black. "About what, exactly?"

*This is it.* Seb needed to get this exactly right or Tim would never believe him. He took a deep breath. "Yesterday, when I said it was no big deal to have you bite me, I didn't realise at the time exactly why that was." Tim huffed and went to pull away, but Seb held on, sliding his hand around the back of Tim's neck. "Listen to me. Please."

"Go on." Tim's body felt tense under Seb's fingers, as though he was poised for the worst.

"It feels like it's no big deal because it isn't, anymore. I want you to be the one to bite me—"

"Sebastian, I—"

"Shh—" Seb covered Tim's mouth with his hand. "—I want you to bite me. I want the change to take, and I want to be mated to you for the rest of my life. Not because there's no other option, but because it's the *only* option that I want. I love you. I'm sorry it took me almost getting bitten by Cam to figure that out."

He pulled his hand away and tried to urge Tim down for a kiss, but he wouldn't budge.

"Are you absolutely sure this is what you want?"

The thinly disguised hope in his voice hurt, and Seb hated that he'd done that.

"When Cam had his teeth against my throat—" Tim's low warning growl startled him for a second, but Seb carried on with a smile tugging at the edges of his mouth. "—it felt so wrong. I want it to be your bite that changes me, your teeth that mark me up, you claiming me as your mate." He tugged Tim forward again, and this time he came willingly. Seb placed a soft kiss on the side of his mouth, wary of the teeth still very much extended. "I—"

Tim stood abruptly, head snapping round to face the door.

"What?" Seb struggled to sit up a little. "Can you hear something? I thought these rooms were soundproof?"

"It's faint, but I can hear." He walked over to the door, pulled it open, and stuck his head out to talk to either Alec or Gareth, Seb presumed. Either way, the conversation was conducted in hushed whispers that Seb couldn't make out.

He lay there, half of him still buzzing with the excitement of wanting Tim to bite him, while the other half got increasingly annoyed with the sudden turn of events. "What the hell is so important that it can't wait?" he grumbled under his breath, more to himself than anything, but Tim immediately turned to look at him.

"They know where Kelly is."

"What?" Seb pushed himself all the way up, but Tim was there by his side before he could get out of bed. "How?"

"The rogue shifter was very helpful, apparently."

Seb really didn't give a shit how they'd got the information out of him. "Is she okay?"

"They're sending Alec's unit out to get her. The shifter said she was unharmed and unguarded, but…."

Tim didn't need to add anything else. Seb knew Kelly's condition could have changed by now, especially since the rogue shifter could be lying. "Okay." He glanced up at Tim, gaze zeroing in on his mouth again. Tim's teeth were almost back to normal, but a hint of sharpness remained, stirring Seb's pulse. "Where were we?"

Tim frowned and tilted his head as though confused. "What do you mean?"

Reaching for Tim's hand, Seb smiled up at him. "We're running out of time." He pointed at the clock on the wall.

"But they've found her. You don't need to do this anymore."

*Oh.*

Tim had tried to hide it, but disappointment coloured his words.

"Tim?"

Tim sighed and ran a hand over his face. "Fuck, I'm sorry. This is great news, and I'm so happy they found her." He met Seb's eyes, gaze flicking down to his neck and back up. "I just…." He shrugged, as if that said it all.

Careful of his back and his ribs, Seb eased himself down against the pillows and stared up at the ceiling. With his sister as good as found, did he still want to do this? Finding her had been a major factor in his initial decision, but now...? His injuries still existed. The rogue shifter was no longer a threat, but what about the rest of P-Pack or the other packs out there? Those were all reasons Seb had thought were good enough to ask for the bite.

But Tim was right. There was only one reason he should be doing this...

"Hey." Seb reached for Tim's hand. "Look at me." He waited until he had Tim's full attention. "I know I don't need to do this for Kelly anymore." Tim's sad smile hurt to see, so Seb hurried to say the next bit, squeezing Tim's fingers. "I need to do it for me. I love you, Tim. I want what Jared and Nathan have. I know there's no guarantee the change will take, but regardless of that, we'll be bonded, right?"

Tim stared at him, wide-eyed. "Yes. The bond will form at the full moon."

Seb smiled big and wide, trying to show him how much he wanted this. "Then bite me."

# Chapter Eighteen

It took a couple of seconds for the words to sink in. Tim stood there, captivated by Seb's blinding smile, almost convinced he hadn't heard correctly. But then Seb very deliberately tilted his head to the side, baring his neck invitingly and raising one eyebrow as if to say "what are you waiting for?"

And that one gesture blew away all of Tim's doubts. He was done second-guessing, done wondering if this was the right thing for Seb. Seb was more than capable of making his own decisions, and Tim needed to respect them. He wanted this more than anything, and he was going to fucking take it.

He stepped closer to the bed and cupped Seb's jaw, drawing him back to face him. "You know, a bite like this is normally done during sex."

Seb grinned up at him. "Is that so?"

"Yeah." Tim closed his eyes for a second, mouth watering at the thought of it. "It'll hurt."

"Ahh. So an orgasm is supposed to take my mind off it?" Seb tried to scoot over a little as he spoke, but he winced as everything hurt.

"Something like that. And what are you trying to do?"

"Make room for you."

Tim laughed softly. "As much as I'd like to do this properly, you're really in no fit state."

Seb winked and reached under the sheet to palm his dick. "There's nothing wrong with this." He rubbed his hand back and forth, eyes closing on a groan, and Tim felt his control slipping.

*Fuck it.* "I can be careful," he muttered, gently sliding his hands under Seb's back and easing him over to the other side of the bed.

"That's more like it."

Tim climbed up beside him and stretched out. His heart raced as he looked down at Seb—still slowly rubbing his cock—and finally let himself believe what he was about to do. "I'm going to ask you one… last… time." He nuzzled the base of Seb's throat, inhaling his scent and growling softly at the heady hint of sex mixed in with it. With his lips brushing Seb's skin, he whispered, "Are you sure?"

Seb pulled his hand out from under the sheets and grabbed the back of Tim's neck, pressing him closer. "Yes." His fingers curled into Tim's hair, gripping tight, and he arched into Tim as best he could. "Do it."

Tim groaned and pressed a kiss to Seb's throat before leaning away to look at him. Keeping eye contact, he slipped a hand under the sheet, searching for the waistband of Seb's pyjama bottoms to take up where Seb had left off seconds before. Seb closed his eyes; his soft gasp turned into a sigh as Tim wrapped his fingers around his length and started to stroke him.

A faint smile curved Seb's lips. "This would have been awkward to do with Cam in front of all the others."

Tim growled and nipped at his skin in what was meant to be a playful warning, but the second his teeth touched Seb's skin, instinct took over. Seb moaned and Tim tilted his head back, mouth open as he let his body take over.

His fangs, already aching with the need to extend, slipped out effortlessly; the pain of altering his jaw barely registered. He felt light-headed, his blood burning through his veins, lighting up his whole body.

Seb pushed into his fist, parting his lips as he watched Tim. His gaze darted between Tim's eyes and his teeth with no fear in his expression, only want and need. That was all it took for Tim to lower his head and set his teeth against the skin of Seb's neck.

Seb tensed, a whimper escaping, and Tim increased the pace of his hand, dragging Seb closer to coming. As Seb's cock pulsed against his palm, he bit down hard, breaking the skin.

Seb cried out, arching off the bed against Tim's hold, striping his belly and chest as he came.

The first trickle of blood hit Tim's tongue. He took a moment to savour the taste, knowing his bite had already started to work its magic on Seb's body. Carefully, he extracted his fangs, licking over the marks he'd left behind. Fuck, just seeing it there on Seb's neck sent a flood of arousal through him. He'd been hard since Seb told him he loved him, and all he wanted was to roll on top of Seb and rub off against him, but Seb had too many injuries for that to happen. Tim thrust against the bed instead, his gaze still firmly fixed on Seb's mark.

"Here, let me." Seb reached out, managing to get Tim's jeans undone with one hand.

Tim lifted his hips, helping to push everything down enough to free his cock. "You okay?" He watched, transfixed, as Seb scooped up some of the mess on his belly and used it to slick Tim's length. "*Fuck.*" He let his head fall onto the pillow.

Seb followed after him, kissing him hard and desperate as he brought Tim off. "I'm good," he whispered, then kissed him again. "So... fucking... good."

With their combined scents filling the air, its nature already changing following the bite, Tim was close as soon as Seb got a hand on him. A few more strokes were all it took. Tim's orgasm rushed through him, and he only realised he had his claws out when the sheets ripped underneath him. Soft laughter tickled his ear as he lay there, floating on the afterglow of what they'd just done. "What's funny?"

Gently easing Tim's fingers out of the bedding, Seb said, "I have to sleep in this bed, remember."

Tim looked around the impersonal hospital room, hackles rising. His teeth were back to normal, but his mouth still tingled with the sense memory of biting into Seb—Seb was Tim's now, marked for all shifters to see, and he'd be damned if Seb was going through the full moon in a strange bed, surrounded by non-pack. "We need to get you out of here."

He climbed off the bed and pulled his jeans and boxers up.

Seb stayed where he was, forehead scrunched in confusion. "What? Why? Surely I'm safe now. We're in a hosp—"

Tim shook his head. "It's not that."

"What is it, then?"

He waved his hand at the sterile surroundings. "There's no scent of pack, of safety, of *us*. I can't have you going through the full moon here." Just the thought of it made Tim's shoulders twitch, his wolf unsettled this close to the full moon. "I need to take you home."

285

Seb eyed him warily. "Would that be my home or your home?"

*Ours.* He swallowed down the word. Something told him they weren't ready to have that discussion quite yet, so he said, "I want to take you back to my flat. It's in Alec's building. It's safe."

For a moment he thought Seb might argue, but he just sighed and then muttered "Fine, whatever."

His eyes fluttered closed and Tim cursed himself for not getting everything organised before biting him. He rushed over to the door, nodded to Gareth and Daryl—Alec's replacement—and said, "It's done. I need to get him discharged."

"Leave it with me." Gareth headed over to the nurses' station while Tim leaned against the door frame.

It didn't surprise him when David came around the corner. What did surprise him was the look on David's face—"pissed off" were the first words that came to mind. David marched down the corridor towards Seb's room, anger rolling off him.

"What's your problem?" Tim asked as David came to a stop in front of him. "I thought you'd be pleased for me."

"My *problem*," David gritted out between clenched teeth, "is that you should've fucking sorted all this before you went ahead and bit him. You're a doctor, Tim. You know better than most how rough this is going to be. And that's without taking into account all his fucking injuries and the fact you bit him on the day of the full moon. For fuck's sake, Tim!"

Guilt hit him like a sledgehammer. "I should have prepared better. I know, okay."

"Do you?" David poked him hard in the chest. "This close to the full moon, it'll have started as soon as you bit him. He needs to stay here."

"No." Tim bared his teeth and let out a low warning growl. "He's coming home with me."

David didn't flinch. "What if something happens? What if his body can't cope with the strain and stress it's about to be put through?" He sighed, and Tim watched him struggle to rein in his temper. "He's still human. A lot of things could go wrong."

The euphoria of biting Seb still clouded Tim's mind, and the nearness of the full moon wasn't helping. He wanted to argue, to say it wouldn't come to that, but David was right. *Fuck it all.* Closing his eyes, Tim breathed in and out. Seb's scent clung to him and he let it calm him enough to think clearly. Yes, he wanted nothing more than to take Seb out of here and back to his flat; everything in him needed to be surrounded by pack. But Seb was already injured, his body battered and bruised as he recovered from the shifter attack, and the next few hours would be intense.

Instinct warred with common sense, but finally Tim opened his eyes, decision made. "Fine. We'll stay."

David let out a sigh of relief and clapped him on the shoulder. "I know this isn't what you wanted, how hard it's going to be for both of you, but it's the right choice. I'll do everything I can to make it as comfortable as possible."

Gareth walked back to them, clearly having heard everything. He glanced at Daryl, who up to this point had been studiously ignoring them. "We'd already arranged for a suite in the ward that

287

deals with the newly bitten. When Cam was going to…." Thankfully he didn't finish that sentence. "Anyway, the soundproofing's better, and only one other room is occupied." Tim nodded his thanks. "I've spoken to Cam, and Daryl and I are free to stay until the change is complete."

Tim glanced between the two of them. "What about the run?" The last thing he wanted to do was shift and run with his pack, but none of them could avoid breaking the law. All shifters were required to run for at least two hours, supposedly to use up excess energy and prevent accidents. They were probably already on thin ice with Seb's documents—usually they took days, sometimes weeks to procure, not hours. All their favours were used up.

David spoke up. "There's a small wooded area at the rear of the hospital. It's not huge, but it's what we use."

Tim vaguely remembered seeing the signs warning about its usage during full moons. The general public tended to avoid wooded areas on those nights, but there were always some who needed reminding.

"Thanks, that'll be fine." Gareth gestured behind Tim. "Let's get Seb moved to your suite and settled in."

"Okay, that's everything." David attached the last monitor pad to Seb's chest and stepped back. "He's all connected up. We'll keep an eye on him from outside, but if you need anything or you think something's wrong, press this call button. Got it?"

Tim nodded, anxious for him to leave. "I know how a hospital works, David."

"I know you do. I'm just doing my job."

"Sorry." With only four hours until it got dark, Tim was on edge; his skin felt too tight and his senses were far too acute with all the foreign scents around them. Technically the moon wouldn't reach its full phase until the early hours of tomorrow morning, but as soon as the sun set, Tim and all the other shifters would feel it more than they were already.

David was no exception, but he seemed to be handling Tim's attitude remarkably well. As though reading Tim's mind, he nodded over at the bed where Seb was asleep—he'd been asleep for the past hour. A sheen of sweat covered Seb's forehead and his skin shone pale under the harsh hospital lighting. "It's worse for you this time because you bit him. You do realise that?"

"What?" Tim couldn't tear his gaze away, intent on watching the slow rise and fall of Seb's chest.

"Wow, doctors really are the worst patients. The full moon is affecting you more this time because you bit Seb and your bond is already starting to form."

That got his attention. Tim snapped his gaze to meet David's. "What?"

David grinned. "Can't you feel it? Whatever the outcome of your bite, whether Seb becomes a wolf or not, you'll be bonded."

"I know that."

"I'm pretty sure, considering how close we are to nightfall, that it's already well underway." He pointed at the empty space beside Seb. The king-size bed gave them plenty of room this time. "Go and lie down with him, close your eyes, and concentrate. I think you'll be surprised." He walked over to the door, but paused before leaving. "I'll make sure you're not disturbed unless absolutely necessary. You have the place for two nights, more if you should need it."

*If he doesn't change.* "Thank you."

David waved him away. "What are big brothers for?" The door closed quietly behind him, taking all the outside noise with it. The soundproofing was excellent. All Tim could hear was inside the suite: Seb's soft snores, the occasional drip of a tap in the bathroom, and the low hum of the electronic equipment connected to Seb.

He walked over to the bed, kicking off his shoes. A damp cloth lay on the bedside table, and Tim used it to wipe the sweat from Seb's brow. He laid the back of his hand against Seb's cheek—hot to the touch; still, Seb had the covers pulled up tight to his chin.

The fever had kicked in almost as soon as Tim had returned to Seb's room. Seb had been in and out of consciousness as he and David gathered up his things and moved him to the suite.

Damn it, he'd never had a chance to warn Seb about what he was going to go through. Maybe Seb had spoken to Jared about it, Tim didn't know, but he should have found time to talk to him, made sure Seb knew exactly what he was in for.

Tim brushed Seb's hair away from his face and leaned down to kiss him. "I love you," he whispered, then kissed him again before straightening up. After removing his jeans and draping them over a chair, Tim lifted the covers and climbed into bed beside him. Keeping to his own side so as not to disturb him, Tim lay on his back, closed his eyes, and tried to do what David had suggested.

He'd read about the effects of a bond, had talked to Nathan and Jared and a few others who'd been fortunate enough to experience it, and each one of them had described an awareness of the other person, a connection they felt deep inside.

At first, as Tim lay there, nothing felt different. A flare of panic threatened, seeping in at the edges, but Tim resolutely pushed it away. This wasn't like Jared and Nathan's case; Tim's bond with Seb was a certainty, not a possibility.

Seb continued to snore softly next to him, and Tim slowed his breathing to match.

His limbs started to feel heavy, as though he was sinking into the mattress, and then he felt it… an awareness of something other than him. He couldn't quite explain it, but it was there in the back of his mind, and it was *Sebastian*.

Tim's breath caught, his fingers curled into the bottom sheet in an attempt to hold on to whatever was happening to him, to *them*. For a good few seconds the bond flared between them, bright and wonderful, and then it faded to a faint background hum.

Tim opened his eyes and grinned up at the ceiling. He didn't even care that it hadn't lasted long, because the bond was still there, he felt it even now, and that one brief flash was the promise of what it would be. He rolled onto his side, startled to find Seb awake and watching him, albeit with half-lidded eyes. "Hey," he whispered. He reached out to cup Seb's cheek. "How do you feel?"

Seb moaned and closed his eyes for a second. "Hurts."

"I know." Fuck, Tim hated that there was nothing he could do to make Seb's experience better.

Seb managed a dry chuckle. "I doubt that. You heal too quick to know how bad I feel."

*Well, maybe he has me there.* "Fair point."

"How much longer?" Seb put his hand over Tim's and twined their fingers. "Thought my ribs ached before… but Jesus." He yawned, taking a deep breath, and immediately winced. "Motherf—"

Tim kissed him, trying to take his mind off the pain. "Not much longer. A few hours."

"Fuckin' ages."

Seb's eyes were closed now, and Tim suspected he was about to drift off again. He quickly kissed him again. "Love you."

"Mmm… you too," Seb mumbled. Then his breathing evened out and he was asleep.

Tim watched him awhile, huge smile in place and their bond happily humming away at the back of his mind. He should probably try to sleep a little, the night was likely to be a long one, but he'd never felt less like closing his eyes.

As the minutes ticked by, their connection got stronger, binding them together. Tim had thought this would never happen for him, had almost come to accept it, but now that it was, he didn't want to miss a second of it. He lay there, occasionally wiping Seb's face with the cloth or soothing him when he whimpered in his sleep, waiting for Seb's body to accept or reject the change.

Despite his best intentions and the pull of the moon, the gentle throb of the bond lulled him, and at some point he must have dozed off because he woke to hands carding through his hair and a soft kiss on his forehead.

"Time's it?" Tim yawned and his jaw cracked.

Soft laughter greeted him. "Eleven fifteen."

*Wow, later than I thought. The full moon must already be—*

He sat bolt upright as his brain finally registered what his senses were telling it. Another breath in confirmed it... *wolf.*

A slow grin spread across his face as he looked down at Seb, now fully alert and smiling back up at him. "You changed," he whispered, awe colouring his tone.

"Yes." Seb laughed again and opened his mouth to show teeth sharper than his human ones. "And I'm feeling kind of... I don't know... jittery? Does that sound right?"

Tim stared at him, unable to fully comprehend that Seb was now a shifter. *Fucking hell.* "Um... yeah... jittery. You'll have a lot of excess energy, especially this first time." He glanced at Seb's previously injured wrist, now free from bandages. The scrapes on his face had healed too. "Just how long have you been awake?"

With a shrug, Seb sat up and leaned against the headboard. "Maybe an hour or so. Why?"

"You should have woken me sooner."

"You looked so peaceful. I could tell you were tired." Seb tapped his head and then his chest, and Tim wanted to tackle him to the bed. "It's pretty great, this bond thing."

Tim nodded, mouth suddenly dry. "It is." The dull hum that he'd fallen asleep with had blossomed into a warmth he felt everywhere, a constant pull inside that let him know he wasn't alone anymore. "How am I feeling now? Can you tell?"

Seb's smile turned sly and he leaned closer. "Oh yeah, I can tell." He licked over the sharp points of his teeth.

Tim shivered, his cock hardening and pressing against the material of his boxer briefs as he imagined Seb's mouth all over him. "And?"

"You're hard, aren't you?" Tim nodded. "Even if I couldn't smell it—which I can, and it's fucking amazing—" His gaze dipped to Tim's lap. Seb let out a soft, whimpery moan that made Tim's toes curl. "Your eyes are all dark, and you keep looking at my mouth, at my teeth, with this hungry expression, and it's taking me all my willpower not to press you into the mattress and bite you."

"Oh fuck." Tim swallowed past the sudden lump in his throat. That sounded... it sounded amazing, but the doctor in him wouldn't let him give in just yet. "We should probably let the others know that you've changed."

"Already sent a text." He gestured to his phone on the bedside table, its cracked screen a reminder of what had happened only yesterday. "Told them I changed, that I was fine, and not to disturb us for a few hours."

Tim's gaze was drawn to the phone again. "And Kelly? Have they found her?"

"Yeah." Tim's face softened. "They took her to Jared and Nathan's. She was a bit shaken up and scared, but otherwise okay."

Tim didn't want either of them to move from this spot, but it would be incredibly selfish of him not to ask. "Don't you want to go and see her?"

"Yeah. But Jared said she was asleep. Exhausted." He reached for the hem of Tim's T-shirt and tugged it. "I thought maybe we could kill a few hours here first."

"Oh?" Tim raised an eyebrow and smiled. "What exactly did you have in mind?"

"This—"

Seb moved quicker than Tim was expecting, grabbing him by the hips and pulling him down until he lay flat on his back. Seb loomed over him, straddling his lap, teeth bared and blue-green eyes shining with excitement. He lifted his right hand, flexing his fingers and slowly letting his claws extend. "Hurts like a bitch, but it's so fucking cool." His smile was contagious. Tim laughed as Seb twisted his hand back and forth, inspecting his claws. Then he glanced down at Tim's chest and back up again. "Are you overly fond of that T-shirt?" His voice came out growly-rough and sexy, and he rested his hand at the base of Tim's throat, claws lightly touching skin.

"Uh—" Tim faltered as Seb trailed a clawed finger down towards the neckline. "No. Hate it."

Seb's smile widened. "Good."

Before Tim had chance to look down, Seb ripped the front of his T-shirt, scraping a red angry line on the skin beneath.

Tim sucked in a breath at the initial sting, and then they both watched as the red faded to pink and then disappeared completely.

"Wow." Seb looked up, awe written all over his face. "That's never going to get old, is it?"

"No." Tim reached up, touching his thumb to the sharp points of Seb's teeth. "Neither is this." He took Seb's hand, fingers tracing over his claws. "Or this."

Finally, he pulled Seb down until their faces were only centimetres apart. "Or this," he said, and kissed him.

Seb growled. The sound went straight to Tim's groin and he arched up, chasing the friction of Seb's body. The full moon set his senses on high alert, his blood raced through his veins, and his wolf was closer to the surface than at any other time.

For Seb, all those feelings would be magnified.

He grabbed Tim's hands and pinned them on the pillow at either side of his head and closed his eyes, resting their foreheads together. "I feel… *fuck*, I don't know. *Alive*, bursting with energy." He pulled back enough to meet Tim's gaze. "Really horny."

Tim barked out a laugh. He tried to move his hands, but Seb growled again and pinned them harder, looking down at him with undisguised want and need, and Tim didn't think he'd ever been harder in his life.

Seb licked over his teeth again, tongue catching on the points. "I want to do so many things to you. Taste you, fuck you, bite you…. Can I?"

"Yes." He kept eye contact and slowly tilted his head to the side. "Whatever you want."

# Chapter Nineteen

Seb's gaze caught on the creamy expanse of Tim's neck, then travelled up to where dark stubble covered his throat. His cock strained against his pyjama bottoms, and his teeth ached to bite, claim, *mark* Tim the same way Tim had marked him. His hand shot to his neck as he realised the bite didn't hurt anymore. To his utter disappointment, his fingers found only smooth skin, no teeth marks. *No mark at all.*

Sensing his distress, Tim cupped his jaw and forced him to meet his eyes again. "Hey. It's still there."

Seb shook his head. "It's not. I can't feel anythi—"

"The wound healed as you changed, but it's still there, under the skin. You can't feel it, but I can see it."

Not that Seb didn't believe him, but he needed to see for himself. Needed the confirmation so badly he was up off the bed before he even registered it. The bathroom door hit the wall with a dull thud as he marched inside and straight up to the mirror, angling his neck to get the best view.

*Thank fuck.*

He let out a huge sigh of relief, fingering the silvery bite mark that seemed to glow faintly under his skin. He traced the outline over and over, marvelling at the shifter magic at work. Then he smiled and spent another minute checking out his teeth. And the rest of him. Nothing much on his body had changed, just a little more muscle definition, but all his injuries had healed: no bruising on his ribs, his wrist was fine, and his ankle and his back too.

It had been such a relief to get that damn cast off. Remarkably easy, too. His newfound strength was taking some getting used to.

"Seb? Everything okay?"

The soft pad of footsteps sounded behind him; he turned in time to see Tim standing in the bathroom doorway.

"You've been a while. I was worried."

Tim looked sleep-rumbled and sexy with his bed hair and his cock still tenting his boxer briefs—good enough to eat. Seb turned and stalked towards him, mirror forgotten. "Everything's fine."

Tim gave him an appreciative once-over. "I see that." He glanced down at the bulge in Seb's pyjamas and licked his lips.

That was all the motivation Seb needed. He backed Tim up against the door frame, using his extra three inches of height to his advantage. Tim slid his hands around Seb's neck, claws tickling the skin there, and maybe for the first time, Seb realised that he was as strong as Tim now. They were equals. The same shifter DNA filled his body, strengthening his muscles and altering everything about him.

He reached down and hooked his hands under Tim's thighs. "Hold on." Tim clutched at him as Seb lifted him up.

Tim wrapped his legs around Seb's waist, laughing. "I could get used to this."

"Good." Seb rolled his hips, pushing his cock against Tim's arse, and he moaned at the thought of getting in there. "It's going to happen a lot."

He leaned in for a kiss, hard and desperate, forgetting about his teeth until he pulled back and saw the blood on Tim's lip. "Shit." Licking at his own, he tasted the telltale tang of copper, and… liked it. He liked the way it looked, too—smeared across Tim's mouth just begging to be kissed. "I want to say I'm sorry for this—" Using his thumb, Seb wiped at the red covering Tim's bottom lip. "—but I kinda like it." He glanced up, meeting Tim's gaze. "Is that wrong?"

In answer, Tim grabbed his hand and sucked Seb's thumb into his mouth, humming in satisfaction. He practically glowed with it. Seb felt it through their bond, strong and possessive, curling around his insides and setting him alight.

*Not wrong. I like it. I want it. Want you.*

Tim let his thumb go with an obscene noise and licked his lips. "Fuck me," he whispered, the words just for the two of them.

They filled Seb's head until all he could think of was getting Tim naked and pushing inside him. He kept Tim wrapped around him and walked them back towards the bed, depositing Tim on it as though he weighed nothing.

"Get them off." He gestured at Tim's underwear, then pulled his T-shirt off and shed his pyjamas to stand naked next to the bed. It felt so good to be able to walk properly; he was half-tempted to jump on the spot, or run, or—

"Sebastian."

His attention snapped back to Tim, now lying naked and stretched out on his back.

"I know you want to shift and run, and we will, later. But right now I need you."

*Shift? Fucking hell, I'm a wolf! A real fucking wolf.*

Closing his eyes, Seb let himself feel it, the primal urge lying in wait beneath the surface, waiting for his say-so to be let loose. The sense of power and freedom it promised was both exciting and terrifying.

"Seb. Come on… *please.*"

Seb looked at him. "You hardly ever call me Seb now."

"Desperate times…."

Tim whined, low and needy, and only then did Seb notice the hand he had around his cock. "No, let me."

He climbed onto the bed and over Tim in one swift move, knocking Tim's hand out of the way.

"Be my guest."

Slowly and deliberately, Seb dropped onto his forearms between Tim's spread thighs, wrapped his fingers around his cock and mouthed at the head until Tim was gripping the sheets, claws out.

"*Seb…*"

Seb pulled off, smiling at the desperate groan the move evoked. He gave Tim a couple of long, lazy strokes, loving the way Tim bit at his lip, the tip of his fangs drawing tiny spots of blood. He wanted to taste it.

The sex they'd had before now had been hot—Seb had no complaints—but this… seeing Tim let go, holding nothing back, was on a whole new level. "I can't wait," he whispered, gaze sliding from Tim's cock to his hole.

Tim spread his legs wider and Seb reached out to rub a thumb over it, pushing in just a little. He dipped low to run his tongue from the underside of Tim's balls to his hole, licking round where his thumb held him slightly open.

"Oh fuck!" Tim arched up. "Thought... you couldn't... wait?"

Seb pushed in with his thumb, going a little deeper this time, before sitting back on his heels and looking round for his bag.

Tim groaned and covered his face with his hands. "*Now what?*"

"We need lube."

"I never thought to—"

Seb hopped off the bed to where his bag lay next to the bedside cabinet. It took him ten seconds to find the bottle of lube Jared had stashed in there when he'd brought his bag in that morning, and he raised it triumphantly for Tim to see. "We're good to go."

Climbing back up next to Tim, Seb paused at the look of confusion on his face. "What?"

"Where did you get that from?"

"Jared."

Tim didn't ask anything else and Seb didn't offer. Instead he opened the bottle, squirted some onto his fingers, and set about teasing Tim all over again—rubbing over his hole until Tim was pushing into his hand for more. When he finally slid two fingers inside, Tim's breath caught but he shook his head.

"Don't need it. Want to feel you." He reached for Seb's shoulder, claw tips sinking in a little as he grabbed on and pulled him up. Seb hissed at the sting. "Sorry." Tim grinned as he said it.

"Yeah, you look it."

Seb settled between his thighs, shuffling close enough to rub the head of his dick against Tim's hole.

301

"'S healed already." Tim's voice came out low and rough, his fangs distorting the words.

When Seb licked over his own teeth, he wasn't surprised to find them just as sharp. A quick glance at his shoulder told him Tim was right. The skin was as smooth as before, the residual smears of blood the only evidence it had happened. A small smile tugged at his mouth. "So, I can do this too, right?" Without more ado, he bent to Tim's shoulder, kissed him once, then sank his teeth in just enough for it to hurt a little. He pushed his hips forward at the same time and the head of his cock slipped inside.

Tim's growled "Fuck yes!" had Seb's wolf preening in satisfaction.

Licking at the mark he'd left on Tim's neck, knowing it was fading already, Seb thrust in all the way and whispered in Tim's ear. "I want to leave a permanent mark on you. So everyone knows you're mine."

"*Yes.*"

"Tell me how?"

He pulled out and thrust in again, making Tim clutch at his shoulders, the tips of his claws teasing but not breaking the skin this time. Seb wanted it, wanted to feel that hurt again. He upped his pace, putting a little more effort behind it, gratified when Tim gasped and wrapped his legs tight around him.

"Hmm?" Tim hummed.

"How do I do it?"

"You need to—*oh fuck…*" Tim faltered, head thrown back as Seb found the right angle and fucked him as hard as he could. "To… bite… hard. Like you mean it."

Seb's teeth ached at the thought of it. His hands under Tim's shoulders, Seb held on tight, mouth resting just above his collarbone as he worked at pushing them both over the edge. Every stuttered breath Tim let out drove them that little bit closer, the sting of claws in his shoulder enough to make his toes curl as the pleasure-pain went straight to his cock.

"Now." Tim's legs tightened around him, his whole body starting to tense up. "Bite me now."

Seb opened his mouth and sank his teeth in, clinging to Tim as he felt the skin give and tasted blood on his tongue. His orgasm hit hard, rushing through him in a wave. Barely aware of Tim crying out underneath him and coming in the tight space between their bodies, Seb held on until they both slumped into the mattress.

Taking great care, Seb retracted his teeth and leaned up enough to inspect the damage. A sharp stab of disappointment drove away his post-orgasmic glow as he watched the mark fade away to nothing. He let his head fall onto Tim's shoulder as he let out a heavy sigh.

Tim immediately carded a hand through Seb's hair and kissed the side of his head. "Hey? What just happened? You went from blissed out to upset in a heartbeat."

"You felt that?"

"Like a sledgehammer." Tim kissed him again. "What's wrong?"

"The bite mark I left on you... it fucking faded already." Tim's soft huff of laughter was unexpected, and Seb was seconds away from pushing him away. "Hey, calm down." Tim shushed him. "I felt it take. It's not gone, I promise." He gave Seb's hair a little tug. "Look again."

Pushing up onto his elbows, Seb met Tim's gaze and gave him a sceptical look. He glanced down at his neck, expecting to see nothing but pale skin, but as he watched, a perfect impression of his teeth began to appear, glowing faintly under the surface just like the one Tim had given him. "Oh…." Reaching out with unsteady fingers, Seb traced over it, smile blooming big and wide.

Tim pulled him in for a kiss. "See, I told you it'd be there. Happy now?"

"Yes." Their bond sang with the contentment spilling out of both of them and Seb wanted to roll around in it. He couldn't help touching Tim's mark again, and then he leaned down to kiss it. "So fucking happy."

"Good." Tim manhandled him until they were lying on their sides, hot sticky messes, and Seb had never felt better. "The others will want to see you soon," Tim told him. "I wouldn't be surprised if they're all waiting around here somewhere."

Seb yawned. Seemed like his earlier boundless energy had vanished. "Later."

Tim cupped his jaw and kissed him—soft yet deep. "We can sleep for a little while, but I need to run." He smiled, eyes crinkling in happiness. "And this time I get to have you alongside me."

"Yeah?" Seb hadn't given the actual wolf part of shifting much thought, which, in hindsight, was probably stupid. Too late now, though, and he wouldn't change a thing, even if he could.

Tim nodded. "Yeah. If you want?"

"I do." Seb reached for him and pulled him onto his chest, wrapping an arm around his shoulders. "I love you."

"I love you, too."

Seb closed his eyes, the warm weight of Tim's body lulling him into sleep, and the bond wrapped around them like a blanket.

This might not have been how he'd previously seen his life going, but lying there, his body thrumming with all the potential of his new shifter genes, his mate in his arms, it was pretty much perfect.

As he drifted off to sleep, a stray thought entered his head. *Nathan's going to be unbearable.*

*Fuck.*


Several hours later, Seb woke to the sound of a text alert, his phone vibrating on silent on the bedside table. Without opening his eyes, he attempted to take in the room around him.

The first and most important thing he noticed was the bond, his ever-present connection to Tim, sitting quietly in the back of his mind, soft and comforting as Tim lay sound asleep next to him. Their combined scents filled the air, and Seb took a long deep breath, his wolf… *content*—that was the only word he could think of to describe how it felt. Or maybe *smug*. Apart from the ambient sounds of the room, the one thing he could hear was Tim, breathing steadily next to him.

Seb opened his eyes and turned to find Tim looking back at him. He was sleep-rumpled, with bed hair and pillow creases on his cheek, but definitely awake.

"I thought you were still asleep?" Seb smiled, and Tim returned it.

"I am." He yawned, his jaw cracking loudly. "Well, I feel it. Are you going to see who that was from?" He nodded at Seb's phone on the bedside table.

"Oh, yeah." Seb turned and reached for it. "Jared," he muttered as he unlocked it. "He and Nathan are down the hall. They've come to see if we want to run with them. Jared doesn't run, does he?" He glanced at Tim expectantly.

"No, but he can be there. As Nathan's mate, he has permission to be a part of it if he wants."

"Oh." Seb had to admit, even though Jared wasn't a wolf, that it would be good to have his best friend there. "I'm going to tell them yes. Is that okay? I mean we have to do it anyway, right?"

"Yeah, we do." Tim reached out to stroke his thumb along Seb's jaw, smiling bright and happy. "And of course it's okay."

Seb quickly typed out a reply, then laughed at what he got back. "Jared says they're coming to our room, and we'd better have at least boxers on."

Tim shrugged a shoulder. "No point when we'll only have to take them off again."

Seb hadn't thought about that side of it. He was no prude, and Jared had seen him naked far too many times to count, but did he fancy getting naked in front of Nathan?

Clearly sensing his doubts, Tim drew him in close for a quick kiss. "We can shift before they get here if you want? I know everything must be overwhelming for you right now."

Seb's phone vibrated again. "Too late, they're outside the door." He moved to get up, but Tim grabbed his arm.

"It's not too late for anything. Put your pyjama bottoms on, and if you're uncomfortable shifting in front of them, then we'll ask them to leave first. No one will mind."

"Okay." He kissed Tim once more before hopping out of bed and pulling on his bottoms.

When he opened the door, Jared grinned and then immediately hugged him tight.

"Oh my God, you're all fixed!"

When Jared let go, Nathan frowned and let out a grumble of dissatisfaction as he tugged him back.

"For fuck's sake, J. Now you smell like those two and sex!" He pulled Jared into his side and raised an eyebrow at Seb. "Showers not working?"

Seb flushed, realising how he must smell to Nathan. Before he could come up with a reply, he felt more than heard Tim move, and a second later Tim was plastered to Seb's back.

"Nathan, Jared." Tim offered in greeting. His voice had an edge to it, and Seb turned his head to get a look at Tim's face. He appeared friendly enough when he said, "You know very well I'd never have let him shower."

Nathan grinned. "*I* know. But he doesn't."

Tim's low growl vibrated through his chest to Seb's back, and Seb had really had enough. "Standing right here, guys." He glared between the pair of them, then faced Jared. "Does this happen a lot?"

Jared laughed but shook his head. "No. They just get a little territorial around the full moon. You'll get used to it."

"Used to it?" Nathan slapped Seb on the shoulder, earning himself another growl from Tim. "He'll be doing it himself. He's now a fully fledged member of the—what is it you two like to call us?—'arrogant, arsehole shifter brigade.'"

"Something like that," Jared answered, smile widening.

*The traitor.*

Nathan pointed his finger at Seb but didn't touch him. "Now that prestigious group includes Seb too."

Seb groaned, unable to take much more of Nathan's smug face. "Whatever. Come inside so the whole hospital isn't listening in." Stepping back, with Tim still plastered against him, Seb ushered them in and closed the door.

Jared put a hand on his arm, and Seb noted that Tim didn't so much as flinch. *Hmm… guess it's just shifters that are pissing him off today.*

"He's your family," Tim whispered in his ear, before moving away from them both. Obviously, Tim understood more about the bond than he did.

"You okay about everything?" Jared gestured to Seb and then to Tim's retreating back.

Seb nodded, still half wondering how Tim read his mind like that. "Yeah. Surprisingly." He wanted to whisper, but the other two would still hear him. *I guess I'll have to get used to having little to no privacy now, too.* "Hey, can you and Nathan tell what each other's thinking?"

He ignored Nathan's snort of laughter and Tim's subsequent grumble.

Jared grinned. "Not exactly. But now I know what to look for, it's easier to pick up on what he's thinking."

308

Tim came up behind him again and slipped an arm around Seb's waist. "You ready? Or do you want to…?"

Seb linked his fingers with Tim's and sighed. This was his life now. He needed to embrace all aspects of it, and if that meant getting his kit off in front of the pack, then so be it. He had nothing to be ashamed of. But… "If we shift in here, we still need to get outside, though, right?" He made a vague gesture at the door. "And is it hygienic? This is a hospital."

Tim smiled against the back of his neck. "They're used to wolves roaming around on the full moon, and this corridor has an outside door for that specific purpose. It opens out into a covered walkway leading to the trees. And Jared can open the doors, remember?"

"Oh yeah."

Seb turned in time to see Nathan shedding his clothes, not bothered in the least by his audience. Okay, then. He hooked his fingers into the top of his pyjama bottoms and was just about to shuck them off when Nathan shifted. For some reason, Seb had never asked how shifters went from human into wolf. He really fucking should have, because it looked all kinds of painful—and not a little terrifying. It happened fast, but Seb still had the sound of bones cracking ringing in his ears.

Oh, but Nathan's wolf was beautiful, though. He was bigger than Seb expected, almost waist height on him, with thick jet-black fur and blue eyes. Seb didn't realise he was staring until he felt Tim's hand on his shoulder.

"You okay?"

"Yeah… I just." He waved a hand at where Nathan had cosied up to Jared's side, watching them. "It looked like it hurt a whole fucking lot, and I just realised I have no idea how to even do it."

His heart began to race, edges of panic settling in. What the hell had he been thinking?"

"Hey, hey." Tim put both hands on Seb's face and forced him to meet his eyes. "Calm down. You can do this." He pulled Seb's head down to rest their foreheads together, his soft sigh brushing Seb's lips like a caress. "Take off your clothes." Seb obeyed, pushing them down and kicking them off to the side. "Now, close your eyes and just *feel*. Your wolf is always there, just under the surface, but tonight more so than ever. He wants to come out, Seb. Relax, open your mind, and let him."

Seb huffed. "You make it sound so easy."

"Trust me, it is." Tim kissed him, lingering for a second before pulling away, giving him space. "Now try."

With his eyes tightly closed to block out his surroundings, Seb willed himself to relax and clear his mind. He felt it almost straightaway, waiting for his command…

*Come out. Run.*

Seb's breath caught as he felt his wolf answer.

For a second his mind froze; the searing pain that ripped through him rendered complex thought impossible, except *oh fuck it hurts*. There wasn't one part of him that wasn't being stretched, snapped, or moulded into some new shape.

Then just like that, it was over. Seb stood with his head hanging down, panting as his faculties slowly returned.

And when they did, it was amazing. Seb breathed in deep; the room was alive with smells, so many more than when he'd been human. Sounds filtered in through the closed door, faint but definitely there.

Seb opened his eyes, startling at a silver-grey wolf that stared back at him. *Tim.*

Seb walked forward and nuzzled Tim's neck; a soft whimper escaped his long muzzle at the familiar smell. *Mate. Mine.*

Tim nuzzled him back, then nudged him towards the door. *Oh, right. Running.*

*But first I want to see what I look like!*

He glanced at the bathroom door, but the mirror in there was too high. Seeing his phone on the bedside table, he padded over and carefully picked it up between his teeth, then carried it over to Jared.

Thankfully, Jared knew exactly what he wanted. He laughed as he took the phone. "Yeah, okay, I'll take a picture."

Jared aimed the camera at Seb and took a couple of snaps, then one of Tim too. Seb was horrified to feel his tail wag in his excitement to see the photo—he hadn't known wolves even did that.

Jared knelt beside Seb. "Not sure how well you can see it, but this is you. You're a beautiful sandy brown colour—fucking typical that you'd look good as a wolf too. Seeing the three of you like this is making me a little jealous." He ruffled Seb's fur and held the phone for him to see.

Seb stared at the image: the surrounding colours seemed a bit off, but the wolf was easy to see. *Wow.* It was so surreal to think that animal was him.

Tim nudged him. Seb turned to look at him, and excitement and anticipation filled their connection.

*Time to run.* The thought was as clear to him as if Tim had spoken it aloud.

*Okay, let's do this.*

He followed Tim towards the door and stood with him as they waited for Jared to open it.

With his mate and his friends beside him, Seb walked out into the corridor, feeling more confident, alive, and content than he could ever remember.

This was the start of his new life.

# Epilogue

*One week later*

"I still can't believe you won't shift for me." Kelly sat staring at the picture of wolf-Seb on her phone.

Seb rolled his eyes. "Three weeks. That's all you have to wait, then you can see."

"Tim says you can do it anytime though. You don't have to wait for the next full moon."

"I know, but…."

"But what?" She set the phone down and looked at him.

Seb shrugged, unsure how to put it into words. "I'd just… rather not. Until I get used to it."

"Okay. Fair enough, I suppose. I'll stop bugging you." She curled into the arm of the sofa and yawned even though it was only half past one in the afternoon.

Seb leaned forward, his hands resting on his knees. "You still having trouble sleeping?"

He'd visited his sister as soon as the hospital had discharged him on the morning after their run. Physically she was fine, but mentally… Seb wasn't too sure.

"No, Seb." She fixed him with a glare that reminded him of their mother. Not that he would ever dare tell her that. "As I keep telling you, I'm fine. I was just up late watching some stupid series on Netflix. Stop worrying about me."

313

"I can't help it, Kel. You were kidnapped by shifters, for fuck's sake. It's bound to have an effect on you."

She sighed and reached over to take his hand. "It did have an effect—I was terrified. But then I was rescued. And now I'm safe." Squeezing his fingers, she sighed again. "It's over now. I just want to forget about it. Please can you try and do the same."

Seb doubted he'd manage that for a very long time. His need to protect his sister was stronger than ever now—but that was another thing he'd never mention. Kelly was fiercely independent and would be none too pleased if she knew he wanted to shelter her from everyone and everything. He couldn't help it, though.

Swallowing it all back, he smiled. "Yeah, okay. I'll try."

"Thank you."

They were in Tim's flat, waiting for him to come back from work. Well, Seb was. Kelly had popped in for a chat and a coffee. He'd wanted her to stay with either him or Jared, but she'd flatly refused.

As soon as they heard the front door open, Kelly stood and smoothed down her skirt. "Okay, that's my cue to go."

Tim wandered into the living room. "You don't have to leave on my account."

She smiled, and Seb wanted to grab her and beg her to stay. "That's okay. I know you two have that meeting this afternoon. Besides, I think I've pestered Seb enough for one day." She walked into the hall, and Seb followed, watching as she slipped her shoes and coat on. "God, stop it. I'll be fine."

"I know. Sorry." When she came in for a hug, he held her tightly. "Text me when you get home"

"Will do." Kelly opened the door and looked back at him. "Good luck at your meeting thing."

"Thanks." He watched her walk along the corridor to the stairwell, then closed the door.

Tim's soft footfalls on the wooden floor were the only indication he was approaching. Seb smiled as Tim reached him and wrapped his arms around him.

"You about ready?"

"I still don't know why I need to be there." Despite being a shifter now, Seb didn't feel like a real part of the pack. Maybe it would take time to adjust.

Tim tightened his arms around him and buried his nose in the crook of Seb's neck. "It was you they attacked, Seb. Don't you want to see Newell's face when Cam accuses him?"

*Honestly? No.* Sitting in a room with two alphas and all their betas wasn't somewhere Seb wanted to be, especially if things started to get heated. "Explain it to me again, because I'm still a little confused about what Cam's going to accuse him of, exactly."

Shifter politics were so weird and complicated. Seb might have zoned out the first time Tim tried to tell him what had happened.

"Really?

"Yes, really."

Tim's exasperated breath washed over the back of Seb's neck, making him shiver. "Listen this time, then, okay?"

"I'm all ears."

"You remember the rogue shifter Alec captured?"

Seb snorted—as if he was going to forget *him* in a hurry. "Yes, I vaguely recall him," he snarked.

Tim gave him a squeeze in retaliation. "Well, according to him, at least some of the Primrose Hill pack were aware of what they were doing, and not only actively encouraged it, but aided and abetted the rogues. He says Newell was certainly aware, and he had contact with Wes and a couple of others, though he doesn't know their names."

"And everyone believes him?"

Tim grimaced, and Seb wasn't sure he wanted to know any more. "I don't think he was in a position to lie. And besides, Cam offered to put in a good word for him with the alpha council, so maybe they'll find him a pack outside the city instead of sentencing him to imprisonment or death." He tilted Seb's chin so their eyes met. "How do you feel about that?"

"About what? That Cam's trying to helping him stay alive?"

"Yes. He was part of the group that tried to kill you and kidnapped your sister. You have every right to want him dead."

Seb closed his eyes and let the memories of that night fill his mind. Yes, he'd been scared stiff for his sister, and being attacked by a shifter was no fun. Maybe, in the heat of the moment, he'd have thought differently, but this was after the fact, and both he and Kelly were fine. *Better than fine.* "I don't want anyone to die on my account."

Tim's lips caressed the side of his neck, and Seb instinctively knew which spot he was kissing.

"Okay."

Tim licked at the bite mark and Seb groaned, leaning back and letting him take most of his weight.

Seb's cock hardened in his jeans as Tim kissed along his throat and up under his ear. "Do we have to go right this second? Surely we can—"

"No." Tim laughed and stepped back, catching him by the shoulders when he stumbled. "I can't make two alphas and their betas wait for me because I was too busy having sex."

"And tell me again why you have to go at all?"

"Because I'm involved. As are Nathan and Jared. They'll both be there."

Seb reached down and palmed his hard-on, now straining against his jeans. God, he'd been so horny since the full moon. Tim said it was normal and would pass, but—

He met Tim's gaze, then let out a frustrated sigh. "Why don't you feel like this? Why is just me?"

Tim moved fast, pinning him against the wall; the answering hardness in his jeans was easy to feel. "Are you kidding me?" He put his head on Seb's shoulder and breathed in deep. "I want you so bad right now, I'm seriously debating pissing off my alpha and risking possible punishment."

That got Seb's attention. "He'd punish you?"

"This meeting will have lasting consequences for both packs. It's about as important as they come." He kissed Seb's bite mark again; a soft sigh escaped. "But you smell so good, and I can feel how badly you want me."

Their bond sang. Seb closed his eyes, revelling in the waves of love and want and need rolling over him. But somewhere in the back of his mind, the word *punishment* flashed loud and clear, and he had a sliver of control left, enough to put his hands on Tim's shoulders and ease him back.

"No." Seb slid to the side and out of Tim's reach. "I'm not going to get you in trouble just because I can't keep my hands off you." He pointed to the door. "Let's go. We can do this later."

Tim stalked towards him, but Seb dodged and Tim stopped, staring at him for a good few seconds before visibly pulling himself together. "Fuck, you're right."

A part of Seb stung with disappointment, but it was definitely the right thing to do.

Tim said, "You can't come with me smelling like that." His gaze dipped to Seb's crotch. "Or with that thing on show."

Seb glanced down, his hard-on easy to see where it pressed against the denim of his skinny jeans. "But I thought—"

"Stay here, take care of that, shower, and join us when you no longer look and smell like sex. I'll explain to Cam. He'll understand. You're newly changed and bonded, so it's twice as bad for you."

"Okay." Seb watched as Tim reluctantly turned and headed for the front door.

He turned back before opening it. "See you up there."

"No kiss goodbye?" Seb teased.

The look Tim gave him did nothing to quell his erection. "If I come near you again, we won't be going anywhere for the next few hours."

"Oh." Seb swallowed. Why had he thought Tim leaving was a good idea? Fortunately for them both, Tim was gone before either of them could change their mind. "Fuck."

Seb stayed where he was, one hand absently rubbing over the front of his jeans. He moaned at the friction, and Tim's scent—their combined scent—filling the hallway made his arousal ten times worse. Tim was right; Seb really couldn't go anywhere without taking care of it first.

After undoing his jeans, Seb shoved them and his underwear down his thighs and wrapped a hand around his cock. Shit, that felt good. Nowhere near as good as Tim's hand would have felt, but enough for him to feel his teeth extend as he let go and stroked himself, tight and fast. Precome pooled at the tip, and Seb smeared it along his length, his orgasm building with every slide of his hand.

With Tim's scent surrounding him, he came hard, spilling into his hand with a choked-off cry.

His breathing ragged, Seb allowed himself a minute to recover before going to the bathroom to clean up. He didn't want to be too late if he could help it. As understanding as Cam might be, Seb didn't want to push it.

Ten minutes later, Seb was clean, dressed, and ready to go. His hair was still wet from the super-quick shower he'd just had, but he could do nothing about that without wasting more time. Rushing out of the flat and down the hallway, he opened the stairwell door and ran straight into Mark from the Primrose Hill pack, sending him stumbling into the wall.

"Shit, sorry!" Seb righted himself and breathed a sigh of relief when Mark laughed, pushing himself off the wall to stand up.

"No worries."

Mark's gaze zeroed in on Seb's neck, and Seb was torn between hiding it with his hand and tilting his head to show it off more.

Mark gestured to the bite mark and grinned. "I'd heard rumours. Congrats."

"Thanks." Seb felt his cheeks heat—he really didn't want to be a blushing bride—and he quickly looked around for a distraction. "Why aren't you up there at the meeting? I'm assuming that's why you're here?"

"Yeah." Mark rolled his eyes and added, "There was nowhere to park, so they made me drop them off outside. Took me ages to find a spot. What the hell's going on around here today?" He started walking up the stairs again.

Seb followed. "No idea." He'd paid very little attention to his surroundings this week. He glanced up as they rounded the bend; Mark's arse was in his line of sight. But it was the tag hanging from his leather jacket that caught Seb's eye. "Hey, your tag's still on."

Mark paused to glance back at him. "What?"

Seb tugged on it. "Price tag's still attached." He laughed. "I'm not surprised you left it on at that price. I'd want people to know too."

"Shit." Mark reached behind him and quickly pulled it off, pocketing it with an embarrassed smile. "I didn't buy it. I reckon your doctor must have put in a good word about me and Will after we came to apologise, because Alpha Newell gave us these this morning as a thank-you from the pack." He beamed, pride obvious in his expression. "I had to put it on straightaway. Guess I forgot to take the tag off."

"That's great." Seb had heard nothing but bad things about the P-Pack alpha. Maybe he had some redeeming qualities, after all. "Is that something that happens a lot?" Seb couldn't remember Tim or Nathan mention Cam doing anything like that.

Mark shrugged. "I don't think so. But then, Alpha Newell does things differently sometimes." He took another sniff of the leather. "I just need to wear it as much as possible to get the smell of other shifters off it."

"Other shifters?"

"Yeah, you get that sometimes with new stuff." Mark tilted his head and sniffed. "I can smell a few different scents, including P-Pack's. It shouldn't take long to get rid of them."

They carried on up the stairs until they reached the correct floor. Seb gestured for Mark to go first, and they walked along the short corridor towards the large meeting rooms where everyone was probably waiting for them.

Figuring he should try and play the good host—it was his pack's building, after all, though it still felt weird saying that—Seb grabbed the door handle. "After you."

"Thanks." Mark stepped through with Seb hot on his heels.

Everyone looked their way.

"Sorry we're la—"

They froze, rooted to the spot as growls and snarls filled the air.

\* \* \* \* \*

Tim stood to the side with Alec and Gareth, watching as Cam and Newell faced each other across the large oak table.

Alpha Newell said, "I understand the rogue shifters are no longer a problem."

Newell's expression betrayed nothing, and Tim wondered what was going on inside his head. Did he not suspect they knew so much, or was he arrogant enough to believe he'd got away with it?

"That's correct." Cam sat back in his chair. Relaxed, in complete control. "But not before they attacked and seriously injured one human and kidnapped another, unfortunately."

Newell shrugged as if that was of no consequence. "These things can't be helped sometimes." He glanced at Tim. "But I understand the eventual outcome was more than favourable."

Tim clenched his fists, wanting nothing more than to wipe the smile off Newell's face.

Cam turned and met Tim's gaze for a second, immediately calming him. "A new addition to the pack is always a good thing."

"Yes, it is," Newell agreed readily.

Tim smiled, knowing something good must be coming as Cam sat forward, resting his arms on the table.

"Which brings me to the point of this meeting…."

Newell had Wes—his newly appointed beta—present, along with three others. He glanced at Wes, then to the door, before answering. "And that is…?"

"I believe you've had a few new additions to your pack recently."

"You must be mistaken. My pack remains unchanged."

The doors to the room swung open, but Tim still caught the smug smile on Newell's face.

Seb and Mark entered, and suddenly Tim was assaulted with a familiar but totally unwelcome scent. Combined with Seb's, it took him right back to the night when Seb had been injured. A snarl forced its way out, and he took a step towards the new arrivals, teeth bared and claws out. Alec's and Gareth's growls sounded alongside his, the warning clear, and it further fuelled his anger. *They smell it too—*

*"Tim!"* Cam's voice cut through the noise, pulling at him like a leash, but just over there by the door was his *mate*. Their bond hummed strong and vibrant, and the smell of the rogue shifter so close to Seb was quickly blanking everything else from Tim's mind.

"You!" he gritted out, pointing a clawed finger at Mark, "why the fuck do you smell like that?"

"Like what?" The tremor in Mark's voice was easy to pick up and it made Tim's wolf hungry for blood.

Seb glanced from Mark to the others, clearly confused. Tim wanted him away from Mark.

"What's going on?" Seb asked.

"Sebastian. You need to move aw—"

Seb was standing close enough to Mark that when Mark suddenly lifted his arm to sniff his jacket, he elbowed him in the side. Seb grunted in surprise.

Tim saw red. Cam's sharp order for him to stop didn't penetrate the red haze colouring his vision as he leapt forward, intent on removing the threat to his mate by any means possible.

Shouts and snarls filled the room, but it was all background noise to Tim. He focused on Mark, who stood staring at him with a stunned expression, seemingly unable to move. As Tim's clawed hand closed on the soft flesh of Mark's throat, something hard and heavy crashed into him from the side, sending them both skidding into the far wall.

*Alec!*

Alec was quickly joined by Gareth, and the two of them pinned Tim to the floor while he snarled and thrashed to get free—to get to Seb.

Alec leaned in close to his ear, his voice low and urgent. "Calm the fuck down. It's a trap. Newell planned this. You're doing exactly what he wants."

Tim heard the words, but his wolf still fought for control, desperate to protect its mate.

"*Tim.*"

Alec's claws dug deep into his arm and shoulder, and the sudden sharp pain snapped him back to his senses. He sucked in a breath. Alec's and Gareth's scents surrounding him, calming him down.

*Pack. Beta. Safe.*

"You with us now?" Alec tightened his grip.

Tim hissed in pain. "Yes. I'm back. You can let go of me now."

Neither Alec nor Gareth let him go, but Alec retracted his claws and Tim sighed in relief as the wounds closed. *Fuck, that hurt.* He shook his head to clear it.

"We're going to let you up, but make one move towards him again and we will stop you."

"I won't."

With Alec and Gareth holding an arm each, they helped Tim to his feet but stayed where they were. Tim shot a look over at Seb to make sure he was okay, their bond a mix of heightened emotions. Seb stood with Nathan and Jared, Nathan's hands gripping Seb's shoulders much the same as Gareth and Alec held on to Tim.

He tried to project that he was okay, that they weren't hurting him. The last thing they needed was Seb trying to protect Tim from their own pack.

Assured that Seb was in good hands, Tim then turned his attention to Alpha Newell, who sat scowling at them. Wes had a pinched look about him, and Tim's stomach sank as he realised how easily they'd played him.

"You need to keep your pack under better control, Alpha Harley," Newell sneered as he glanced at Tim and then gestured to Mark, still standing in the same place by the door. "He would have killed him given half a chance."

"Yes, he would." Cam looked around the room, gaze finally settling on Mark, who seemed to shrink under it. "And why is that, exactly?"

"Because your pack is full of disobed—"

"I wasn't talking to you," Cam spat, halting Newell mid-tirade. He beckoned Mark over to him, at the same time addressing Tim. "Why did you attack him?"

Tim forced his teeth to retract before answering. "He smells like the shifters who attacked Sebastian."

"That's ridiculous!" Newell shouted.

But Cam ignored him. "Alec, Gareth, you were there that night, is that correct?"

"Yes," they answered in unison, and Cam smiled.

Cam's voice was soft, but his tone was like ice. "I'll ask you once more, Alpha Newell, and I'd like the truth this time. Tell me about the new pack members you acquired recently."

Newell bared his teeth. "I already told you my pack is unchanged."

"I have a shifter in this building who says differently." Cam turned to Mark, casting an eye over him. He stood and stepped in front of him, then gestured to his jacket. "May I?"

Mark hurriedly took it off and handed it to Cam, jumping when Newell growled under his breath. He looked from one alpha to the other, clearly terrified, and Tim felt a wave of sympathy for him. He was probably as much an unwitting pawn in all this as Tim was.

"Get over here and keep quiet," Newell barked, and Mark rushed to obey his alpha.

Cam studied the jacket. Now it wasn't attached to Mark anymore, Tim could easily tell it was the jacket that carried the scent, not Mark. "This is new, right?" He held it up, directing the question to Mark.

Mark looked to Newell, who glared and shook his head.

Seb stepped forward, Nathan followed, close but not touching him now.

Tim went to go to him, but Alec's claws threatened a repeat performance and he halted in his tracks.

"Stay put for now," Alec whispered.

Tim grumbled his displeasure, but stilled.

"Alpha Harley," Seb began. He then glanced at Mark as if asking permission, and Tim could swear he saw Mark give a tiny nod. "I spoke to Mark on the way up here. He said the jacket was given to him by Alpha Newell as a thank-you from the pack."

Newell pointed a clawed finger at Seb. "That's a fucking lie. How dare you—"

"Silence!" Cam's roar echoed around the room.

Newell snapped his mouth closed, rage dripping off him. Tim could smell it across the room.

"Alpha Stephen Newell," Cam intoned. "I hereby accuse you of attempting to cause bodily harm and/or death to members of this pack, with the intent of discrediting the alpha and taking the pack for yourself. I also accuse you of putting a member of your own pack in danger to help facilitate this."

"Based on what evidence? The word of a newly turned and a rogue shifter?"

Cam raised an eyebrow and carried on. "As is my right, I will take this to the alpha council and ask them to rule accordingly."

"They'll laugh you out of court." Newell abruptly stood, his chair flying back across the room. He pointed at Nathan and Jared. "If you do this, I'll be forced to tell the council about them."

Cam nodded. "As is *your* right."

"Add that to your latest illegal pack member—" Newell turned his attention to Seb, and Tim immediately stiffened. Gareth and Alec weren't letting him go anytime soon, though. "—coupled with your other transgression, the council is going to be far more interested in you than me."

He looked far too smug for Tim's liking.

"The council will find all the paperwork was in place before Mr Calloway was bitten."

Newell narrowed his eyes. "That's impossible. There wasn't enough time to—"

"How would you know exactly how much time we had?" Cam walked over to him, stopping just out of reach.

Newell paled slightly as he realised what he'd almost implied. "It was on our doorstep. Naturally we heard about the attack. We were watching out for Calloway, as agreed by our packs."

"So where were your men?" Cam glanced at Wes and Mark, but neither spoke. Not that anyone expected them to. "Where were *they* when an innocent human was attacked?"

"I'm sure there's a—"

"And how was it that my men managed to get there first, when, as you say, it happened on your doorstep?"

Cam's expression betrayed nothing, but Tim couldn't stop his smile from appearing. They fucking had him, and Newell knew it.

"I'll see you at the council meeting."

Cam smiled. "You will."

Newell turned to Wes, nodded, and then scowled at Mark. "Let's go."

"Daryl and Mike will see you out."

Newell grunted but followed Cam's betas out the door.

The room fell silent as they left, the echo of their footsteps fading as the doors closed behind them.

"*Fuck.*" Seb let out a harsh breath, cheeks immediately colouring as everyone turned to look at him. "Sorry. It's just, that was…." He looked over at Tim with a "help me out" expression, but it was Cam who went over to him.

Careful not to touch him—Tim was far too on edge for anyone to touch his mate, even his alpha—Cam met Seb's gaze. "No need to apologise. That was incredibly tense, and while necessary, not what I wanted for your first pack meeting."

Seb visibly relaxed.

Cam's soothing tone changed the mood of the whole room. Gareth and Alec let go of Tim's arms, and he immediately hurried over to Seb, crowding him against the wall. No words were needed. With his nose pushed into the crook of Seb's neck, and Seb's scent filling his lungs, Tim's wolf settled, and Tim could finally relax. He felt Seb do the same, the tension leaving both of them on a sigh.

"Is it over now? Am I safe?" Seb whispered.

Tim nodded. "Yeah, I think so." He felt Cam's hand on his shoulder, the touch of his alpha now more than welcome.

"With my accusations now raised with the alpha council, Newell will be under too much scrutiny to try anything else. Neither he nor his pack will be a problem."

As Cam finished speaking, a familiar scent drifted into the room—*P-Pack*. All heads turned to the door. The firm knock had Cam raising an eyebrow. "Enter."

A slightly terrified-looking Mark came in and stopped. "Alpha Newell ordered me to come back for my jacket." His gaze drifted to where Cam had left it on the table.

"I'm sorry, Mark. But you're going to have to tell your alpha that I'll be keeping that as evidence for the council."

Mark didn't look all that surprised. "I thought as much. But I had to ask." As he turned to leave, Mark paused; he set his shoulders and then walked back into the room a little.

He faced Seb. "I probably shouldn't be saying this, but I'm sorry about what happened to you, and I want you to know I had no part in the attack or the business with the jacket. I didn't recognise the scents on it as belonging to one of the rogues. I'd never have worn it if I had."

Seb smiled. "Thanks."

"I suspect there are a lot of your pack who are innocent in all of this," Cam said, drawing Mark's focus.

"Yeah. But I can't say any more than that."

"I understand."

Mark hesitated before walking farther into the room towards Alec. "I wanted to thank you."

"For?" Alec gave him a slow once-over.

Mark's gaze dropped to his feet for a second. "I know you were just protecting Tim, but you saved my life. So thank you."

Alec nodded, and to Tim's surprise, a small smile appeared. "You're welcome."

Mark lingered a little, looking up to meet Alec's eyes, then seemed to remember where he was. "I better go, they'll be wondering where I am."

With a deferential nod to Cam, he turned and walked quickly out the door.

Tim watched him go. Hopefully that was the last they'd see of P-Pack members for a while. Not that he disliked Mark now that he knew he wasn't involved, but their pack scent had started to leave a nasty taste in his mouth.

Seb's hands gripped his waist, pulling him closer, and Tim relaxed into him, P-Pack already forgotten.

"Take me back to your flat."

Seb's voice was a little huskier than it had been seconds before, and when Tim breathed in, the faint trace of arousal tickled his senses. *Fuck.* "Watching you attack him was scary-hot, and now that it's all over, I'm leaning towards just plain hot." He nudged his thigh between Tim's and the firmness in his jeans pressed against Tim's hip. "Come on."

Tim groaned softly; the bond was a warm glow getting hotter by the second. He cleared his throat, ready to make his excuses, but Cam beat him to it.

"Go. I don't expect to see you for the rest of the day." He grinned at whatever he saw on Tim's face and waved them away.

Nathan winked at Tim, and Jared patted Seb on the shoulder, much to Seb's apparent disgust.

"Mate sex is awesome," Jared mouthed.

Seb rolled his eyes and let Tim lead him out the door.

As soon as they were back downstairs and out of earshot, Seb said, "Jared's right."

"Hmm?" Tim concentrated on fishing out the key to his flat.

"Mate sex is the best. I don't know why I ever thought it wouldn't be." Seb draped himself over Tim's back as Tim tried to open the door, fumbling the key twice. *Stupid fucking lock.*

When he finally got the door open, Seb manhandled him inside and pressed him up against the wall.

"Especially as now I can do this—" Grabbing Tim's thighs, Seb lifted him easily, and Tim obliged by wrapping his legs around Seb's waist. "—and this." Tim tilted his head, knowing what Seb wanted.

Seb sucked and licked at the bite mark; each press of his tongue sent a shiver down Tim's spine, their bond magnifying the feeling until all Tim's focus was on Seb, everything else forgotten.

"I love you," Tim whispered, head leant back on the wall as Seb kissed his throat and rubbed off against him.

"Love you, too."

Tim came with the tips of Seb's teeth sunk into his skin, their bond fully open, letting him feel everything as Seb followed him over the edge.

This was what he dreamt about, what he'd yearned for these last few years.

And it was every bit as good as he'd imagined.

# About the Author

Annabelle Jacobs lives in the South West of England with her three rowdy children, and two cats.

An avid reader of fantasy herself for many years, Annabelle now spends her days writing her own stories. They're usually either fantasy or paranormal fiction, because she loves building worlds filled with magical creatures, and creating stories full of action and adventure. Her characters may have a tough time of it—fighting enemies and adversity—but they always find love in the end.

https://annabellejacobs.com/
Twitter: @Ajacobs_fiction
Facebook: Annabelle Jacobs Fiction

Email: ajacobsfiction@gmail.com

# Also by Annabelle Jacobs

The Choosing

Torsere Series:
Capture
Union
Alliance

The Lycanaeris Series:
The Altered
The Altered 2
The Altered 3

Toy With Me

Will & Patrick Series:
A Casual Thing
A Serious Thing

Christmas Stories:
Magic & Mistletoe
A Christmas Kiss
Not Just For Christmas

Chasing Shadows

Always Another Side

Maybe This Time

The Regent's Park Pack Series
Bitten By Mistake
Bitten By Desire

Bitten By The Alpha

All Hallows' Eve

Butterfly Assassin

38354947R00199

Printed in Great Britain
by Amazon